THE TRAP

To Caroline —

Enjoy!

Andrew Steele

2/27/22

THE TRAP

A WILSON STEELE

MOUSE HOLE FARM PRESS
DURHAM, CONNECTICUT

ISBN: 978-0-578-55740-3

In this novel, every effort was made to accurately depict the historical events surrounding the fictional story. The characters are fictional, and any resemblance to persons alive or dead is coincidental.

Cover design by Andrea Steele and Willis Steele

Dragon illustration by Cai Steele

Printed in the United States of America
Signature Book Printing, www.sbpbooks.com

To my husband, Willis Steele, the man who, many years ago, changed the trajectory of my life.

ACKNOWLEDGMENTS

I am grateful to the many friends and family members who followed the book's progress and read the manuscript. Your feedback was both stimulating and essential.

I thank my friend and editor, Gillian Belnap. Her skill and experience as an editor and knowledge of the business of publishing helped guide a complex storyline to completion. Working on such a personal, passionate, and creative effort as a novel, requires a special kind of collaboration. Gillian's countless editorial improvements are noted and appreciated. I look forward to our next endeavor.

Prologue

Tübingen, Germany, 1920

"I lied to my mother this morning."

"What about?"

"Remember that secret I told you about my family?"

"Yes."

"She asked again if I ever told anyone. I said no."

"Don't worry, I will never tell. Come on, we will be late to school. I'll race you to the oak tree."

1

A town near Tübingen, Germany, 1995

"Come on, damn it!" Albert listened as the phone rang. "Pick it up!"

"Hallo."

"It's me, where's Egon?"

"Albert! Where are you?"

"Is Egon there?"

"I don't know."

"Damn it, woman, just go see if Egon is in his rooms."

"Why, what's the matter?"

"Verdammt, just do as I say!"

She never understood the hatred behind his voice, but he was right, it was too late to question him now. She placed the phone down quietly on the table.

He heard Helga's high-heeled footsteps as she walked across the wood floor. Albert spent more time away from their home these days; she knew he was with another woman. There had been many women over the years, but this time felt different.

Helga couldn't get used to the fact that they had been husband and wife in name only for some time. Even so, she wanted to be treated with respect. If nothing else, she felt she deserved that.

Albert fidgeted nervously while he waited on the line. His mind raced back over all the problems their son had caused. He had wanted to commit Egon to an institution many times, but his wife and all the doctors were convinced that Egon was the victim of a dysfunctional family, not the cause. Given space, therapy, and medication, he would be able to work through his problems and lead a normal life.

"Das ist Unsinn!" Albert knew Egon had always been out of control and now he was violent.

Egon was an unusual child from the time he was born. He topped all the early childhood charts that recorded the development of muscle strength and responses to sounds, along with the obvious "firsts" such as walking before nine months and speaking in sentences before he was two.

At that time Albert and Helga were proud to talk about his progress. The accolades continued until his fifth year when interaction with people outside the family was evaluated. That's when everything went haywire.

His social skills were notably awkward. To say he didn't play well with others was an understatement. He presented outright hostility. With that came blame. Albert condemned Helga for being overly protective while Helga criticized Albert as a distant father who paid little attention to his son. These back-and-forth accusations continued until he was seven years old.

That's when they bought him a dog so he could interact with another being and learn responsibility. At first he seemed to love his new friend, but the puppy disappeared within weeks. Helga and Egon walked the neighborhood for days looking for the pup with no luck finding him.

Egon showed no interest in another pet, so they didn't buy one. Then, months later, their gardener brought Helga into a wooded area behind the garage. He was dumping clippings from the garden and came upon the skeletal remains of small animals in a grouping surrounded by rocks. This was definitely not a random or natural way to find the bones of dead creatures.

Helga was unnerved. She could see animal skin and hair still stuck to some of the bones. There was no doubt that those belonged to Egon's puppy. It was shocking to know that her son was killing these little creatures. But walking back to the house, Helga fell back into denial. She instructed the gardener not to tell Albert or anyone else about the bones. She rationalized that she would get help for her son and that revealing this discovery would only make things more difficult.

But Helga never followed through. She said nothing to his doctors. Egon's high I.Q. distracted her and the medical professionals from dealing with his psychosis. Instead, Helga asked for Egon to be advanced a grade in school. She believed her son needed a more challenging curriculum. The teachers half-heartedly complied. But that only compounded the social issues.

Egon was small for his age and looked even more so when mixed in with older children. A year later, his public school had had enough and expelled him.

His parents enrolled him in a private school geared for high achievers. But within weeks, the same issues surfaced. The new school insisted that their psychologist develop a profile on Egon. Both Albert and Helga had to agree in order for him to remain at the school.

The psychologist diagnosed Egon with conduct disorder, a precursor to sociopathic tendencies. The school demanded he receive psychiatric care. Albert knew that Dr. Erma Haase, the daughter of one of his research assistants, was a psychiatrist; she began counseling Egon weekly.

Now, all these years later, Albert fumed while waiting for Helga to return to the phone. There had only ever been one way to stop Egon right from the start. Rehabilitation was a joke.

Albert wished he had killed Egon himself. He'd thought about it. It would creep into his mind at the most inopportune times. Once, he was walking with Egon down the huge staircase at the school. The principal had summoned Albert to meet with the psychologist after his son had a "breakthrough" therapy session. He considered pushing him down the stairs, visualizing his son's body tumbling head-over-heels four or five times before landing face down on the stone entranceway. But that might not have killed him.

THE TRAP

There was another time in the car. Albert was at the wheel and saw Egon in the driveway through the rearview mirror. He revved the engine thinking he could back over him and claim it was an accident. No one would think otherwise and, even if they did, who would convict him of murder? No one could prove it. But no, when it came right down to it, he couldn't do it. Albert believed himself a coward.

Finally, Helga returned to the telephone. The house was large in its own right, but when Egon reached the age of thirteen, he took the rooms above the garage. The doctors claimed, "It will help him separate from the anger he feels toward you and your wife."

"Albert?" Helga's voice sounded breathless.

"Yes!" he shouted.

"He's taken off again. His rooms are a mess, his rucksack is gone. Clothes are gone. The computer is not on his desk. Where has he gone? Why do you want him?"

Helga spoke as if Egon was a normal son with normal reasons for his father to call him. She heard a click on the phone and the line went dead.

Albert couldn't bring himself to blurt out what her son had done, not over the telephone. He would deal with Helga later.

Albert was an awkward-looking man. He was tall and fine-boned with a somewhat crooked spine that over time had made one shoulder slightly higher than the other. His angular face might have been chiseled out of granite. He had high cheekbones, sunken cheeks, a long straight nose, and thin lips on a wide mouth. Egon looked like him without his

7

height. At twenty Egon was small, often mistaken for a much younger teenage boy.

Albert was not well-respected at the university, but he was content to teach the requisite classes that the other professors were bored with. This was the singular reason for his existence at the school and why they tolerated the whispers about his political views.

His passion, in fact, was writing about politics. He maintained an extensive research library at his country home. The author of twelve books, he had a large cult following for his work. Many rooms of his once-elegant manor home were now converted to warehousing all his research material.

Albert headed a group of like-minded individuals who called themselves "historical researchers." But their research and writing was narrowly focused. The Holocaust loomed heavily over Nazism and Fascism. Deniers sought many different angles to cast doubt on it; they tried to rewrite history. In their eyes, this was the single issue that impeded efforts to revive any type of National Socialism in their time. They were all neo-Nazis.

It wasn't unusual for someone from the group to be working at the house at any given time. Helga hated the intrusion but knew her opinion meant nothing. Instead, she just ignored anyone in the house and kept to a small group of rooms off the kitchen where she wouldn't be disturbed.

Egon was a member of the group. A genius by all accounts, with an I.Q. of 161, he grew up an office boy tethered to his father's duplicitous beliefs over one of the darkest chapters in human history. The only access Egon had to his father was through the work conducted in the library, and he enjoyed being given grownup jobs.

No member of Albert's group advocated violence in their writing. They promoted a return to National Socialism as an ideal system of government. The writers, however, trained to deceive their audience, captured the attention of Egon's troubled mind in a way they couldn't perceive. He was on the fast track to madness from a young age, trapped within a propaganda mill.

Now an adult, Egon checked many boxes for his therapists: impulsivity, frustration, and mood disorders were his highlights. His childhood diagnosis of conduct disorder escalated into sociopathic behavior with paranoid personality disorder. Over the years he tried medications like risperidone and quetiapine, but he never continued any treatment for a sufficient time because he claimed the drugs inhibited his mental acuity. One of his doctors suggested an experimental herbal treatment made from ashwagandha, passionflower, and lemon balm, which were intended to help his body produce more natural amino acids beneficial for brain function and anxiety relief. But like all the other treatments, Egon didn't use it long enough to feel any improvement in his condition. In Egon's mind he didn't have a problem. He rejected the notion that he should behave differently toward the people in his life.

Working in the library seemed the best medicine for Egon. When he was younger, he loved being in the library filing and making copies. Then, as he grew older, his job turned into fact checking, editing, and statistical analysis. Given his age, members of the group disregarded his quirks, which at the time, were mainly displays of rudeness.

Over time, Egon's work in the library fostered the development of brilliant writing skills, which Albert saw as positive growth. The library was a place where being odd was okay; he gave Egon a free rein.

But this period of seeming stability didn't last long, and Albert had to tighten the rein on Egon. His eccentricities spiraled into disdain for everyone in the library. He took pleasure in demeaning people. Members of the group walked on eggshells around him in order to maintain a functioning workplace. The parameters of his involvement had to change.

Albert told Egon he must now send his editorial comments via the computer mail system on the library server. Group members would make requests for research information in the same fashion. Egon spent less time in the library and worked more and more from his rooms above the garage. He had no direct contact with people. This produced a period of tranquility…until Egon discovered the power of the Internet.

During the nineties, people began posting hypertext links online, which enabled all sorts of content to reach a seemingly unlimited audience. This caught Egon's attention. Not only was he able to connect with like-minded peers, it exposed him to militant extremists. This only emboldened Egon and created even more distance between him and any degree of normalcy. He became obsessed with the Internet as a weapon to connect and recruit people to the cause in a way that his father didn't understand. Learning to use this new technology to his advantage was foremost in Egon's mind. He cloistered himself in his rooms to read and write. He stopped taking his meals with his mother. Instead, he insisted that she bring food up to his room, leaving a tray outside his door. She complied.

Egan came to see his father's work and that of the rest of the group as a huge waste of time. He dropped out of school to write a neo-Nazi-themed novel targeting the minds of young people at an age when they were most vulnerable to influence. Without the structure of the library's propaganda topics, his writing turned even more dangerous. Organizing a book's content differed greatly from his father's style of propaganda. His novel quickly ballooned to seven-hundred pages of incoherent ramblings from a disturbed mind.

Albert became aware of his son's Internet activity through one of his students at the university. Soon after that things exploded in a confrontation at the library with members of the group in attendance. The extent of Egon's mental illness was now clear to all. It was like watching a freight train barreling toward an obstacle on the tracks with brakes failing... it had to end badly.

2

Hartford, Connecticut

The air was heavy. The July temperature had soared to ninety-five degrees by the early afternoon. Everything felt sticky. It was 1995 and Alana Eastwood rushed to Gate 4 at Bradley International Airport just north of Hartford, Connecticut. She was booked on Lufthansa's flight 1052 to Munich.

As usual, she would be the last person to board the flight. This time even her baggage was labeled with a big orange sticker *LAST BAG ABOARD*. She dreaded flying, and it seemed no matter how hard she tried to be on time, the results were always the same: She was late.

Conrad knew the flight to Germany was fully booked. Doubtful that the seat next to him would remain vacant, he picked up his attaché case and stowed it in the overhead bin. When Alana boarded after the crowd had thinned, he felt sure she would take the seat next to him. He figured her to be in her early thirties and taller than average, perhaps five foot eight. Conrad always noticed height before any-thing else, because he was so conscious of his own five-foot-six frame. Even more than tall men, tall women intimidated him.

Alana was slim, dressed in a cream-colored linen shirt with khaki trousers and a thin brown leather belt, a fashion understatement to say the least. Her hair was long, dark brown, and pulled back with a barrette at the nape of her neck, accentuating her facial features. Her skin tone made Conrad curious of her heritage. Was it what was called a Mediterra-nean complexion he wondered? People rarely got it right. Alana never wanted to be put into any box; she took pride in being enigmatic.

As she came closer, Conrad could see that her only jewelry was a simple gold chain around her neck. Everything about her appearance said she was a quiet and unassuming person. Conrad found her attractive, but she was not the sort of beauty that was likely to turn other heads. Alana felt his eyes on her as she neared her assigned seat.

That feeling of being on display was the reason she carried only a small bag onboard any plane. She never wanted to make a spectacle of her arrival. She'd seen it too many times, some pompous person barging down the aisle at the last minute, trying to squeeze a large bag into an already stuffed overhead compartment. That wasn't her style.

When she came to her row, she greeted Conrad with a pleasing smile. Trying to read his expression, she hoped he wouldn't be the type to talk the entire flight. She wasn't sure.

Not long after takeoff, Alana reached for her shoulder bag and pulled out a paperback. She had purchased it the night before at the convenience store in her small town of Durham. They hadn't much of a selection, but it didn't matter because she could never settle on a plane to do any serious reading. This book was a mystery thriller that she hoped would distract her attention from the flight. She just wanted to keep her mind off other things. Atlantic crossings were long, and there was a lot troubling her.

Alana had just lost her job as the branch manager of a small regional bank when it was bought out by one of the big national institutions. "Nine years!" she thought. Nine years she had worked at that bank. It wasn't a long time by current standards—people seemed to change jobs frequently in the 1990s—but it was her first real career job and she loved it.

The new manager said, "It's best for the whole transition team if you leave today." They didn't even give her time to complete what files she had open on her desk. "We'll handle it," they said. She had worked at some kind of job ever since she turned sixteen; even through college, she had always been employed. She couldn't bear to think of herself as jobless.

Alana understood the banking business and how the mega-banks eyed the loyal deposit base of small banks. While the industry was ripe for deal making in 1995, she thought the structure of her bank would have made it an unattractive takeover target for many years to come. Driving home that day, she realized that her thinking was misguided. It all came down to ROI (Return on Investment) for the stock-holders, and this particular buyer was willing to pay a premium.

The eight investors who had formed the bank in the late 1980s all expected a takeover, just not at this time. But once the bank was in play, there was little they could do to stop it. They made a lot of money and negotiated the best possible severance packages for their employees impacted by the sale; Alana received three-weeks pay for each year of service.

But crossing the Atlantic wasn't about losing her job nor was she going on vacation. Her German grandfather had taken ill. Despite their long-distance relationship, Kirk Augsburg was the only family Alana had, and she felt incredibly close to him. They seemed to be soul mates of different generations. Kirk was it, and they both needed each other now.

Alana lost her father at a young age. He died of a massive heart attack in 1984 when she was a junior in college. Alana loved her father and losing him so suddenly was a shock. Oddly enough, he had rarely talked about his own family; his childhood background was a mystery. All she knew was that he was originally from the South and that her parents had settled in Connecticut only on the promise of a job when he left military service. She remembered a phone call when she was about eight years old telling him of his own father's death. But she couldn't recall if he went away to the funeral.

Growing up, some of Alana's playmates had big families with brothers and sisters, aunts, uncles, and grandparents. It was always so busy at their houses. Occasionally, that fun-loving environment made her jealous, but more often it made her appreciate the solitude of her own home where it was only ever her, her mom, and her dad.

Alana enjoyed spending time with her father. He had continued target practice after he left the army, and when Alana turned fifteen, he invited her to go to the shooting range with him. To his surprise she enjoyed the experience, and before long they were skeet shooting together. They were both fast and each had a good eye.

Much to her own surprise, Alana joined a shooting club in college. She had never been in any club before. It wasn't that she was antisocial or didn't want to be a team player. She was artistic and had spent most of her extracurricular time alone in front of an easel or with a sketch pad in hand.

Her talent had been evident as soon as she picked up a pencil as a young child. Growing up without siblings, her spare time had been spent sitting in the yard or in her room drawing and painting. Once in school she was told she had an "artist's eye," so she enthusiastically explored the techniques her teachers introduced to her. As the years passed, everyone who knew Alana knew of her talent.

She entered college as a fine arts student. In her small-town high school, Alana's artistic ability had defined her and had been highly lauded. But when compared to the work produced by other art majors, she saw things differently. Her work was average. This prompted her to enroll in as many business classes as art classes in order to develop the skills she would need to support herself financially as an adult. She came to see her art as a calling rather than her career. It would never pay the bills, so she would need a "regular" job.

Alana graduated with honors with the unlikely double major of economics and fine art. She came back to her hometown and accepted a position at the local bank, becoming a manager within two years. The job ticked all the boxes she set had for herself.

But most of all, it meant she could live in the historic town where she grew up. She found a loft-style apartment in a renovated nineteenth-century factory building that was large enough to provide a small studio for her art projects.

Alana's mother had chronic health issues. She had suffered with debilitating arthritis throughout her adult life. Years of abusing the medications she needed to function eventually lead to kidney disease. The doctor predicted that dialysis would be the next step.

Although mother and daughter got on well, theirs was not the "best friends" relationship Alana saw among others her age. But now that her mother was widowed and in declining health, Alana knew living nearby was the correct move after college. She was sure that her father would have wanted her to oversee her mother's care, which she did diligently for many years until her mother gave up the will to live.

Now on the plane to Germany, Alana turned a page of her book, but she wasn't really reading. She put it in her bag and leaned back into her seat. In a rare extravagance, she had booked into business class. She wanted to sleep, however unlikely that would be, but each time she closed her eyes her mind focused on her grandfather and they filled with tears.

Kirk had been taken to the hospital two days ago. He had been so healthy and active all his life that it was shocking to learn of his collapse. After he retired from his medical practice, Alana had convinced him to get live-in help. Luckily, he found a college student willing to assist him at home in exchange for room and board. Her name was Marta Voss.

When Marta returned to the cottage after shopping for that day's meal, she walked in to find him lying disoriented on the kitchen floor. She called the ambulance and then Alana. That was all Alana had been told.

Kirk and Alana wrote long newsy letters to each other on a regular basis. Unlike most of her generation, she had mastered the art of letter writing and took both the time and the effort to keep her grandfather abreast of all the things happening in her life. She joked with people at the bank about how she could make her life sound so interesting. She also talked to Kirk on the telephone on the first of every month. Kirk always timed the calls so Alana didn't spend too much.

Alana used electronic messaging at the bank. A new company called America Online was making "email" a popular way for everyone to communicate via the World Wide Web. All you needed was access to a computer and an Internet connection. She was anxious to see what was available to Kirk in his town in Germany. She had wanted to buy him a computer and teach him to use it, so they could email every day, but now that seemed unlikely or at least delayed.

Alana tried to tell herself that Kirk's condition might be nothing serious and that he would be himself by the time she arrived. But her family story was very different. Her father had died from his heart attack, and her mother seemed to deteriorate with every doctor visit. They both went to the hospital to die, not to get better.

The first memory of her grandfather was from 1966 when Kirk visited Connecticut. She was a small child then. Later, she found it difficult to separate any real memories from the stories of his visit that had been repeated so many times. Then in 1986, when she graduated from college, completely out of the blue, a round-trip airline ticket arrived inviting her to spend three weeks with him in Germany. The card read: "Your education is not yet complete. Let me show you your German heritage and the marvels of this beautiful country."

They were a compatible pair, Kirk and Alana. She related well to older people. And Kirk, a rebellious thinker all his life, was bored by people his own age. Always trying or reading about new things, he said he never wanted to be "… too comfortable in life. I want to keep pushing all the buttons!" He reveled in the company of younger people. He would often say, "Being surrounded by youth fills me with the energy to stay active in body and mind. Youth is an infectious state of mind."

So, for three weeks in the summer of '86 Alana shared a storybook vacation in Germany with her adoring grandfather. He turned seventy-four that year, yet he appeared to be—and had the energy of—a much younger man. In fact, he had never been quite truthful about his age, not wanting his patients to think he was too elderly to practice medicine. He had only recently retired from his medical practice.

They spent every day on long treks around the towns and countryside, taking in all the sights that tourists do. They passed most evenings quietly in Kirk's comfortable cottage just minutes outside the town of Tübingen in southwest Germany in the state of Baden-Württemberg.

But some nights, when they weren't too tired, they would walk arm in arm down the hill to the rathskeller in the village to drink beer with the locals. From the outside, the bar was postcard perfect. In fact, they sold postcards at the bar. Once inside, however, the restoration necessary to bring an eighteenth-century building up to twentieth-century safety codes looked shoddy and unfinished.

Still, there was the traditional sawdust on the floor, which Alana found charming. Tables lined the outer stone walls, but most everyone sat at the long U-shaped bar in the center of the room. It resembled the popular show *Cheers* on American TV—a place where everyone knew each other's names. She had never experienced such comradery. After several evenings, she even opened up to a few strangers and wished there was a place like it in her hometown back in Connecticut.

There was aloofness about Alana. Those who knew her liked her, but she didn't let many people in to understand her or share her life. Some found her unfriendly but that wasn't true. She was guarded and wanted to know something about a person before letting them into her sphere—and even then, she didn't let everyone in.

In addition to keeping her friends at arm's length, Alana felt detached from her own life at times, like a spectator eavesdropping on what she was doing. She interpreted this as her mind examining situations on a different level, such as an artist studying a subject to properly compose what they see.

She liked her close-knit world, despite the quirkiness that came with it. She knew who she was, and she was comfortable in her own skin. But now with Kirk in Germany, she saw an outgoing side of herself that she didn't know existed. Was this her "skin" too? Should she bring this Alana home with her?

Another aspect of Alana's makeup was her unusual dreams. As a child, her mother explained these dreams as nightmares. She told Alana that she shouldn't be frightened because they weren't real. But, as she grew older, that explanation didn't hold up. She would dream about things that she would later learn were true. Those dreams disturbed her parents too. She overheard them talking one morning that such dreams were not normal for a child her age, or for anyone really, at any age.

In an unguarded moment, her father revealed that his grandmother experienced similar dreams. "Members of my family said she was clairvoyant. People started coming to the house to ask questions about their lives." He rolled his eyes, "It was a freakin' sideshow. He always held there were other explanations for unusual dreams."

Her father didn't believe in clairvoyance—he said his family was just gullible. It was one reason he joined the army after high school. He wanted a different life and thought if he'd stayed in Mississippi, his life would have been squandered.

Alana heard what he said and didn't want him to think that way about her. From then on she kept her dreams to herself. She didn't want to investigate her dreams; she didn't want the dreams at all. She didn't want to know if she was psychic or clairvoyant. She wasn't even sure what those words meant. But she didn't want it to be either; she grew up without ever examining her situation. This left her a private and introverted person.

But the one thing she couldn't ignore was that as she got older the dreams grew more intense. Some day she would have to face the fact that she might indeed have some sort of psychic ability.

That time came in 1986, sitting with Kirk in the German rathskeller. They had arrived early and found themselves alone at the bar. She had dreamt about Kirk and she wanted to ask him about it.

Since her arrival, Alana had been curious about the sleeping arrangements at the cottage. Kirk gave her the master bedroom; he slept in a smaller bedroom, which seemed to be his permanent room. Could it be that even though Kirk's wife had died forty years before, he still couldn't bear to sleep in the room they had shared?

Then, while sleeping in her grandparent's bed, she had a dream in which she saw Kirk coming home from the Second World War to find his wife pregnant with a child that Alana thought couldn't possibly be his. She woke and stared at the ceiling for the rest of the night.

Could that dream be true? Did sleeping in her grandparents' bed somehow connect her to their past? Alana assumed that this unborn child wasn't a mere figment of a dream; surely the child had to be her mother. Had she discovered a truth about her mother and grandmother? She felt the need to talk about the dream but didn't know how to approach Kirk. Since she was going home soon, it was now or never.

To start the conversation, she told Kirk that she might be psychic in some way. He listened intently as she recited some of her earlier dreams about something that had happened in the past that she could have no knowledge of. But when it came to talking about her recent dream, the one about him, she couldn't do it. How could she discuss it with her grandfather—because if true, it meant he wasn't her biological grandfather at all. She just couldn't take the conversation further.

Kirk didn't know what to say to Alana. He was a medical doctor, a man of science. Yet he didn't dismiss her. He used words like "interesting" and "thought provoking." Soon the bar filled with a rowdy group of soccer players, which made further conversation on such a delicate topic difficult, so they decided to go home.

On the walk up the hill Kirk told Alana he didn't know how to react to her dreams, but he wanted her to know he believed her and took what she had told him seriously. He told her that she could be tested for clairvoyance and offered to introduce her to someone at the university who would know about such testing.

THE TRAP

Alana thought there would be no point to speak with anyone in Germany since she was going home in a few days. But she said she would consider it in the future. They didn't talk about it again, and she never looked into any testing. But the question of her bloodline was something she couldn't erase from her mind.

Alana married her high school boyfriend after she returned from Germany. Many friends had already tied the knot. It seemed the appropriate next step in her life, and she was excited about the prospects of starting a life with her husband. Unfortunately, her husband wasn't as happy in the marriage. When it came time to celebrate their third anniversary, Alana realized there was nothing to rejoice in.

Their anniversary fell on a Saturday. A few weeks earlier he had said he was going out on a fishing boat with his "buddies" on Long Island Sound. "When I agreed to go, I didn't realize it was our anniversary. Let's plan on a late dinner to celebrate. We never go out late so it will be special," her husband said.

She went shopping for a dress and waited for him to come home. At nine o'clock he called, saying he hadn't known that the boat wasn't expected in port until morning; she didn't have to be psychic to know there was a problem in their marriage. It wasn't the first time he had lied to her, but it would be the last time she believed him. Alana tried hard to keep up appearances, because to her, marriage vows were for life.

But that wasn't the case for her husband. After another year, which seemed much longer, he packed his things and moved in with a woman in a nearby town. Alana questioned if she really knew how to love or be loved and, for a period of time, went even deeper into her shell.

They had no children, nor did she see her ex-husband again. She reclaimed her family name of Eastwood in the divorce. Because her mother was in declining health, Alana moved back home to help her.

Caring for her mother meant she didn't have much time for friends. The people she had known as a married couple were more her husband's friends than hers, and she withdrew from all of them. Her few friends from high school had moved away after college. She found she didn't have friends outside of work and the people at work weren't really friends after work.

In 1993, her mother started dialysis. Then, without warning, she declined rapidly. She was admitted into the hospital and died within a week. Losing both her parents left Alana empty inside. In the course of two weeks, she had gone from the all-consuming care of her mother to living alone and detached from friends.

While some artists produced their best work in times of emotional turmoil, that was not true for Alana. She could never be creative in times of stress; instead, she immersed herself in her job. The bank was upgrading its computer system, so it was easy to avoid everything else and give 110 percent effort to the installation. The next six months passed quickly, and Alana received praise from the bank for a smooth transition.

Kirk had consoled her then from 4,000 miles away. Now she was on the plane to console him in person. She wanted to make sure he would be healthy again. In her mind, Kirk would still be as youthful as when they walked arm in arm touring Germany in 1986. It had been the happiest time in her life.

"Excuse me," the flight attendant said. "We're serving dinner now."

Alana jolted in her seat as she was abruptly brought back to reality. "I'm sorry?" She looked up.

"I apologize, I didn't realize you were sleeping. I have your dinner."

"Oh, I wasn't sleeping, just deep in thought. Thank you."

"We have three selections for your entrée: Beef involtini with a tomato sauce, honey-glazed salmon, or Indian vegetarian curry." Alana asked for the salmon and nodded when the attendant said, "Would you like a mixed greens salad with soy and sesame dressing to begin with?" The salmon dinner came with sautéed broccoli and rissole potatoes. There were crème brûlée cookies on the tray for dessert. The gentleman seated next to her prepared his table as Alana was being served. He had chosen the beef involtini.

"Thank you." Alana heard his voice for the first time.

"Hello, I am Conrad, Conrad Strasser." He smiled at her.

"Alana Eastwood. I haven't flown in business class before. The menu is impressive and the dinner smells great." She smiled back at him.

Conrad agreed. "I fly regularly and actually look forward to the meal. Tell me Ms. Eastwood, what brings you to Germany? Are you on business or vacation?"

"I'm visiting a relative," Alana spoke tentatively, already divulging too much information to a stranger.

"Sprechen Sie Deutsch?"

"A little." She thought and then added, "nur ein wenig."

"Ja." Conrad smiled.

Alana's body language deterred Conrad from further the conversation. After dinner she retrieved her book and pretended to read, again thinking how good it was to have upgraded to business class. Before long, she drifted into a deep, undisturbed sleep. She awoke hours, later hearing the bustle of passengers as they neared their destination.

"You had a good rest?" Conrad asked.

"Yes." Alana arched her back and stretched her body in her seat. "I was exhausted."

Within an hour, they were on the ground.

"Enjoy yourself in Germany." Conrad insisted on helping her retrieve her carry-on bag from the overhead compartment.

"I'm sure I will; it was nice meeting to you."

"Auf Wiedersehen."

"Yes." She smiled, "Auf Wiedersehen."

Alana landed in Munich and navigated customs without undue stress. She rented a car for the three-hour drive to Tübingen. Kirk's cottage was in a small village just outside the town.

Tübingen was still the picture-book German town she had visited eight years earlier. And not much had changed in the hundred years before that. She remembered Kirk telling her that the town had not been bombed during the Second World War. It was a university town, and the historic center was a hub of dynamic activity.

The synagogue, however, had been destroyed in the Kristallnacht of 9 November 1938, when, in a two-day period, called "the night of broken glass," Jewish businesses and synagogues were burned throughout Nazi Germany. Knowing Kirk and the wonderful German people she had met, she found it difficult to fathom such hateful destruction. Nor could she possibly know how those events of the past would impact her life in the weeks to come.

Just a kilometer or so outside of Tübingen, Alana was in the village where Kirk lived. She drove past the Catholic Church and saw the familiar row of shops in the village center. When she came upon the rathskeller, she looked right to navigate the sharp turn in the road up to the cottage. Her rental car strained on the hill, reminding her of how Kirk's car roared when he had accelerated up the same hill. As the car leveled off, she took her foot off the pedal to turn into Kirk's driveway.

She looked over the unkempt hedge at the weeds shooting up between the rose bushes beneath the windows. The cottage paint was peeling and the exposed wood had weathered a dampish gray. It wasn't 1986 anymore, but she was back with Kirk at last.

The front door opened and a young woman walked out over the high grass. Marta Voss was the college student Kirk had hired. The deal was cooking and cleaning for room and board, and it made Alana feel secure knowing Kirk had companionship. Thank goodness Marta had been there when Kirk collapsed.

"Alana! It is good you have arrived, yes?" Marta came up to the car with a smile. Her English was better than Alana expected.

"Hello, Marta," Alana got out of the car. "After all this time, it is so good to meet you."

"Ja, it is good to see you as well." Marta was tiny. She projected a cute child-like appearance. Yet in contrast to her image, Alana knew her to be mature. "I am sorry for this." Marta gestured to the condition of the garden. "I cannot do it all."

"There's more to worry about, Marta; I know you do your best. Please don't apologize." Alana opened the trunk to retrieve her luggage. "Has there been any word on Kirk today?"

"Ja, he will come home with us."

"Come home? I don't understand. Do they know why he collapsed?"

"They just called and said he would come home. I think that you be happy, no?"

"Yes, of course, but I don't understand. Did you speak with a doctor?"

"No. I am sure they will talk to us when we get to the hospital."

Once Alana was inside the cottage, it was as she remembered, although the kitchen had been updated. "Which room am I in?" she asked.

"Kirk said the main bedroom next to his room. I have taken this cozy little room off the kitchen," Marta gestured to her room.

Alana took her bags and threw them on the bed. Marta had the room ready for her. "Thanks for all you've done, Marta. I don't know what would have happened without you here. This is probably not what you planned for when you took the job."

"No, please, I am glad to do what I can."

"Can we go to the hospital right away?" Alana pulled the band from her hair and immediately tied it back again into her signature ponytail.

"Yes, I can take you. But should you not rest first?"

"I can't rest until I see Kirk."

"That's good, because I was confused about the time of your arrival. I think Kirk will wonder where we are."

Within minutes they walked back outside. "I will drive." Marta loved to drive Kirk's Mercedes and, because she was used to the local roads, she drove quite fast. It was 10 kilometers, skirting around the town of Tübingen, to get to the hospital; despite her jetlag, Alana's eyes were riveted on the road.

"I can't remember Kirk ever being ill," she said. "Did he take any medication?" Marta explained that Kirk didn't want to worry her, so he didn't tell her that he had taken blood pressure pills for many years. But a few months ago, he slipped and fell in the garden. "He refused to go to the hospital; you know they say doctors are the worst patients.

"When the pain didn't go away, he said it must be a nerve." She explained, "He started taking a drug for nerpatic pain." Marta struggled to pronounce *neuropathic*. "But he was not quite himself taking the pills. He agreed with his doctor to try a different

31

medication a few weeks ago. I had made an appointment for him to go back. It was planned for tomorrow, but of course he went to the hospital. I think the new pills may have caused him to fall in the kitchen."

"Thank you again for being so kind to my grandfather. Now that I'm here talking with you, I'm sure there aren't many people your age who would care for Kirk the way you have. You're a special person to be so kind. I'm sorry I didn't come back to visit him over the years."

"No, please do not thank me. I feel like Kirk is my grandfather. I felt this way ever since I moved in. We have been as family."

Earlier at the hospital, Kirk asked to wait for Alana in the sunroom. The nurse helped him dress and took him there in a wheelchair. "Are you sure you want to go out there now? When is your granddaughter coming for you?"

"She will be here soon. I have my book." He said pulling an old medical journal to his chest. He had asked Marta to bring several journals from the house. "I just want to go home." He dragged the word out. "I'm an old man, there's nothing wrong. I feel cooped up here. My granddaughter is coming soon. I'll keep myself busy in the sunroom."

Marta pulled the car into the parking lot. Alana followed Marta's fast pace into the hospital. As they approached the nurse's station, Alana grew cold.

"Frau Augsburg?" An older nurse with graying hair and a somber look walked out from behind the counter and held out her hand.

"Yes." Alana didn't correct her; it wasn't important considering the look on the nurse's face. She felt tears come to her eyes.

"I'm afraid we have terrible news for you, my dear."

The nurse put her arm around Alana's shoulder and began to walk her down the hallway. "Your grandfather has passed away, dear, just about an hour ago." She held her other hand out to Marta, "I'm so sorry for both of you." She looked at Marta, "I could see how much you cared for him."

A tear rolled down Alana's cheek. "I don't understand. What was wrong with him? I don't even know why he collapsed?"

"There is nothing I can tell you. I know that's not what you want to hear, but that's all I can say right now. I've called the doctor to come and talk with you."

Kirk's body had been brought back to his room and rested on the bed. The nurse partially opened the curtain that surrounded his bed. "You can stay as long as you like. But if you would prefer to wait for the doctor in the lounge, it is just down the hall."

Alana's heart sank deep into her chest as she stared at the frail man on the bed. There was barely a resemblance to the Kirk she knew. She had thought her being there would make him well. She expected to take him for drives in the country and have lunches in the local villages. Reality, however, was quite different. She didn't even know the old man lying on the bed.

Alana touched his lifeless hand. It was warm. Studying his face, she finally found the likeness to the man she remembered. Then, she couldn't look away, trying to come to terms with the fact it was Kirk and that he was dead. She sat on the bed and sobbed, pressing her face down onto his fingers.

"Why has this happened?" Alana looked up and cried out to Marta. Realizing Marta was crying too, she reached around and grabbed her by the hand. "Oh, Marta, why has this happened?"

A tall man in a white coat entered the room. "I'm Dr. Weiss," he announced. Looking at Marta, he asked, "Are you Fraulein Augsburg?"

"No, I'm Dr. Augsburg's granddaughter." Alana stood up and turned to face the doctor, but his manner was so abrupt it did not prompt a hand-shake. "My name is Alana Eastwood."

In a matter-of-fact explanation, he proceeded. "I'm sorry for your loss Ms. Eastwood. My assess-ment is that your grandfather died of heart failure. I spoke with his Hausarzt, I'm sorry, I should say to you his primary care provider, and she said this had been coming on for some time."

The doctor looked at his chart, "His high blood pressure was not responding to medication as well as expected. It took several adjustments to get it to an acceptable level; still, it was not an optimal reading. Then the fall in the garden required pain medication, which could have made him unstable on his feet, causing him to fall again in his house. But it was just a matter of time. His heart was failing."

"But you were letting him go home?"

"Yes, for the simple reason we couldn't treat him here once he was stabilized. He could not stay at this hospital; we could have transferred him to a nursing home, but he wanted no part of that. In fact, your grandfather became so agitated when I brought up the topic that I thought it best to wait to speak with you privately.

"There is nothing more we can do outside of an autopsy, and that would be irregular given his age and medical record." The doctor fiddled awkwardly with his clipboard and pen. "Is there anything more I can do for you?"

"Well, I guess not." He had managed to make Alana equally uncomfortable.

"Right, then," the doctor pulled the clipboard to his chest, "The nurse will be in to take care of some formalities, after which I suggest that you go home and let us take care of the body."

Alana couldn't help thinking this communication would have been better had she been fluent in the German language, allowing the doctor to speak in his native tongue. She couldn't imagine a doctor being so intentionally cold.

They sat quietly with Kirk. The nurse brought them coffee, after which Marta drove slowly back to the cottage. She explained that she knew Kirk took blood pressure pills, but it was such a common medication among people his age that she thought nothing of it. Unaware that the pills weren't working well, Marta said, "I assumed his blood pressure was under control. He never told me there was any problem with his heart."

Kirk was in terrible pain after the fall he took in the garden. Again, Marta thought it was a good thing that he agreed to take something for the pain. She continued, "Alana, I would have called you right away if I thought anything was truly wrong.

"Kirk didn't want me to worry you with what he told me were nothing more than routine problems. He said he was the doctor, and I should not worry, and not to worry you when you were so far away."

"Don't feel you need to explain. Perhaps he knew what was happening to him," Alana told her. "Kirk enjoyed having energy and an active mind. I don't think he wanted to grow old without a healthy body." She thought but didn't say: Maybe he didn't want me to see him as an old man.

Over the next few days, Marta was such a help to Alana. She knew how to arrange funerals, but in a foreign country with her limited German vocabulary, it would have been a nightmare without Marta.

The funeral differed greatly from those held for Alana's parents. There was no High Mass, no catered gathering back at the house, no people calling to pay their respects, no flowers, or homemade dishes brought to the door each day with cards of sympathy for her loss. The people that knew Kirk over the years didn't know Marta and, even if they knew Kirk had a granddaughter, they wouldn't have known Alana was in town.

It was a simple Catholic ceremony at the village church followed by a short walk to the gravesite. The turnout overwhelmed Alana and Marta. People from the town, from the rathskeller, many of his former patients, and some of his medical colleagues all came to pay their respects. Alana reconsidered her opinion of Dr. Weiss when he appeared at the gravesite with flowers.

As they left the church, the sun came out, and although autumn was close at hand, it warmed their faces as if to assure them that better days would come. It was a dignified way for Kirk to leave the place he loved. Who could ask for anything more?

Certainly not Kirk, a man who lived through the trauma of war and the sorrow of a young wife's death; he never looked back on misfortune, only forward to the future and what it would bring. Kirk would not have asked for anything more.

That afternoon, Alana sat at the wooden table in the kitchen of his cottage and began to mourn. She decided that since she had no job or no one to go home to, she would stay in Germany for a while to clear up her grandfather's affairs. There were no other relatives she knew of, and she couldn't expect Marta to do any more than she had already done.

Alana knew Kirk had bequeathed everything to her in a will. She was sure she would find a copy in the house. It would leave her comfortable, but she was already financially secure. In her head she knew she would find work when she returned home. But in her heart, she was sad: no job, no family, no life to go home to.

Why had she stayed away so long? It was one of the few times in her life she felt scared—alone and scared.

Hours later, Marta came in to find her still sitting at the table. She put a bag on the table and pulled out sandwiches and a bottle of wine. "Have you had anything to eat?"

"No, I'm starving."

Marta had time before the new term started at the university, so she helped Alana pack up Kirk's clothes and personal items. Everything that couldn't go to Catholic relief services went into the trash.

As the days passed, it became easier for Alana to relax. Marta's English improved each day and with that came a friendship between the two women. Marta was easy to like, and Alana's respect for how Marta had helped Kirk allowed her to open up in a way that she would normally find difficult.

As she listened to Marta telephone family and friends about losing Kirk, it was saddening for Alana to realize there was no one she was close to at home. No one to call to say Kirk was dead. There were people at the bank of course, but she had been fired. That door was closed for now. Maybe later, when she got home, she would feel differently.

Before long, there was just one room left to clear, Kirk's study. Marta only ever cleaned around the stacks of papers covering every surface in the room. Kirk always insisted he alone would sort through his papers—one day. It was a lifetime's accumulation of documents and personal keepsakes that Alana thought would tell the story of Kirk Augsburg.

There was a desk in the middle of the floor with its credenza against the wall. A bay window took up one wall that overlooked the front garden and fields beyond. Another wall had French doors, opening onto a latticed terrace and the back garden. The terrace, which once had filled the room with the fragrance of potted flowers, was now bare and gloomy.

Flanking each French door were antique sea trunks. Alana opened each trunk to find them filled, like the rest of the room, with books and files. The final wall provided a backdrop for two comfortable-looking overstuffed chairs covered in a floral chintz fabric, separated by a striking round table about twenty-four inches in diameter. But clearly the most eye-catching piece was a large hand-carved sideboard under the bay window. It was the magnificence of the carving that dominated the room.

The top of the sideboard displayed a dozen or more framed photographs of family and pets. There were pictures of Kirk and his wife, Elsa, another of Alana's parents' wedding at the local church, Alana as a baby, and several of dogs from different stages of Kirk's life.

When he lost his dearest little white dog, Britta, last year he just wasn't up to another pet. He told Marta that the thought of a dog outliving him and not having any home to go to was more than he could bear. Alana smiled at the picture of Britta thinking how Kirk would convivially ask his dog to bark a hello to Alana when they spoke on the phone.

In the middle of the collection was a photo of Kirk and Alana arm in arm outside the rathskeller in 1986. The writing along the bottom of the photo said *Thank you for a wonderful summer. Love, A.* She picked it up remembering when she had mailed it to him. She ran her finger over Kirk's face. Suddenly, she needed air and walked out to the terrace.

Alana spent the next week weeding the garden and trying to make the cottage look presentable. A painter was replacing rotted boards before applying a new coat of paint. He was also arranging for new doors and windows. As soon as the work finished, she would list the house for sale.

One evening over dinner, as she poured the last of the wine from the bottle, Marta opened up about her family. "My mother and father divorced five years ago," she explained. "My father moved away shortly after. I do not see him much now, once or twice a year. Kirk was, how do I say, a father, grand-father, and friend to me.

"I am not so much a friend with my mother. I moved out of her house when I started college. I make a point of going to see her, but it is not so good. She complains about everything I do. Why do I go to college? Why do I not get job and find a man to marry?

"It is as if a whole generation has just passed her by! She thinks I should be married with babies by now. I loved being here with Kirk. He was the one to encourage me. He wanted me to get an education and think about what career I would enjoy. He had faith in me and treated me in the way I wished my parents had treated me." She wiped tears from her checks.

"Kirk was a voice of reason for me too," Alana said, sipping her wine. "I've never asked what you are studying at school."

"I am getting a business degree. I like computers and take all the programming classes they offer. I hope to be a computer technician. Kirk said there is much time to decide. But that would be a good background for me to start a career."

"I agree. Besides, sometimes you just fall into a path that is right. Precise planning doesn't always work well. You just need a good direction forward."

"Did you plan to work in banking after college?"

"Gosh, no! I started out as a fine art major. I wanted to be a sculptor." She rolled her eyes, "but I didn't want to be a starving artist, so I switched to a business degree in economics.

"Sometimes I pictured myself working at a big multinational corporation. The theory called cross-currency arbitrage intrigued me. But I think I was delusional in school. I'm not a high roller candidate for a Fortune 500 company. I took the job at the bank because I knew I could do it well and still have time for my art.

"My mother had health concerns, and I thought I should be there to help. Then I found I really liked working at the bank. It is something I still find hard to admit, but I'm better at business than art. Whenever I have any doubt of that, I remind myself that almost no one earns a living as an artist, right?"

"Well, I don't know about that, but I'm glad you are happy at your job."

"Absolutely, I love my job." She paused, "Well, I loved my job. I didn't tell you, but I lost my job just before Kirk became ill. The bank was sold and they let me go."

"Oh no, I am so sorry. It is awful for you. Why did you not tell me before now?"

"I don't know. We've both had too much to think about. It didn't seem to matter."

"How long do you think you will stay here?"

"Not much longer. I'm not on a schedule, but once I get the house ready to sell, I'll make plans to leave."

"We have not talked, Alana, that I will start school soon. I think I will find a room for myself near the university. I don't think I can get into a dormitory at this late date."

"You are quite welcome to continue to stay here at the cottage until it sells, even after I go back to the States. Who knows when this place will sell?"

"That is kind, but I do not think that is a good idea. I do not feel comfortable to stay here alone when you have gone. I will stay until you leave. I will not leave you on your own. But I need to have a place to go when you leave. I have started to look at what is available."

Alana leaned back in her chair, pulling the band from her hair. "I guess you're right, we've both got to get on with our lives. I've been hiding out long enough." They sat for a while in an uncomfortable silence until Alana sat up in her chair wrapping the band around her hair. "Let's call it a night, I'm tired."

For the first time since Kirk's death, Alana was thinking about going home. She thought about her house in Connecticut. Suddenly she missed her own surroundings. But first, she had to sort through the papers in Kirk's study. Perhaps she had postponed that task to avoid the more personal history of Kirk's life. But the time had come. She had to face it now.

The following morning Alana opened the door to the study and planned her attack. She went through the bookcases first. Kirk had been an avid reader throughout his life and seemed to have kept every book he read. She divided the books into three piles: one to donate to the local library, another of medical books that were probably too old to be useful, but she would see if the university library wanted any of them, and the third pile would go straight into the trash bin.

She threw away the magazines and most of the papers and, depending on what she could determine from the letterhead, Alana set some papers aside for Marta to translate. Some of them dated back fifty years and were a curiosity if nothing else. It made sense to have Marta's help before throwing them all away.

As expected, Alana found Kirk's will and set it aside. The law firm had already contacted her after his death. She had scheduled a meeting with them the following week.

When Marta came in about dinner time, Alana was sitting in a chair drinking tea. "That's it, Marta, I'm done for today. Let's go out to get something to eat."

Later that night, lying in bed, she remembered going through her mother's belongings. She avoided that for the longest time as well. Closing out someone's life is challenging; it stirs up memories and takes a toll on whoever's doing it.

She felt lost amidst all the papers in Kirk's study. When she started, she was both curious and uneasy about reading Kirk's personal correspondence, but everything she found was simply mundane. The pile readied for the trash was overwhelming. Then, with tears filling her eyes, she turned on her side and hugged the pillow. No, Kirk had no need for these things any longer. Besides, how important could any of the old papers be?

They were dead, she cried, thinking of her family. Keeping bits and pieces of their lives doesn't make them less dead and throwing things away won't make their memories less dear.

Alana had bottled up these feelings too long. When she finally drifted off to sleep, it seemed to close the door on her grief, and not just her grief for Kirk, but her grief over the loss of her dad and her mother. She had been carrying a lot of baggage around with her. It seemed Kirk's death had allowed her to come to terms with death itself, perhaps even her own mortality.

Years before, a concerned priest had told her, "Mourn the dead, then let them go. Life is for the living. Grieving too long casts a shadow over life that can be difficult to escape." Alana knew all of that was true, but she just hadn't been able to make it happen. It was time to move on. And the only thing between her and moving on now was emptying the beautiful sideboard in Kirk's study.

3

Tübingen, Germany

Usually a slow starter in the morning, Alana had no trouble awakening on this day. The release of pent-up feelings the night before now energized her. She was focused on going home and what she had to do to get there.

Alana called out for Marta as she walked to the kitchen. Then she saw the note clipped to the door, *Back by 2:00*. Alana prepared tea and toast and went to the study to start her task.

She stood in the doorway looking at all she had accomplished the day before, the stacks of boxes, bundles of magazines, and best of all, the empty shelves. Lowering the cup from her lips, she walked over to the sideboard. She wanted to take one piece of furniture back to Connecticut; this would be it.

The sideboard was impressive. You might see such an elaborate piece in an elegant country house or in a sophisticated hotel. The pale creamy wood was from the horse-chestnut tree. The intricately carved design on one door represented the tree in spring with its large showy conical blossoms. The other door showed the tree in autumn when it bore fruit, called conkers, enclosed in a spikey husk. The decorative leaves that outlined each door were carved to precision.

Alana knew the tree by its botanical name, *aesculus hippocastanum*, because Kirk had one growing in his yard and that was how he referred to it. His medical training required him to learn both the botanical and the common names of medicinal plants. Alana was sure Kirk relished giving his patients additional information on the homeopathic preparations or the synthetic pharmaceuticals he prescribed.

Unfortunately, Kirk hadn't been too careful with any of his furniture. The top of the sideboard was badly scratched. Alana ran her fingers along the lines, thinking she wouldn't change a thing. Every mark would remind her of Kirk.

She remembered the sideboard from her visit in 1986. On one cold rainy day, when Kirk took the opportunity to nap, Alana had done a little snooping. She opened the sideboard and saw a pencil signature on the back of one door.

Nine years later, she opened the same door again and there it was. Just as in 1986, she couldn't make out the name of the cabinetmaker, but the date was clear, 20 August 1912, as was the location, Tübingen, Württemberg, Deutsches Reich. It had been made by a local artisan. In 1912, the German states had different names. She thought this connection made it even more special. It would be like bringing part of her family history home. These thoughts reminded her of her dream of Kirk's home-coming from the war. Did she even know her family history?

Alana loved antiques. Almost all of the wood furnishings in the cottage appeared to be antique, probably handed down by Kirk's family or maybe his wife's. Like the furniture, the cottage had stood the test of time, even if that meant having a few scrapes and scratches.

Yes, the outside needed maintenance and some repair now, but inside all the original woodwork was in good condition. While problems were inherent in a hundred-plus-year-old house, Kirk had kept all the mechanical systems, like the heating and hot water, all up to date. He had remodeled the kitchen and bathrooms just before Marta moved in. In a word, the cottage was lovely.

Alana's mother had talked about renovating her house for years. She enjoyed watching *This Old House* on TV and imagined what she would do to fix up her own house. While those plans never materialized, it was Alana's house now and she was inspired to modernize it when she returned home. She knew exactly what she would do first: Take down the wall between the living room and the kitchen, creating what the 1990s called a "great room."

The design promoted casual living, and Kirk's sideboard would provide the ideal transition between the kitchen and living areas. All of this gave Alana even more enthusiasm to return to the States.

But she was in Germany now, and she had to clean out the sideboard and arrange shipping to Connecticut. She opened the top drawer to find a single box. It was difficult to remove because it only just fit from front to back within the drawer. With some effort, she pried it loose and pulled it out.

The box was made of smooth dark wood, maybe a foot wide and half again as long and four inches deep. There was a simple design carved on the lid that resembled, but wasn't, a fleur-de-lis. Alana grasped the lock mechanism, which released quickly, and the lid opened easily between her fingers.

Looking inside, she had a familiar feeling. It was the feeling of being a spectator snooping in on a past life. A chill traveled up her spine and her fingers tingled as she sifted through the contents of the box. Was she about to connect to Kirk's life in a way she couldn't explain?

Inside the box, she found a tattered but neatly folded red armband that Alana supposed was a medical identification. There were several keys, a Catholic cross, and a well-worn pocket Bible with a soiled leather binding. Tucked inside a page of the Bible was a medic badge. All of these items seemed consistent as keepsakes from Kirk's past, and she felt privileged to have finally found such personal items.

But when she read the inscription inside the Bible and looked through the loose papers and letters, she got a surprise: Nothing belonged to Kirk at all. The name in the Bible and on the birth certificate was Helmut Augsburg. The papers and letters as well, were all addressed to Helmut Augsburg.

Alana knew Kirk had an older brother named Helmut, but he never talked about him. She thought Helmut had died before her mother was born. The birth certificate showed he was born in 1910, which made him two years older than Kirk. As she looked at the other documents, the entire contents of the box appeared to belong to Helmut. Was this box sent to Kirk after his brother's death?

She picked out a document emblazoned with the swastika of the Third Reich. It made her cringe. She couldn't bring herself to even attempt to read it at this time. She believed that Helmut had been killed in the war but couldn't remember how she knew that. Probably her mother had told her. As close as she was to Kirk, there were two topics he never discussed: the war and Helmut.

Kirk was a man who dedicated his life to healing people. It seemed impossible that Kirk could have been a Nazi; surely he was just a German doctor caught up in events that were out of his control.

She pulled one letter from its envelope and tried to decipher the old writing. The date was 14 May 1939. The ink had faded and the paper had yellowed; she couldn't read the writing easily. She left it open on the top of the sideboard and flipped through the other envelopes.

She opened a second letter dated 20 June 1939. The handwriting appeared the same but was more readable. It was addressed to Helmut and talked about waiting for him to return from somewhere; she couldn't read all the words because the paper was ripped along the fold, but she was able to get the gist of it.

The letter went on about mundane things: "My father is having another flare up of gout. Do you remember when it happened last year? This time is much worse. His foot became so swollen he couldn't fit it into his boot. Yesterday he insisted on taking care of the cows, but today…" Alana had to skip several unreadable lines until the topic continued. "The doctor is coming to the house, but I have already applied a poultice to reduce the swelling."

The remaining words were again too difficult to read as the paper had also frayed. The letter seemed to be from a wife or girlfriend. Then she saw the signature, *Liebe Elsa*—Elsa was Kirk's wife's name. Would she sign a letter to Helmut, *Love Elsa?* Other letters, in the same handwriting, seemed to be love, or at least affectionate letters, but, she reasoned, that didn't mean there was any connection to Kirk's wife. Alana thought… it was just the same name, right? After all it was and is a common German name. Nevertheless, it was an intriguing coincidence. But Alana was a practical person and didn't believe in coincidences. She found it difficult to separate this "Elsa," obliviously involved with Helmut, from Kirk's wife. Yet she convinced herself she was being silly.

Other envelopes were addressed to Helmut at the cottage, which made sense because the cottage had belonged to Kirk's parents and their parents before. But the letters she read from Elsa were addressed to Helmut in another town.

She continued looking through papers in the box. Then, wait, she spotted an envelope that was still sealed. She picked it up and dropped it immediately! She felt consumed with dread. It was as if her blood had turned to ice. Instinctively, she picked it up again. The chill returned, numbing her finger tips. She examined the envelope back and front.

THE TRAP

It was stamped by the Reichspostministerium on 10 April 1945. The ink on the postmark was smeared, and she couldn't make out where it had been mailed, but Alana knew history, and that date was just before the fall of Berlin and the end of the Second World War in Europe. She was astonished that there had been mail service throughout such turbulent times.

But why had it not been opened? She reflected. Helmut may have already died. But wouldn't Kirk have been interested in opening it? The feel of the letter in her hands was stimulating all her senses. She walked over to the chair, tapping the letter in the palm of her hand as she sat. She wanted to open it, yet at the same time she was fearful. But there was no question that she must open it.

Alana went to the desk for a letter opener. With the envelope upright between her fingers, she gently poked the tip of the opener under the flap and sliced upward making a clean slit. She returned the opener to the desk and sat back in the chair. She slipped a single page out of the envelope and unfolded it carefully. A musty odor reached her nose. Stains on the paper looked like blood. Her preternatural senses elevated. What impressed her first was the writing. It was beautiful, artistic in fact, almost calligraphy, and with even her modest level of German, she could translate most of it.

Alana was so fully engrossed in the letter that she hadn't heard Marta come home and enter the study.

"I've got ebäck (pastries) if you're interested." Marta saw the stunned look on Alana's face. "Are you all right?"

"Look." Alana leaned forward, handing her the letter. "I found this in the sideboard. It's never been opened. I just opened it now. It was addressed to Kirk's brother, Helmut." Marta put the pastries on the table between the chairs and sat to read. She could decipher the German script faster and more accurately than Alana. "This is so weird," she said. "What do you think it means?"

"Marta, read it aloud in English. I want to write it down." Alana grabbed a pen and writing pad out of the desk and prepared to take down every word.

29 March 1945

My dearest friend Helmut,

I pray you are alive and that this letter finds its way into your hands. It seems that fate brought us together again when you came to my home in Berlin some years ago. When you saw what we used to call the trap, we reminisced how, as children, we would hide things inside.

I have discovered the most unbearable realities of the Third Reich and to know I took part in such inhumanity is more than I can bear. It now shrouds my very existence. We all live and die by our choices, and I prepare to die for mine.

Berlin will soon fall and there is no one here I can trust. I have hidden a secret in the trap, and I must ask you, my friend, to reveal it to the world. I can't write what it is for fear this letter could fall into the wrong hands. But people must know, and you are the only person who will know where to find it.

I am sorry to burden you with such responsibility. I will cry aloud before I die, I am Jew and I am German!

Your friend,

Franz

The letter unnerved both women. They kept reading it over and over again. Marta asked, "What could it mean… revealing a secret that is hidden in a trap. How mysterious."

Alana walked about the room continually tapping the envelope in her palm. Other than with her mother and father when she was a child, she had never discussed her psychic experiences with anyone except Kirk. She knew that people would treat her differently and most would consider her a kook. She couldn't share all she was feeling with Marta.

"Who do you suppose Franz could be?" Alana asked. "There's no last name. Did Kirk ever mention a Franz to you?"

"No, he never even talked about Helmut. I did not know he had a brother." Marta sat in one of the big chairs with her legs pulled up underneath her as if to provide comfort.

Alana told Marta, "I read letters from someone named Elsa. There was no last name and no return address."

"That was Kirk's wife's name, no?"

"Yes, but it's a common name, right? This Elsa appears to have been Helmut's friend. Maybe a girl-friend, or even a wife. Everything in the box I found belonged to Helmut and everything was dated well before the war. Everything except for this letter from Franz dated 1945."

Alana asked, "Marta, look at this badge; I found it inside the Bible."

Marta knew it immediately. "My grandfather was a medic in the war and had a badge like this with the snake on it. His was a blue arm band; the one in your box is red. That tells me there were different ranks of medics. But I think Helmut must have been a medic of some sort during the war."

Marta left the room and Alana sat thinking that nothing else in the box gave her any unusual vibes. It was just the Franz letter that roused her senses. But also puzzling was the question of Elsa's identity.

Later that evening, Marta came back into the study to find Alana sitting with a glass of wine in one hand and the letter in the other. "Yes, I'm still thinking about the letter," Alana admitted, throwing it down on the table between the chairs. "Maybe it's the artist in me, but I keep dwelling on the handwriting. It is so beautiful, yet this Franz person was in obvious distress. Marta, I think the discolored areas are blood spots.

"Someone else in such dire straits might have scribbled the words. That tells me he was incredibly disciplined. I don't know, I guess we could speculate anything about him but what good would it do. I am just so moved by how emphatically he writes about whatever this secret is and that it must be revealed."

"I think of something to do." Marta took the chair next to Alana, "We could show the letter to my professor at the university. He knew Kirk; he told me to come here for the job."

"Yes, that might be a good idea. He would offer an objective view. I was going to ask if you knew of a friend or acquaintance Kirk might have mentioned. Is there anyone who would have known the family when Kirk and his brother were younger, before the war or during the war?"

"I know that Kirk has gone to several funerals since I have been living here, including for the two men he considered his best friends. He was quite sad when they passed within months of each other. He never mentioned anyone else to me."

"I feel sad that he never told me about losing his friends. In hindsight, I guess our chats were more about him asking after me and my life. I would think of things to tell him for entertainment value. That seems pretty shallow now. I wish I had asked about his life as well." Alana sat quietly for a time, then said, "Besides Kirk's will, I found no family papers anywhere in the house, just those belonging to Helmut that were in the box. There was no birth certificate for Kirk, no marriage certificate to Elsa, no death certificates for his parents, Elsa, or Helmut were amongst his papers. I think that's strange, don't you?"

Marta just raised her eyebrows and shoulders in an expression of "I don't know."

"Do you know where I could go to get copies of family records like that?"

"No." Marta shook her head. "I could call my mother and find out. I'm sure she would know. I have seen a family history center in Tübingen, but I do not know if they provide those certificates."

"How will you get in touch with your professor?" Alana asked. "School isn't in session."

Marta was tired. She bent down in the chair, putting her head in her hands. She then looked up at Alana, wiping her eyes. "Oh, I am sure he will be in his office during the day. It is almost time for the classes to begin. It's not far; we could drive there tomorrow. I'd like you to see the university anyway."

"Fantastic." Alana stood up and picked up her glass. "Why don't we call it a night, I'm exhausted and so are you."

Marta nodded. "Do you think we make too much of this letter?"

"No." Alana said sharply.

"Well, if you think okay, we can drive over to the university in the morning and talk to my professor."

Alana said slowly, thinking of the words in the letter as she spoke. "Yes, I like that idea. I'll say good night now."

She went to bed thinking what if it wasn't just the box that belonged to Helmut. Was the sideboard his? Perhaps the furniture came to Kirk on Helmut's death. Would that explain why Kirk left the contents of the box untouched? She tried to clear her head to fall asleep, but the feeling of dread she experienced when she touched the mysterious letter weighed heavily on her mind.

Following a restless night, Alana was late rising. It wasn't until 10:30 that they were on their way to the school.

The University of Tübingen now extended throughout the town. Marta's business classes were located in the area called "old town." The university dated back to the fifteenth century, and the town had grown up around the school as each college expanded. Today the town and university intermingled to form a vibrant environment for everyone: locals, students, and tourists.

Some of the streets were now cut off to traffic, allowing venders and cafés to create a festive atmosphere in a town built in a simpler time, adapting as best it could to the late twentieth century.

On the campus, there was a lot of activity with repairmen finishing up summer maintenance and renovations. Alana wondered what student life must be like at a school like this. Perhaps she should have come to Germany for her education. Living here with Kirk could have changed the direction of her life. But that was silly to contemplate because, while she had experienced the sadness of losing people and a failed marriage, she was content with her life. She had never looked for any new direction.

Of all the professors Marta knew, Dr. Altmeyer was the only one she would even consider dropping in to see unannounced. Marta guided Alana across the campus.

As they walked passed a building Alana said, "Look at this charming old building, it's beautiful!"

"No!" Marta said with a laugh, "the others are old, but this one is new! They build this just two years ago. In your country they make everything to look new, but here we build to look old when they are finished!" She grabbed the handle and pulled open the heavy door. "This is where most of my classes are, this is the business center."

They walked into an empty hallway and climbed several flights of stairs. Alana lost count of how many, but she was breathless at the top. Nerves she thought: I am not out of shape!

At the top, they turned into the hallway and made their way to the other end. Marta stopped in front of an opaque glass door that read *Dr. Valdemar Altmeyer, Business Management Department.* She didn't knock. She just pushed softly on the door and peeked through as it opened, "Professor?"

"Ja." An elderly man swiveled in his chair to see who was asking. Peering over the glasses resting on the tip of his nose, he said, "Ach, Marta, wie geht es meiner besten Studentin?"

"Nein, wie werden sie mich nennen, Herr Altmeyer, wenn ich dieses Jahr noch besser bin?"

Alana stood behind smiling at the professor. Marta showed the kind of friendship toward her teacher that Alana never did when she was in school. She had completed her education anonymously. She was sure none of her teachers would even remember her. Marta fit into any situation in a way Alana believed she never could. That was one thing Alana wished she could change about herself. She would like to be more self-confident when meeting people.

"Hier ist meine Freundin aus Amerika, Herr Altmeyer, Alana Eastwood. Sollen wir English sprechen?"

"Kein Problem."

Hearing her introduction and Marta's request for English, Alana squeezed into the small office and held out her hand. "Hello Professor Altmeyer."

The professor stood up and greeted her with a warm handshake. He was a pleasant man, wearing a heavy knit sweater. Even though the day was warm, the office was cold; the professor appeared dressed to work in comfort.

Alana had a good feeling about him and was glad they had come. He readjusted his glasses and asked,

"Now what can I do for you ladies? My students rarely drop in to just say hello, not even you, Marta." He chuckled.

"You are right, Professor, we do want something. We want advice. Did you know that Dr. Augsburg has died?"

"Oh my goodness, yes, I read that in the newspaper."

"Alana is Dr. Augsburg's granddaughter."

"I was very sorry to hear it. Kirk Augsburg was a good man. I must admit I didn't know him well, but he was well respected. If I remember rightly, didn't I tell you about Kirk when he was looking for a housekeeper? I think we listed the position here at the university."

"Yes, you did, Professor, and I am grateful." Marta looked over to Alana then back to her teacher. "After he died, when we were cleaning out his home, we find a letter that is strange. It is from World War II. We would like to show it to you if you have time."

"Of course." He removed his glasses, which had slipped down his nose, and pulled a handkerchief from his pocket to give them a wipe. "You know I like Marta very much," he looked at Alana, "she is a good student."

Alana pulled the letter from her bag and fidgeted with it in her hand, waiting for the professor to stop cleaning his glasses. "The letter was unopened," she said, "well, I mean I opened it for the first time."

He looked at the letter in Alana's hand. He was obviously a slow and methodical man. In his own time, he reached for the letter and laid it on his desk.

"Well, let's have a look." He put the handkerchief back into his pocket and placed his glasses on his nose.

Picking up the envelope, he examined it back and front before pulling out the letter. He sat still so long it appeared to Alana that he read it twice. Then he looked up right into her eyes. "Wie seltsam," then in English, "A mystery can be exciting. What kind of advice do you expect from me?"

Suddenly Alana felt silly for coming, but Marta wasn't bothered.

"Professor, the letter was sent to Dr. Augsburg's brother who we believe died in war. The letter was in a box, along with a few personal effects, hidden away in an old cabinet all these years. Remember, it was never opened—no one will have found what this man has hidden. We want to find out who Franz is. We want to learn what secret was hidden in the trap. We want to know what it all means."

Marta kept on, "This Franz person was emphatic that this secret be revealed to the world. That sounds pretty important to me." Marta was talking like an excited schoolgirl. It surprised Alana how confident she was with English now. She looked at Alana, "Is *emphatic* the right word? I think I heard you say that."

"Yes, it is." Alana smiled.

The professor didn't say a word. He looked back at the letter. He turned the paper over and examined the back of the page that was blank. Alana wondered what he could be looking for, perhaps a watermark on the paper. He looked again at the envelope, rotating it in different directions in a seeming effort to read the markings on the stamp.

"Amazing," he looked up, "the whole of Europe was in shambles and letters got delivered!" He laughed and shook his head at the same time. "It's true you know, and it wasn't unusual, the mail finally got through. I believe this stamp says April, and of course the mail did end in May—there was no more Reichspostministerium after Berlin fell.

"Look at this imprint here." He showed them. "This means the letter was mailed in April—that ink is smudged—it didn't arrive in Tübingen until the mail was handled under the French occupation. I can't make out that date, but it could have been weeks later, perhaps many months later." He rambled on as he opened the letter again.

Neither of the women spoke until Alana broke the silence. "We found the letter disturbing, Herr Professor; we can't stop thinking about it. This poor man sounds desperate. I know it may sound silly to you, but as Helmut's relative I feel almost obligated to follow through on this. Perhaps I could locate a living relative who would understand the meaning of the letter."

The professor removed his glasses again, this time laying them on his desk. "Oh my dears, I don't think you are silly at all. I just don't know what I can do to help you. If I were thirty years younger, I would join your search myself.

"I understand your fascination. Oh, the thought of unraveling a mystery like this! But I'm afraid these days it is all I can do to get myself in here and home again at a reasonable hour. It takes everything out of me, and there is nothing left over.

"But there is another professor here who is a World War II historian of sorts. Do you know Dr. Schmidt, Marta? He is in the history department."

"No." Marta sat half across the corner of the desk to make more room for Alana to stand. The cramped office was made smaller by the stacks of new books piled on the floor waiting for the upcoming school session.

"May I keep this until tomorrow?" The professor looked at Alana. "Our copy room is closed for the day because a new machine is being installed ahead of the school year."

Alana hesitated, and he could see she was uneasy.

"It would give me a chance to discuss it with Dr. Schmidt. It is quite possible he would be interested in helping you. I would send you to see him yourselves, but quite frankly, he's a bit of an odd person. I would prefer to talk to him first and then give you an introduction if he is willing to assist."

Alana could see he was genuinely trying to help them and replied, "Yes, I would be most grateful to you Dr. Altmeyer, thank you very much."

"Right, then let's plan to meet again tomorrow. Shall we say about this same time? Call me in the morning before you leave your house just to make sure I have been able to arrange something." The women agreed and turned to leave.

"Oh! Wait a minute, just wait a minute." The professor opened the top drawer of his desk and shuffled through a stack of business cards that were held together with a rubber band. "Just a second," he abandoned those cards and rummaged through the drawer, "ah, here."

He turned around and using both hands he gave Alana a business card. "Just in case Dr. Schmidt can't suggest anything, and you are really serious about this, you could get in touch with this firm. They do all sorts of research. Perhaps they would at least point you in the right direction. They have done research for us here at the university. I'm told that they are nice people."

Alana looked at the card; it read, in German, Griegg Informationsdienst und Forschungsbibliothek, Hochbaumstrasse 94, Zurich 3436. The back of the card was in English: Griegg Information Services and Research Library. "Thank you." Alana put the card in her pocket.

The professor tucked the letter under his sweater and pushed it into the breast pocket of his shirt. Flattening the sweater back down and patting his chest where the letter rested. "It's safe here." He said with a smile.

"Oh!" He reached back to his desk and handed Alana his card, so she would have his number to call him the next morning.

"Thank you again." Alana said. "I appreciate you speaking with us."

"Oh, the envelope," the professor noticed that it was still on his desk, "I won't need it, why don't you hold on to it." He handed it back to Alana. "I'll see you tomorrow." Then looking at Marta, he said, "Auf wiedersehen."

Leaving the university, the women went into the town. Allowing the professor to keep the letter served to put some distance between them and the mysterious Franz. Alana was able to shut off her deeper feelings and enjoy herself for the afternoon.

Marta showed her the apartment she had her eye on. It was a bed/sitting room set up with a kitchenette in one corner. They weren't able to go inside, but they climbed up the stairway to a small porch and peeked through the windows. Alana wanted to give Marta some things from Kirk's cottage, and she spotted a place in the room that would be perfect for one of the sea trunks. She would give her both of them if she agreed.

There was no sadness that afternoon. Marta felt she was on her way into the next phase of her life, and Alana felt a little closer to getting home. Perhaps with Dr. Schmidt's help, they might find the meaning of the strange letter. It was such an innocent, well-meaning thought. They had no way of knowing the inescapable consequences that would befall such a quest.

Over lunch, Alana asked Marta what the word *Erstvollzug* meant. "That is a prison. I think it is for first-time offenders." Marta explained, "A place they send people for just a few months confinement for minor problems. Why do you ask?"

"I told you about the letters in the box that were from a woman named Elsa, right? Those letters were addressed to Helmut and the word *Erstvollzug* was written on the envelope. I can't pronounce the name of the town without looking at it in writing, but I'm sure I've seen road signs for it as I've been driving around."

"Does that mean Helmut committed a crime?" Marta wondered.

"It would seem so. Although I guess he might have worked there. But the content of the letters seemed to indicate Elsa was updating him about what was going on at home while he was away. I think he was in prison."

Later that night at the cottage Alana packed the final boxes of Kirk's belongings. Other than the items in the box, nothing else appeared to have any connection to Helmut or the letter.

She was looking at Helmut's letters again when Marta came in. "My mother tells me that marriage banns are published in the local newspapers. Now that I think about it, I think we will also find arrests and convictions in the papers as well. The library at the university has all the newspapers on microfilm so we could find answers. I know how to do that." Marta offered.

"I'm realizing that I know little about my family history. It might be fun to do some investigating while I'm here. Helmut can't have done anything too terrible if it was just a short-term prison. Do you want to go to the library when we go back to the university in the morning?"

"Yes, I agree with you, it might be fun to do some investigating."

They reread the letters from Elsa and were convinced that they were romantic in nature. None of this was connected to the Franz letter, but Alana wanted answers. She went to bed that evening feeling her work in the cottage was wrapping up. If there were ways to check into her family history, then perhaps they would get help on the mysterious

Franz letter as well. She fell asleep as her head hit the pillow.

At the university, Dr. Altmeyer realized he had worked much too late again. Everyone else had long gone home. He was just getting ready to leave his office when the telephone rang.

"Hello?" he said, placing his keys back down on the desk. "Yes, I was just leaving." There was a pause while he listened. "Don't be silly, Herr Schmidt, I'm not in any danger." He paused again. "Well, all right, yes, I'll wait for you here. Okay, ten minutes, yes, I'll see you then."

Dr. Altmeyer put the receiver down on its cradle and pondered the strange call. He heard a noise and turned toward the darkened hallway. A figure was lurking in the shadows. "Yes, can I help you?"

"I want the letter." The voice was male.

"What are you talking about? Who is out there?"

A small man walked from the shadows into the office. He had a ski mask pulled over his face. He pushed the professor down into his chair.

"Look, I heard you on the phone. I don't have much time. Give me the letter!"

The voice sounded crazed. The professor tried to stand, but the pressure of the man's hand was too strong for someone his age to resist; he couldn't move.

The strain of trying to get up made his chair roll off its mat and hit up against a file cabinet with a bang. The old man flailed his arms around trying to grab hold of his assailant. He wanted to pull off the mask to see the face of his attacker. Just as he was able to grip the mask, the chair tipped sideways to the floor and pulled the professor with it. The mask held tight between his fingers. He looked up into a young man's face.

"Why? Why are you doing this?"

"You stupid old man, you don't have a clue as to what you may have."

"Guter Gott, what are you talking about?"

Something snapped within the deranged assailant. He rummaged about the desk. "The letter, you fucking idiot, I want the letter those women brought you today."

The professor, wedged between the desk and the chair, looked up. "What? How do you know about the letter?" He tried to stand. "Get out or I'll call the police!"

The old man heard a click, then saw the long thin blade before his face. Struggling, his head hit the file cabinet and the room went black. An incredible surge of pain burst inside his chest. His whole body contracted with one great reflex, and then there was nothing.

The attacker looked at the professor's body as it slumped lifeless on the floor. The wheels of the up-turned chair clicked rhythmically in the otherwise silent building. Blood seeped through the professor's sweater as his heart exploded with its last beat.

"Stupid man! Why didn't you listen to me?" He couldn't believe what he had done. He smashed his forehead into the file cabinet as if to make his brain focus on the situation. He came for the letter and then killed the only person who could help him. He swung his head at the file cabinet again.

He grabbed the mask from between the dead professor's fingers and stuffed it into the waist of his trousers. He wiped the stiletto blade against the man's knee and clicked it back into the handle.

Why had he killed him? He never intended to use the knife. He'd never used his knife before. But he just couldn't control himself. Before he knew it, the stiletto plunged deep into the man's chest. He re-lived the sensation, how the knife went in easily, how he jerked it upward in some sort of instinctive killing motion. Maybe he had seen it done that way in a movie. He felt his own heart pumping hard. But forget about all of that now; he needed to find the letter!

He shuffled through the papers on the desk, but it wasn't there. He pulled drawers open with such force that they detached from the desk and dropped onto the professor's body. He had panicked and killed the man before getting what he came for! He couldn't focus his mind. He bashed his head again.

The attacker pushed the chair out of the way, rolling the professor onto his back. He couldn't move within the cramped office space. "Calm down," he thought, "calm down!"

Bending over the body, he felt for anything in the pockets. He felt something and pulled the sweater up. And there it was! He grabbed the bloodied paper from the professor's pocket so frantically that it ripped into two pieces. The knife had sliced through the paper, and the blood had made it unreadable.

Was this what he had come for, that he had killed for? He thought so, but he couldn't read it. There was too much blood. Then he saw the name at the bottom, Franz. He knew that it was the letter and that he had to get out of there—now!

He pushed the letter into his pocket and pulled the mask down over his head. He ran out into the dark corridor, sprinting the down the long hallway to the door illuminated by the exit sign. As he pulled the door open, he caught a glimpse of light coming from behind him. Someone had entered the hall from the other end. He had to make it out fast!

He flew down the stairs. He knew who was trying to stop him, but that wasn't going to happen; he was in control now. He skipped two and three steps at a time hanging onto the handrail for support and momentum. He had never felt so high.

His heart pounded like a war drum inside his chest. He felt invincible. He swung around the last corner to see the door leading outside. With arms outstretched, he pushed against the bar and sped into the crisp night air.

Albert Schmidt stood before the open door of Dr. Altmeyer's office, looking down at his bloodied body. "Oh my God! What has Egon done!" Albert turned and ran from the building.

4

Berlin, Germany, 1936

"Hello Papa." Monica entered her father's study, stopping at the gilt-framed mirror to the right of the door. She played with stray hairs, then smoothed her hands across her stomach, turning slightly to admire her figure in her new tennis costume.

"Monica, what are you so cheerful about?"

"I'm in love, Papa."

Now at his side, her father didn't move or interrupt his work. In a rare show of affection, she gripped the broad frame of his uniform.

"Who is it this time?" He never kept track of the young men his daughter brought home. In fact, he had met but a few of them.

Monica left her father's side. She ran her fingers along the mahogany shelves that lined the walls of the stylish room. At the window she cast her eyes down upon the busy Berlin street, yet the activity didn't draw her attention; she was preoccupied with her own thoughts.

She looked at her father to see his reaction. "I'm going to marry him."

"Has he asked you?" Otto questioned without raising his eyes or lifting pen from paper.

"No! He doesn't know he wants to yet."

"Come here, Monica." He stood up. "How can you be so sure of yourself?"

Monica didn't move from the window, so he walked to her. "I wish I had your determination when I was your age." He joined her in gazing out the window, realizing that his statement was ridiculous. When he was young, the world was embroiled in the Great War. His only resolve then had been to survive.

Before the war Otto von Rutler was in university and exempt from conscription. His father was in the munitions industry, employed by Deutsche Waffen und Munitionsfabriken (DWM) to oversee the production of the MG09 machine gun for the German Army. Otto had interned with his father while in school and was considering a career at DWM. Life was good.

But in the summer of 1914, his father appeared at Otto's school without notice demanding he enlist in the army without delay. An imperialistic arms race had been in play for years, and most of Europe believed war was inevitable. With DWM's connections to high-ranking military officials, Otto's father could all but ensure him a position with rank and a non-combat assignment should war come. Otto was reluctant, but his father was insistent and would not take no for an answer. He frightened Otto; a week later Otto capitulated and signed up.

Within weeks Germany was at war, and Otto was training conscripts in everything from how to drive a military vehicle to the use of a variety of weapons. As more men were needed, older Germans were brought in to do the training, and Otto moved into a supervisory role for the duration of the war.

Every person deployed in the war effort, from supply clerks, to nurses, to the soldiers on the frontline, regardless of nationality, lost authority over every aspect of their lives. Otto appreciated how his father's foresight had landed him in the best possible position; he would learn what he could and make the best of his situation.

He concluded that a career at DWM would be a wise choice. Believing the war would clearly position Germany as a major power, and under the tutelage of his father, he would have a successful career and a rewarding life. Otto's assignment kept him away from the brutality of the battlefield, which fostered this optimistic view for his future.

But none of that happened. Germany lost the Great War, one of the deadliest conflicts in human history. And the deaths continued long after the fighting ended. From the armistice in November 1918 through the signing of the peace treaty in June 1919, the naval blockade of Germany, already in place at the end of the war, continued to isolate the German economy and the German people. It was months before Allied ships were allowed to deliver humanitarian aid. This delay prolonged the suffering of the population; disease and starvation threatened the entire nation.

Otto's father was a casualty of that period. He died from a wound to his leg, incurred as he tried to navigate rubble in the streets of Berlin. He had no access to antibiotics. It was a tragic accident that should never have happened.

The arms restrictions placed on Germany after 1918 had companies like DWM scrambling to stay solvent. Without his father there to guide his career, Otto had no opportunity for a job in the arms industry. He took the path of necessity.

Otto never went back to university to finish his education. Instead, he found work as a laborer in Berlin. His priority was to care for his grieving mother, who was now destitute. But just as he had become a capable manager in the army, he rose quickly through the ranks of peacetime construction.

Otto prospered as the construction industry flourished. He married a fashionable woman, and a year later his daughter, Monica, was born. Unfortunately, Otto married in haste. The war itself forced most women to postpone marriage. At the same time, eligible men were dying in huge numbers. When the long-awaited peace arrived, it played matchmaker to unlikely couples. Otto quickly discovered he had little in common with his beautiful bride.

By 1925, Germany's economic woes turned into a boom. During *Goldene Zwanziger* or Golden Twenties, the country experienced an exhilarating period of financial stability similar to the Roaring Twenties occurring in the United States. The Greater Berlin

Act of 1920 expanded the geographical foot-print of Berlin, making it one of the largest municipalities in the world. It was easy for Otto to immerse himself in his work and ignore his wife.

She shared the unspoken acknowledgement of their mismatched marriage. Since love was not to be, she was content to raise her child alone with a husband who did little more than fund the household. They went through the motions of being husband and wife without ever revealing any problem in their relationship. Her husband's detachment, however, gave her independence. Their lives were separate but equal, a rare marital division for German women at that time.

As Hitler came to power in the 1930s, Otto saw even more opportunities for his career. He joined the Nazi Party. When Hitler announced his master plan of urban transformation, the Führerstadt, Otto reenlisted in the army and became a liaison between private construction companies and the Führerstadt projects. He was now poised to reach the pinnacle of his career.

During this time, Otto's wife fashioned a role for herself that benefited his career. As an attractive spouse, she enthusiastically supported him at social events. While this added a new dimension to their marriage, it was more of an intellectual affiliation than an affectionate bonding.

In Monica, Otto saw the mirror image of her mother. It was a constant reminder that his beautiful bride was the wife he was unable to love. It disturbed him to have his daughter stir such feelings, so he simply kept his distance. But as Monica now talked of marriage, he realized she would soon be out of his house to live her own life, and he wanted a different type of marriage for his daughter.

"Well," he fixed his eyes on hers, "perhaps I should meet this man of yours." In another rare sign of tenderness between them, Otto wiped a hair from her forehead. "My dear, you are just seventeen years of age with your whole life in front of you. You have time to pick a man that will make you happy and give you a good life. There is no rush to marry at your age."

"But there is a rush. A huge rush! I have so many plans. I don't want to wait to see what life brings me. I want to make my life happen, the way I want it to, and I want it to happen now."

To Monica, her father was a commanding figure, larger than life in the uniform he always wore. There were no casual days at the von Rutler home. Otto worked for Germany seven days a week. She respected that and wanted to marry someone with those same qualities. She never once suspected her parents were not deeply in love. She wanted the life she believed they lived.

Otto was uncomfortable with intimacy, and he found even these "chats" with his daughter more than difficult. It was a relief that his marriage had produced no other children. Not even a son would have been welcomed. He thought he should ask Monica to tell him about her young man, but he remained silent.

As Monica walked to the door, her voice took on a serious tone, causing Otto to turn. "My man, his name is Franz. He's coming to dinner tonight. You know Mother's friend Gertrude? Franz is her son. He has just graduated from university." She left the room shouting from the hallway, "He was first in his class! You'll love him." She used these theatrics to entertain her father. It was a game she had learned as a child and as she grew older, she couldn't stop. It was their only form of communication.

Monica went off to her tennis lesson where she dutifully hit the ball for an hour, trying hard not to exert herself. She then spent three hours at lunch with friends. Her social circle was comprised of daughters of Nazi Party officials like her father.

Monica and her friends were all taught from an early age that a proper German woman should marry young to a diligent, hardworking German. Her task would be to clean his home and bear his children. Monica's circle saw this as an exciting future.

Many German women once held important jobs in medicine, law, and education, but by the mid-1930s it was rare for a woman to hold any of those positions. Women had been systematically cut from the workforce; the indoctrination of new societal norms had taken hold.

Although not political *per se*, Monica believed she was the only one of her friends to fully understand the Nazi vision of Germany. They were all good Germans, but she was fixated on Hitler. She once paraphrased his vision: The ideal world will come once the racially superior people govern and the lower races restrict their activities accordingly.

Monica focused that day's lunch conversation on what she elatedly called "her" party to be held that evening. She intended to stun everyone: Her classic

Aryan features would be exquisitely set off by the black dress she had purchased for the occasion. In keeping with the fashion of the day, it had a military look, with a fitted bodice adorned with two rows of brass buttons and a sleek skirt that ended just below the knee. She would look mature and sophisticated. It was a fashion statement to demonstrate to Franz and her father that she was old enough and ready to marry.

Despite Monica's aim to make the party about her, it wasn't. It was a long-planned dinner to bring four Americans closer to a business deal with Otto. Monica's mother chose to include Franz that night in a calculated move to showcase the superiority of Germany's next generation. Surely the Americans would invest their money in a country with such a bright future.

This was tricky because America's economic boom during the Roaring Twenties had ended with the stock market crash in 1929. By the time of "Monica's" dinner party, America and the rest of Europe were in the depths of the depression. Yet Germany was still building and building big. Investment capital from America continued to flow into the country, but cash was scarce, and both Otto and his wife were well aware of how she could advance each of her husband's business transactions.

American men were easy to flirt with. They were caught up in Olympic fever, clean streets, and the proverbial trains that ran on time. Most German women had relinquished any role in business, but Otto's wife liked being a participant at the table. She was well versed on current events and instinctively knew the art of conversation with ambitious men. Most importantly, she knew to avoid topics concerning certain changes in German society. As always, she meddled in her husband's business whenever the stakes were high and the outcome in doubt.

Germans like von Rutler were seduced by the growth of the country under Nazism. Their belief that Germany was unfairly treated after the Great War helped Hitler spark an electric atmosphere of German socialistic nationalism. For the industrialists, each contract fed on the next, and the sky seemed the limit. Otto was happy to seat Monica and Franz at the table to underscore just how blue the German sky would be for American investors.

On the way to the dinner, Franz received careful instructions. "Yes, Mother, I have heard this all many times." His voice became irritated. "You don't have to worry. I will mention nothing of our past life." He threw his hands in the air. "As far as the world will ever know, I was born at the age of seventeen, when we arrived in Berlin." He looked out the taxi window, believing no one would have reason to check into their past.

"Don't joke with me, Franz. Of course you can have a history prior to Berlin. Just let there be no doubt that there are topics that can never be talked about. Monica's father is an important man to know. Never feel close enough to anyone to share our family secret. No one must know! Do you understand me? That includes Monica. You are a man now, I needed to say it one last time."

Not waiting for a response, her voice and expression changed in an instant. She smiled and patted her son's knee. "But don't be shy about your accomplishments. Monica's father needs to hear about your ideas and ambitions." She hesitated, "If von Rutler likes you, he could introduce you to all the right people, even bring you into a government job." She continued, "A young architect would do well with our government. Just think about the grand projects you could be part of. Germany is changing, Franz, and you could create a name for yourself.

"I think you were born at just the right time in history," Gertrude continued, speaking as if she were jealous of his future. "Think of how wonderful your life will be. I'm proud of what we have achieved since leaving Tübingen. There would have been only one job for you there, and now, here in Berlin, you are positioned for a great career... and with Monica at your side, well I don't have to tell you how happy that would make me."

Tired of listening to his mother, Franz rolled down the window for air. But the exhaust fumes from the city street were as irritating as his mother's conversation. The odor compelled him to roll the window back up. "Mother, you act as though Monica and I are to be wed." He looked at her. "You seem to be forgetting something," he tilted his head to look directly into her eyes, "I haven't asked her, and I don't know if I will." He paused and softened his voice as if talking to himself. "Or if she would say yes."

Gertrude heard him. "Of course she will say yes," she said confidently. "You will wed." His mother patted his knee, "She adores you."

THE TRAP

Gertrude was a handsome woman, but was not particularly feminine. She was tall and slender, and even as an older woman she still wore clothes like a fashion model. She looked ethnically German with blonde hair and bright blue eyes. Her son did not share her Aryan appearance, and it had concerned her as she watched him grow through his teenage years.

Franz favored his father. He had a dark olive complexion and thick black hair that required ample tonic to hold it in place. Thankfully his eyes were blue, albeit pale, more gray than blue. The combination of dark hair with light eyes was quite acceptable, whereas people with dark hair and dark eyes had a difficult time under the current Nazi belief in Aryan supremacy.

Franz hadn't known Monica long, perhaps six months, maybe less. However, Gertrude knew her well enough. Not because they had spent much time together; in truth, they hadn't. It was because they seemed cut from the same cloth. She knew the type of wife Monica would be, and she believed Franz needed someone like Monica to propel him into a successful career. Above all Gertrude wanted her son to be prosperous. As a widow, it had been a challenge for Gertrude to raise Franz and see him through a university education. They survived on a meager benefaction from a sympathetic cousin in Austria.

Over the course of the next decade Franz would realize how much his mother and then Monica had directed him in ways to support their own ambitions. He had allowed the manipulation: First, to have a peaceful life with his mother, then, for a peaceful life with his wife. He had permitted himself to be guided down a certain path, but once on that path, he was determined to succeed at all costs. In the end, he would pay dearly for those choices.

The taxi pulled up in front of the von Rutler townhouse. Franz looked up at the stately Baroque façade and the elaborate entryway. He thought he caught a glimpse of Monica pass by a window. Glancing back into the taxi, he watched his mother check her face in her compact mirror. She powdered her nose and reapplied her lipstick. He smiled at her as she tucked a loose hair behind her ear, "Let's go Mother, we don't want to be late."

What Franz couldn't foresee on that festive evening in 1936 was just how far he would stray from his vision of his career. He was an artist in his heart. He displayed his artistry in his elegant penmanship every time he attended to his correspondence. He chose a career in architecture to bring beauty, efficiency, and balance to structures that would enhance the lives of the German people.

He believed that the job of an architect should be nonpolitical. But it suddenly occurred to him that if, as his mother suggested, he took a position with the government, he might have to join the Nazi Party. Would they allow anything to be nonpolitical? No, everything about the Nazis was political.

5

Death Links Disparate Lives

Like Albert, Helga was the child of a Nazi officer, but unlike Albert and her son, she thought nothing of politics. She was born during the war that killed her father and five other family members. To Helga, the word Nazi represented death and destruction. She wanted no part of it.

Albert had joined the university within a few years of their marriage. At the time, Helga thought she had a perfect life as a professor's wife, as baby Egon's mother, and Frau of a country estate that was purchased with an inheritance she brought to their marriage. It was a time when women of means made a career of their social obligations, and she found her position in life ideal.

But, when problems with Egon surfaced, everything changed and she became reclusive. Obsessed with Egon, mother and son stayed alone in their home. One by one she dropped her outside activities as her son's illness progressed. Even the local grocer began delivering food and household supplies each week. In recent years, she had rarely left the house at all. It was during this time that Albert moved to the bedroom next to his study.

When they stopped sleeping together, she was sure he sought the company of other women. Little did she know that it had started years before. He wasn't what you'd call a "catch" for an extramarital affair, but she thought he could surely find a woman in need of anonymous companionship from time to time. Just recently she suspected that he might have found a woman who wanted more.

To make up for her loss of intimacy, Helga took to drink. She drank alone, since that's how she now spent all of her time. Egon stayed to himself, and when Albert did come home, he brought meals in with him and rarely came out of his private rooms.

By that time, Helga's only companion was a local woman who came in to clean twice a week. When she arrived and found Helga in a drunken stupor, she called the doctor. Helga let her go.

Even during periods of sobriety, Helga refused to seek help. Albert denied any responsibility and even declined the doctor's calls. Unlike Albert, Helga always felt responsible for the way Egon turned out. That burden of guilt became a heavy load for a mother to bear.

When Albert arrived back at the house after his frantic call to Helga regarding Egon's whereabouts, he went straight up the back staircase into his son's rooms. Helga heard him come in and ran behind begging him to tell her what was happening. "He's my son Albert. Please talk to me." It was obvious she'd been drinking; Albert ignored her condition.

Swastikas, Nazi paraphernalia, pictures of Hitler, and other heroes of the Third Reich covered the walls of Egon's rooms. This was the first time Albert had been in his son's quarters. The display neither surprised nor disgusted him. "Get all this stuff the hell off the walls and burn it."

"Albert!" she was crying. "Please talk to me!"

"Burn it! Then we'll talk. I want everything gone."

Like an obedient soldier she followed his orders.

Albert walked down to his study, his sanctuary. He closed the door and with his hand still on the knob behind him, leaned back against the door as if it could block out the turmoil he faced.

He stared at the chair where Egon had sat the day before, listening to Dr. Altmeyer on the speaker phone discuss the Eastwood woman's letter.

Albert told Altmeyer that he had an interest in the letter and would send an associate to pick it up the following morning. He also agreed to meet with the women later that next day, just after their planned meeting with Dr. Altmeyer.

When that conversation ended, Albert called Horst Wilhelm and asked him to go to the university to pick up the letter. Horst was a long-time friend and a member of Albert's group. He was someone Albert trusted and could depend on.

Hearing his father ask Horst to do the job, Egon went wild. They argued. Egon cursed his father for his lack of confidence in him as his research assistant. It was true.

It had come to a head a few weeks prior when Egon had edited an article written by his father and then published it under his own name. "This is not your work, Egon." Albert had thrown the pamphlets at him. "This is my work. You have no right to it." His eyes flared. "Know your place. You're only here because nobody knows what to do with you. Try this again and I won't care what happens to you. Do you understand me? You'll never set foot in my office again." Members of the research group witnessed the argument.

Oddly, Egon left his father's office that day with a feeling of superiority. He believed his father ignorant compared to his own brilliance. He believed he didn't need any of these people any longer.

Egon knew the day would come when he would break from his parents. In preparation, he'd been stealing from his mother for years. When he couldn't grab her cash, he took silver and gold items from the house and turned them into cash. He had thousands of Deutsche Marks stashed away. If he had to leave now, so be it.

Albert fought back exhaustion. He had searched for his son most of the night before. There were only a few places he thought Egon might go. When he couldn't find him, he parked outside the Augsburg cottage just in case Egon showed up. He didn't want more violence.

Albert wasn't a vicious man, but he had strong convictions and dogged determination. One might have believed he was desperate to find Egon because he was his own flesh and blood. But in reality, Albert had to find his son to save his own reputation and his own future. Egon could destroy him, and Albert would do anything to keep that from happening.

Albert thought about all of this as he leaned against the door of his study until he felt the weight of someone pushing from the other side.

"Albert!" Helga cried out.

He listened. He knew he would have to let her in and talk to her. He dreaded the conversation but couldn't put it off any longer. He let go of the doorknob as he walked forward. Helga came into the study and followed him through to his bedroom. He asked her to sit. "Helga," he tried to remain calm, "I believe Egon has killed a man."

He could smell alcohol on her breath. He was unaware of when she became an alcoholic. He just knew she was one. He wanted to be civil, even show kindness toward her. But as the words came out of his mouth, he couldn't help himself. It wasn't in his nature to be kind or calm; he held nothing back. She showed no emotion as he spoke.

"Egon is insane," he yelled, "and if it weren't for your miserable whining, I would have committed him to an institution years ago." He walked about as he spoke, throwing a suitcase on the bed and tossing clothes inside. "Now a man is dead." He glared at her. "Dr. Altmeyer at the university is dead because of you and your stupid doctors!"

She sat with her back straight upright in the wooden chair, without crying or speaking. It was as if she hadn't heard a word he said. She kept smoothing the hem of her skirt across her knee.

"I'm going after him, and God help him when I find him." He closed the case and picked it up. "I don't know when I'll be back. Why don't you go to your sister's?" He didn't expect an answer.

"Did you go to Galiena last night?" Helga asked, with a tremor in her voice. "I'm not stupid, you know. I have known about Galiena for some time."

"Do you not hear me, woman? Egon has killed a man! Why are you concerned about Galiena now?"

"Suddenly it matters I guess; I want to know if you went to her last night instead of coming home."

"No, I did not. I was looking for your son to stop more violence. Galiena should be the least of your concerns." Suddenly, Albert felt light-headed. He couldn't seem to bring enough air into his lungs. He stood still momentarily as the feeling passed. He cursed Egon for causing him such stress.

"Are you going to kill Egon?" Helga questioned calmly.

"I've got to find him before the police do! I've got to salvage what will be left of my life! My career! He's just destroyed everything!" Albert walked to the door.

Helga hadn't moved the whole time and now sat facing in the opposite direction from where Albert stood.

"I don't know what I'll do to Egon," he said. "I just know I've got to find him. The police will come. I don't know what evidence they'll have, but sooner or later they'll be here." There was a pause; Albert held his chest again. "I don't care what the hell you tell them." He walked out, looking back over his shoulder. "I'm taking files from my library, and then I'll be gone. If you haven't already burned all of Egon's belongings, do it now. I want everything connected with that monster destroyed before the police arrive. At least that will give me time to find him before they do."

Albert didn't care about the police finding the content of his research library. He'd taken a few boxes of special files, but there was nothing they could read that would bother him.

Helga sat in the chair in Albert's makeshift bedroom for the longest time. She didn't cry. She just sat. The booze caused her thoughts to spin around inside her head. They were the memories of her life, her husband, and her son. Her thoughts drifted back to her own childhood after the war. Her mother had remarried. Her stepfather was a man of means and growing up with her sister was a happy time. She was quite distant from her sister now; they hadn't spoken in years, but nothing unpleasant entered her mind.

Helga pictured two teenage girls laughing and joking on the lawn of their stepfather's home. They lived in the country with several horses and ponies. They would jump on the backs of the ponies and chat about school, or friends, or make up stories as the ponies grazed in the field.

Then Helga remembered holding Egon for the first time. She thought how proud Albert had been of his young son. They had made so many plans in the years following his birth. But now she couldn't remember what any of those plans were.

She felt herself running her hand over the hem of her skirt again and again. It wouldn't lie flat across her knee. When she was at school, the teacher made all the girls sit and straighten their skirts across their knees, tucking the loose material beneath their legs.

"That's the way young ladies do it," said the teacher But today the skirt she wore wouldn't lie flat. She wanted someone to help her. Her hands trembled. The schoolteacher would be so upset by what had become of her, she supposed. She tried to quiet her mind to all these thoughts.

In robotic fashion, she stood up and went back to Egon's rooms. She gathered up his few remaining possessions—the local newspaper, a *Musikmarkt* magazine, some items of clothing, all things that carried no symbolic meaning, just ordinary things found in any son's room. But it didn't matter; she knew Egon wasn't coming back.

Helga collected them all and carried them down to the incinerator behind the garage. She walked by the spot where Egon had killed his puppy. She hadn't thought about it in years but now wondered if telling someone would have made a difference.

The first load she had brought down was now reduced to red ash in the bottom of the incinerator. She filled the bin again; it ignited the moment she placed the lid on top. She felt the warmth on her legs. Her job was done.

"Destroy everything connected to that monster," she muttered under her breath. She thought Albert was the real monster. She wondered if he wanted to marry Galiena. She thought nothing of Altmeyer. She was self-absorbed in what had happened to her life.

She stumbled back into the kitchen and picked up the bottle of gin from the counter. Albert was gone. She had heard his car leave when she was at the incinerator.

Helga sat at the table and drank as she did most days. The first time Egon ran away she tried to drink herself to death, but she only managed to break her arm falling down the five stairs leading to the garage. She didn't want to go through that again. Albert raged like she'd never seen him before. "Oh, Egon, what have you done? I can't protect you anymore."

She walked to the dining room and took a Steuben goblet from the china cabinet. Tucking the gin under her arm she walked out to the garage. She opened the door to her Mercedes, slipped inside and started the motor. The CD played *Romance* from Shostakovich's *The Gadfly*. The music calmed her mood: She drank and closed her mind to any more thought. She couldn't endure any more thought. As fumes swirled around the garage, some seeped through a slight opening in the car window. Helga took a deep breath like someone craving a cigarette and sensing second-hand smoke in the air. She said, "Yes, Albert, I have gotten rid of everything for you." She willed all energy to drain from her body.

Egon drove for hours when he left the university after killing Dr. Altmeyer. He had no destination. He just turned from one road to another. His head felt as if it was clamped in a vise. The pain would have stopped another driver, but Egon had learned to live with the pain and he continued on.

His mother had purchased the vehicle for him years earlier, since she was often inebriated and couldn't drive him to his doctor's appointments.

Egon chose a utility van and put a mattress in the back, telling his mother it gave him a place to rest and relax when his mind became overactive. He never bothered to get a driver's license.

But now the van was old and had never been properly maintained. The shocks and brakes were bad. Egon's head pain and his fatigue further compromised his ability to keep the van straight in the lane.

To avoid main thoroughfares, he was navigating dark and narrow country roads. Still, he continued on dangerously fast. He was incapable of making a connection between the poor condition of the van and the speed at which he was traveling. He shifted between hard on the gas or hard on the brake. There was never a middle ground for Egon in any aspect of his life.

It was past midnight when his mind reeled back through the events of the last day. He repeatedly banged his forehand on the steering wheel when his brain activity overwhelmed his thinking process. He drove himself like he drove the van—full on despite a defective system.

Killing Altmeyer was a mistake. Egon didn't know how it happened. When he was in the office, he became confused. He wanted to show the man the knife, so he would give him the letter. Then the man was dead.

Egon couldn't feel real remorse even though he recognized that the killing wasn't helpful to his cause. As his mind fixated on his mistake, he felt the right-side tires hit debris on the rocky shoulder of the road. He yanked the wheel to the left and, as the van steadied on the road, he banged his forehead against the steering wheel again. "Focus," he told himself, "focus."

Egon found a place to pull the van off the road. He backed into the woods out of sight from passing cars. He had to think what to do next. There had been no plan to kill the professor. There was no plan at all. But now he knew he needed to concentrate on the letter he had snatched from the professor's pocket.

He climbed into the back of the van and flopped on the mattress. Lying flat made him nauseous as the van's interior spun inside his head like a hallucination. He opened the sliding door on the side of the van, hanging his head out to vomit. It was cold outside. Barely able to pull himself back into the van, he wrapped a blanket around his shoulders and leaned against the cold hard frame of the vehicle. He fell asleep from sheer exhaustion and slept through most of the next morning. He woke about the time his mother climbed into her car in the garage.

Alana and Marta saw the police cars as they pulled into the parking lot at the university. They had talked the whole drive over and hadn't turned on the car radio to hear the news: Professor found murdered at local university.

They got out of the car and walked toward the building where Dr. Altmeyer had his office. They saw that the police were turning people away.

"Was ist passiert?" Marta asked a student as she passed.

"Es gab einen Mord. Mehr weiss ich nicht." The young woman kept right on walking.

They continued toward the building when Marta recognized a student; again she asked, "Weisst Du wer ermordet wurde?"

"Marta, es war Herr Altmeyer!" the woman cried. "Er wurde erstochen." She pointed to a police car with the doors open. "Kathrina fand die Leiche."

Marta looked to see Kathrina in the back seat of the police car talking to a policewoman.

"Oh mein Gott, Alana. What should we do? Someone has murdered Professor Altmeyer! My friend Kathrina found his body!"

"Come on, let's get out of here." Alana shouted.

"But die Polizei, we should talk to them. We should tell them about the letter, right?"

"I don't know." She grabbed Marta's arm and pulled her back to the car. "I've got to think."

They sat in the car watching the activity. Marta saw a friend and called out to him. "Stefan."

"Marta, isn't it crazy that someone would kill Dr. Altmeyer?"

"Do you have time to talk to us?" Marta asked.

"Sure." He climbed into the backseat of Kirk's Mercedes. "But I have little information. All I know is that Kathrina was to meet with Dr. Altmeyer and saw his body on the floor."

"We met with Dr. Altmeyer yesterday and we were coming back to see him again today." Marta looked over to Alana, "Stefan, this is my friend from America Alana Eastwood."

"Hallo." Stefan smiled at her.

Alana nodded her head.

"We expected Dr. Altmeyer to introduce us to Dr. Schmidt." Marta asked, "Do you know him?"

"Ja," Stefan leaned back, "he's a fucking idiot."

"Ja, I thought you were a history major so you would have taken classes from him."

"He's a descent teacher but not a good person. What do you want with him?"

Alana interjected, "I have an old letter that we wanted to show him. It concerns something that happened during World War II. Professor Altmeyer said Herr Schmidt had the expertise to help us."

"Expertise? The guy is a Nazi! He has a whole group of Nazis writing propaganda outta some big freakin' mansion in the country. They all think it's a secret, but everyone knows what they are up to." Stefan spoke with anxiety in his voice. "All history majors have to take Schmidt's classes because nobody else teaches them. But it's appalling that we have to even talk to him."

"I did not know any of that." Marta said with surprise. "You hear stories about people like that, but I knew nothing about neo-Nazis here on our campus."

"Don't you remember the rally in town a couple years ago? It was a small group. People like Schmidt don't show their faces because they want to keep their jobs. But these rallies do happen. Schmidt's propaganda comes out under a pseudonym, and the university looks the other way.

"Look, we will study the rise and fall of Nazism forever. You know after the war most ex-Nazi Party members accepted the reality of defeat and showed no interest in promoting neo-Nazism as a political party—even if they still held personal convictions for the philosophy. All but a few of those people are dead now. Those still alive are too old to cause any problem.

"People continue to join the cause for Nazism in countries all over the world. Why anyone wants to stir that crap up again is beyond me. If you look at our grandparents who were of age during the war, who fought in the war, only a minority ever believed in true Nazism. They were just demoralized after the resolution of the first war and got caught up in the events of the day.

"They wanted a better life. But nobody wanted the outrageous actions of the Nazis or the horror of the Holocaust. I know it devastated my grandparents; remorse hung over them the rest of their lives. It can never happen again.

"Nevertheless, a few sick people have picked up those disgraced political views and now garner about 1 percent of the electorate in each election cycle. But that is not what the other 99 percent of people think. I'm sorry. I know I get carried away when I talk about people like Schmidt." Stefan flopped back into the car seat. "I'll shut up now. I just hope Schmidt had nothing to do with Altmeyer's murder. That would be a stretch even for me to believe. I doubt he's a killer, but regardless, I don't want any disgrace brought to our college."

"I'm glad to talk with you Stefan. We worried the professor's death might have had something to do with our meeting with him yesterday," Alana said.

"You see, the letter I have may concern those 1 percent views you mention and why he wanted us to talk with Schmidt."

"But I don't think Dr. Altmeyer knew Schmidt was a Nazi." Marta said.

"Marta, everybody knows." Stefan said firmly.

Alana just sat quietly, taking in the conversation.

Stefan continued, "Here's how Schmidt and the others around the world like him are successful: By the late eighties, when it was clear that neo-Nazi views held no widespread appeal, they purposefully aligned themselves with mainstream groups on both the left and right of the political spectrum. They wanted to find impressionable people that they could hook into a small piece of their ideology.

"The organizations they target are diverse—everything from Christian congregates to ecological organizations. Take environmentalists for example: Nazis are against foreigners, but if you rebrand that as opposing foreign-owned mines that are polluting any particular country's eco-system, all of a sudden you get an awful lot of environmentalists listening to you. A certain number of them will follow you to another level of distorted nationalism. Don't get me wrong, there is nothing wrong in having pride in your country or wanting policies that benefit its citizens over citizens of other countries. But these folks twist definitions to suit their own political needs."

"Yes, I know what you mean, because every now and then you hear similar things in the American news as well," Alana confirmed. "The Klu Klux Klan will have a rally. It's difficult to believe anyone holds those racist views, but like you say, it is that tiny percentage of the population that does, and then they prey on others to expand their reach. I guess for some it becomes a cult-like following."

"Right," Stefan continued. "Schmidt's writing denies the Holocaust. They have to do that because otherwise they'd lose any sane person in a heartbeat.

"They claim no documentation exists that shows Hitler ordered or even knew of any mass killings. They also claim the numbers of deaths have been distorted and that what we are told were gas chambers actually served other purposes. Numbers are easy to manipulate; they claim that tests within the buildings said to be gas chambers have shown no traces of cyanide.

"I could go on but you get the picture. It's easy to cause impressionable people to question if anything governments tell them is true. No one fully trusts people in authority, and that's what allows these creepy individuals to do what they do. Luckily, their numbers haven't increased, and I really doubt they ever will. People are not stupid… 99 percent of them, anyway."

"Thanks for talking with us, Stefan. You've given me a lot to think about."

"Sure, bye-bye. I want to catch up with my friend Kathrina." Stefan left the car but looked back through Marta's open window and said, "You know another thing about the war that is of interest—what happened to all the looted wealth? The gold, hard currency, artwork, and the like—it has never been found… not all of it.

"Maybe not Schmidt, but perhaps others like him are, in effect, treasure hunters. As they say, follow the money! Think about it. They get 1 percent of the population through grassroots operations at little cost. What if people like Schmidt had great wealth backing them? The Nazi Party took over Germany with the backing of just 30 percent of the German people, and I would say many of that number were coerced. Could it happen again with financing from an untold treasure?

"I'm not saying treasurer hunters hold Nazi views, that would be preposterous... but some might. It's something to ponder."

Alana thought about the feeling she got when she first touched the letter. What was the letter telling her? Was the warning from Franz a cry for humanity or could it be, as Stefan proposes, about the spoils of war? She was in the driver's seat and, without a word, she turned the key and backed the car onto the road.

"Where are we going?" Marta asked.

"Back to the cottage." She looked over at Marta. "What would we tell the police? We don't know that the doctor's death has anything to do with the letter. We may be overreacting. Let's hear the news report. We just don't know."

Alana drove recklessly back to the cottage. She jammed the gear shift at every turn and came off the clutch fast. Marta just stared out the window. When they arrived in their village, Marta jumped out and bought a newspaper while Alana kept the motor running.

She read aloud in German as the car pressed up the hill to the cottage. Then she looked at Alana and repeated in English. "There was no apparent reason for the killing. Anyone with any information should contact the police immediately."

Inside the cottage, they sat at the kitchen table and read the full report, which included a hotline number to call. "Alana, I know he was your grandfather and maybe the letter is your property, but I am involved too. I think we should call the police."

Alana got up and walked over to the phone, folding the paper so she could hold it easily in one hand as she reluctantly keyed in the number for the police station. She held the phone out to Marta. "Perhaps you should talk to them or ask for someone who speaks English well."

Because the women had met with Dr. Altmeyer and had another meeting scheduled for that morning, the police elevated the call to a high level. Within a few hours, the police arrived at the cottage to question them.

Alana opened the door to see two detectives, a man and a woman. They had their badges ready for her. "Inspektor Stark," the woman said, "und das ist Detektiv Brandt. Können wir reinkommen?"

"Ja, sicher. Sprechen Sie Englisch?" Alana stood to the side and gestured them to enter.

Inspector Stark was a tall and somewhat heavy woman in her early-to-mid-forties; she had the hard look of a veteran crime fighter. The detective was a good-looking young man in his late twenties with an athletic build. They both seemed to fit the stereotype for their presumed years on the force.

Alana took them into the sitting room. "Would you like tea or coffee?" They both declined anything to drink, so she immediately began reciting the events as though she had practiced the lines for a play.

"May I speak English?"

"Of course."

"My name is Alana Eastwood. I arrived here last month to visit my grandfather who had taken ill."

She introduced Marta at the appropriate place. No one interrupted her as she gave a nearly flawless rendition of finding the letter and taking it to Dr. Altmeyer the day before and learning of Dr. Schmidt as someone who might help them understand it. Her training at the bank as well as her artist's eye made her keenly aware of every detail.

As Alana spoke, Detective Brandt wrote details in his notebook. Inspector Stark observed her intently. When she came to speak of the letter, Alana handed the inspector a copy that she had rewritten just before they arrived. Her recount ended with Marta Voss persuading her to phone the police when they arrived home. "But I really don't know how this could have any relevance to Dr. Altmeyer's murder. How could it? It's a mysterious letter, yes, but no one knew about it.

"We called Dr. Altmeyer's office before we left for the university this morning. When there was no answer, we decided to just drive over. We don't know if he ever talked to Dr. Schmidt."

"Well, thank you, Ms. Eastwood. We don't often meet someone with such precise recall. The letter is intriguing. But, as you say, no one knew about it.

Still, you did right to call us." Inspector Stark looked at Marta, "Do you have anything to add?"

"No Inspector, I don't." Hesitating to muster the nerve to contradict her friend, "except, who would kill the professor if it wasn't to do with the letter? Nothing makes any sense. He was just a nice man who taught business classes at the college. Who would want to kill him?" Marta asked.

Stark looked back at Alana. "We will be in touch." Hearing those words, the detective stood up and inserted his pad and pen in the inside breast pocket of his stylish jacket. The jacket looked posh for a detective's wage. Alana always observed details.

Listening to Marta challenge her view, asking who would want to kill the professor, if not for the letter, made her rethink her position.

"Inspector," Alana asked, "did the police find my letter in Dr. Altmeyer's office? We left the original letter with him so it should be there. I would like to have it back."

"I don't have an inventory of the office yet. Our investigation is still in its early stages. If we find the letter, you can have it back when the investigation is over."

Alana watched their car drive off down the hill and out of sight.

"They didn't seem too concerned," Alana said as she walked back into the sitting room.

"You can never tell with the police," Marta added. "They never let anything show."

Inspector Stark checked her watch. "Drop me off in town. I've got to do some errands. Get yourself some lunch. Then we'll pay a visit to this Dr. Schmidt and see if the American's story checks out."

It was several hours before they returned to the university. They went up to the crime scene to check on the forensic team. "Oh, by the way," Stark asked, "did you come across any letter? It would look old, dating back to 1945 or sometime around then. It would be one handwritten page."

"No, I haven't seen anything like that in here." The officer turned to see if the medical examiner had left. "But, it's funny you mention that, because the ME said there were fragments of paper on the shirt around the wound. No paper in the pocket though, so he asked us to look for a torn piece of paper. It would be blood-soaked, not something we'd miss. But we have found nothing."

"Okay, let us know. It may be nothing. It's just something of interest at this point." She turned back, "Who's got a map of the campus?"

One of the other officers said, "I've got it, Stark." He walked over. "Who are you looking for?"

"A Dr. Schmidt, in the History Department."

"Ja, Schmidt. He'd be here," pointing his finger to the map, "This building directly across the courtyard, room 145 Inspector."

They tried to open Dr. Schmidt's door, but found it locked. They knocked with no answer. Brandt called headquarters for Schmidt's home address.

"Did you get an address?"

"I did, but the captain wants us at the station first, they're having a meeting. He's being pressured into holding a press conference this afternoon."

"Christ! Can't they wait until we have something to report?"

"Are you going to tell them about the American woman and the letter?"

"For what?" They hadn't been partnered together long. Brandt irritated her. He had worked for the Bavarian State Police for nearly two years and had already transferred between stations and changed partners twice. "We haven't got our heads around this one yet," She said. "I find it best to keep my mouth shut until I know what I'm talking about."

"But the letter is missing." Brandt didn't expect an answer. Stark remained stolid until she understood where the investigation was headed.

"Marta, how long does it take to drive to Zurich?" Alana asked.

"Oh, about four hours, I guess. I never drive there. You could take the train."

"No, I'd rather drive." Alana couldn't settle, and she couldn't share all of what she was thinking with Marta.

"Why Zurich?"

"Do you remember the professor gave me a business card?"

"Yes, that is right." Marta replied, "You did not say that to the police."

"Well, it didn't seem relevant. But I was thinking I could go there and see what they would make of the letter. Marta, I can't just sit here."

"What about Dr. Schmidt?" It surprised Marta that Alana would want to go to Zurich at this time. Wouldn't she want to hear from the police… see what would happen with the investigation? "Let's call on Dr. Schmidt and see what he tells us."

"No, I want nothing to do with Dr. Schmidt after listening to what your friend Stefan had to say." She sat next to Marta. "Besides, we could leave now and be back tomorrow."

"We? No, not me, Alana, I can not go." Marta shook her head intently.

"Why not! I need you!" She depended on Marta because of the language.

"No, I am concerned about what the police will do. I think I should stay here in case they ask more questions. Besides, I have to see about the apartment tomorrow. If you go, you have to go by yourself."

Alana didn't press further because it was obvious she wouldn't change Marta's mind. Traveling alone would challenge Alana, but she realized Marta was right. Having her stay at the cottage would allow her to be there for the police. She could call Marta to stay abreast on what was happening in Germany.

"I'm going to get ready to leave. I will call you once I am in a hotel. I'll be back tomorrow."

The inspector pulled the car up to the Schmidt's house; there was no answer at the door. The house was large, so Stark decided to walk around to see if someone was in the yard. She sent Brandt in the opposite direction. As she walked past the garage, she heard a motor running. She ran over and pulled open the door.

Covering her nose, she ran to the car. She saw a woman behind the wheel with her head cocked back. She opened the door and reached to turn the engine off. She felt the woman's neck for a pulse. There was none.

Stark coughed her way out of the garage, hanging her head down to catch her breath. Grabbing onto a light post for support, she saw Brandt approach. "Damn meeting! Damn stupid press conference!" she declared, gasping air. "Go public to tell everyone nothing—while this stupid woman is here gassing herself!"

Brandt walked over to the garage holding his handkerchief to his face even though he never went inside.

"Well, what are you staring at?" Stark said.

"Nothing."

"No, you're staring at me and I want to know why!" This wasn't the first time he had shown contempt towards her. She'd let it go before, but it's funny how literally looking death in the face can bring things to a head.

Life wasn't easy for Stark, either personally or professionally. There had been women on the local police force for years, but she was the first with rank. Even so, not all the men in the force treated her as an equal, not even the captain who had encouraged her to take the detective exam and had promoted her. The demands of the profession, many of which were self-imposed, had made it difficult for Stark to have a social life. She now resigned herself to the fact that she had become one of those women married to their job.

"Well, if you must know, the press conference wasn't the only thing that kept us from getting here sooner." Brandt's expression was smug as he looked downward, not at her face.

"Oh, I get it; you're blaming me because I stopped in the village." She walked over to him. "Is that correct?"

"The fact is, you went shopping. If you hadn't, we would have come here before the press conference."

"The fact," she glared into his eyes. "You want facts? Well, the fact is I've logged sixty hours a week for the past month. How many have you logged? The fact is, my parents are celebrating their fiftieth wedding anniversary today. The fact is, I probably won't make it to the party this evening, so the least I could do is drop off a card and a gift when I drive by late tonight."

Brandt said nothing.

"If you think that makes me responsible for this woman snuffing herself, well fine, that's your business. Just don't play all righteous with me, college boy, because we both know you're not in this job for the long haul."

She let it all out: "This is just a stepping stone for you. And it's a good thing too, because I'm a damn sight better out here than you are, and I think you know that, don't you? Inside here," she pointed to her head, "You'd never admit it, but you've got to know it." She walked back to the car to report the death and request the medical examiner.

Brandt stayed in the yard, avoiding Stark until the forensic team arrived. Even though this looked like a clear suicide, the connection between Altmeyer and Schmidt warranted a forensic sweep to be sure. At one point Brandt looked through the doorway at Helga's body in the car. He stepped back and looked at the house and gardens surrounding it, thinking he'd like to have such a place of his own one day.

Brandt wasn't a bad cop. But Stark was right; she had more instinct for police work than he ever would. And just as important, she had passion for the job. It was her life.

6

Zurich, Switzerland

Alana drove nonstop, arriving in Zurich at four o'clock that afternoon. To her surprise, she found Hochbaumstrasse with little difficulty and parked the car in front of the Griegg office at number ninety-six.

Zurich's historic center was charming, and the area around the Griegg office was equally so. The buildings on Hochbaumstrasse were old four-story stone row dwellings that now housed professional offices.

Number ninety-six was much like the other buildings on the quiet side street. A stone walkway led from the pavement to the doorstep. Rows of red geraniums flanked the walkway and a decorative iron railing kept them from spilling out onto the side-walk. The door was painted a shiny black with a bell in the center.

Alana tried the handle, but it was locked. A small brass plaque under the bell read *Bitte Klingeln*, which she translated as *Please Ring*. She pushed the button and in a moment a voice said, "Wie ist dein Name?"

"Alana Eastwood," she stumbled, "ah… sehen Griegg ah… Informationsdienste."

"Step back a little, please." The voice recognized the language difficulty and spoke in English.

Within a second she heard the click of the door unlocking. She pulled the handle and walked through into the foyer. It was impressive. She walked across a mosaic tile floor toward a wide mahogany staircase.

An ornate chandelier cast a welcoming light around her. Why had the voice asked her to step back? Was it to see her face on a camera feed?

There were doors on each side of the staircase. The door to her left said *Griegg Informationsdienste*, to her right the door was labeled *Forschungsbibliothek*. She started to walk left when the door opened and a man came out to greet her.

He was tall and thin, a studious-looking type wearing an argyle vest. He spoke to her in his native Oxford English, "May I help you?"

"I hope so, but the reason for my visit is rather unusual. My name is Alana Eastwood. I'm sorry not to have called for an appointment, but I don't speak German well, and I wasn't sure if I could have communicated my problem adequately over the phone. Dr. Valdemar Altmeyer from the Tübingen University referred me to your company. I would like to see Mr. Griegg."

"And what is your business with Mr. Griegg?"

Alana felt on the spot. How could she explain in a few words all that had happened—the complicated reason for her visit? All of a sudden the thought of telling the story again became frightening. Would they believe her? She still wasn't sure what the police thought of her. Did they laugh when they got back into their car?

Noting Alana's hesitation, the man said, "I'm afraid you can't see Mr. Griegg unless you convince me that it is appropriate." Realizing he intimidated her, he changed his tone. "Why don't we sit down," he pointed to the bench beside the door. "My name is Ian Stewart, please take a seat."

"Thank you, Mr. Stewart. I am hesitating because I'm trying to think how to relay a complex situation in just a few words."

"Well then, use as many words as you like. Take your time. I'm a good listener."

It was clear that she would have to recount the whole story if she wanted to move forward. She cut a few corners, omitting her psychic visions, and handed him an English copy of the letter and went through much of what she had recited to the police. She hadn't told the police about her visions either. She also left out of her decision not to meet with Albert Schmidt and why.

"Dr. Altmeyer suggested I come here if I was serious about finding answers. Then, when he was murdered, I didn't know what else to do."

Ian could see she was quite shaken. He looked at the letter and paused slightly before handing it back to her. "Please excuse me. I will be back shortly."

Alana sat there, pondering what might happen next. The foyer was quiet, so quiet she wondered what could be going on behind the closed door. Were there groups of people working busily or was it just Mr. Stewart and Mr. Griegg back there? What type of people came to the library? Alana spotted a portrait of a pleasant-looking woman on the far wall. She walked over to read the nameplate: Corinne Aurelie Griegg 1913–1964.

After about ten minutes, a man came out of the door marked *Forschungsbibliothek* and walked out onto the street without looking in Alana's direction. A few more minutes passed before the left-side door opened and Mr. Stewart said, "Mr. Griegg will see you, please come this way."

She followed him into a conference room that featured a large oval table with eight chairs. There were doors at each end of the room. Bookshelves lined the walls except for a small space reserved for a beverage cart next to the door in the back of the room. Alana stood uncomfortably at the table when the back door opened and a man walked through.

"Thank you, Ian, I'll take it from here." Sigmund Griegg was a good-looking man in his mid-forties. His hair was dark brown, almost black, graying at the temples. His eyes were a steely gray-blue; his dark blue suit fitted him to perfection. He exemplified that classic European look.

"Ms. Eastwood, I am Sigmund Griegg." He held out his hand to greet her and then held a chair for her to sit. He spoke in clear English, perhaps the result of an English education. There was just a hint of an accent that she couldn't place. "Would you like a cup of tea or coffee, water?"

"Either tea or coffee, thank you, whichever is easier. Just black is fine." Alana normally took milk, but she didn't see any on the cart. Because she was uneasy meeting new people, she kept things simple. Settling at the conference table to discuss such bizarre events was challenging enough.

Sigmund poured two cups of coffee, placing one cup in front of her. Before he sat down, he removed the chair between them so that the space was comfortable for an informal conversation.

"I know you have told your story to my associate in some detail, but I should like to hear the whole account again." He held his cup to his lips and sipped. "No detail is too small, Ms. Eastwood. I must hear the narrative in full."

Alana repeated almost verbatim what she had told the police. She added a few details that she had omitted when talking to Ian Stewart. Like Inspector Stark, Griegg sat quietly without interrupting. Alana gained confidence as she spoke.

"Your story is quite interesting, Ms. Eastwood. But how do you imagine our service can help you?"

"I don't know really what your service is, Mr. Griegg. Professor Altmeyer gave me your card and I...." She felt awkward, "I just didn't know where else to turn."

"There are many questions from the war that cannot be answered or explained. I could tell you countless stories of families who have tried.

"Look at your position. You are away from home, you've suffered a terrible loss, and now you face what looks like an intriguing mystery. I understand the temptation to learn what the letter means, but, as I said, you don't realize how many others have faced similar circumstances.

"I've tried to help many of them myself, so I can tell you for a fact that in almost every instance the circumstances turned out to be misleading, or insignificant, or else impossible to solve. I thought it only fair to hear you out in case my associate had missed something of particular interest."

"What about Dr. Altmeyer's murder? Doesn't that make my situation different?" Alana interrupted.

"You did the right thing to notify the police and tell them your story," Griegg spoke from experience. "My suggestion is to give them time to investigate the murder before you jump to the conclusion that your letter is involved. You might even go back to America. Forget about the letter. Get on with your life."

Up until this point, Alana had been reserved in recounting the events of the past days. But the man's outright dismissal irritated her. Out of desperation, she felt impelled to convince him to help. Who else would there be? He seemed her only link to finding the truth. She now spoke forcefully.

"Mr. Griegg, I can't go back to the States and forget what's happened. First of all, this is my family. I feel obligated to do something to right what could be a terrible wrong. This all happened because my great-uncle died before reading the letter." She paused and took a breath. "Second, the moment I touched that letter I was overcome with a sense of purpose. I have to see this through to some sort of resolution. I can't explain to you how or why, but I know I am responsible for Dr. Altmeyer's death.

"I must come to terms with the meaning of the letter before I can, as you said, get on with my life."

She stopped talking but maintained eye contact with Griegg. She could see he was unconvinced... he wasn't going to help.

"Look, I don't talk about this because I know people will dismiss it. It's difficult to explain, but when I touched that letter, my life changed." She searched for better words. "You see, I have dreams, and then I find out later that they're true. But they are not really dreams at all. It's as if I become connected to something that happened in the past, and I see it, I see it happen all over again. I don't know if that makes me psychic; I don't know what I am.

"But I know I'm connected to that letter, and I know it is difficult to understand what I'm saying. I wouldn't believe it myself, if it hadn't happened to me." She paused and looked around the room. "I can't go home until I get some answers. Whether you help me or the police help me or I'm on my own, I've got to try.

"Maybe you're right. Maybe there will never be an answer, but I..." A tap on the door interrupted her. The door opened about six inches. Sigmund turned his head and gave a nod.

"Please, Ms. Eastwood, excuse me, for just a moment." He stood up and walked through the door. The door almost shut behind him, but Alana could see his fingers still holding the edge. She hadn't seen who called him out of the room, but she heard the whispers of several people conversing.

She was really shaken now. She had confided in a stranger that she had unusual dreams. What would he think of her? Then, the last thing she said to Griegg, about finding answers on her own, was frightening. How would she find any resolution for the letter on her own? It seemed an insurmountable task—where would she even start? She knew she wouldn't go to Dr. Schmidt. Was Griegg right? Should she let the police do their investigation and not get involved? Should she forget the letter and go home to Connecticut?

She stared into the cup on the table, its contents now cold. She thought back to Kirk. Why hadn't he opened the letter? Why had he left all this for her to face on her own!

Alana considered slipping away before Griegg re-entered the room, but she heard the door close and when she looked up, he was back. He took his seat and clasped his hands together on the table. "Well... it seems I will help you after all."

"I don't understand."

"My associates believe that someone followed you here today. There is someone on the street. One of my colleagues thinks the gentleman is an Israeli agent, we're not sure. There's no reason for him to be out there, if not for you." He left a long pause. "Have you told me the whole story Ms. Eastwood?"

"Yes!" She glared back at him. "I can't imagine anyone following me. Could it be the German police?" There was a pause. "But I never told them Dr. Altmeyer gave me your card. It didn't seem relevant.

"I thought I would be back at the cottage before they contacted me again." She became animated, "They just didn't seem concerned, and I didn't know what to do! I just couldn't sit there. That's why I came here."

"Ms. Eastwood, the German police are not in the habit of sending Israeli agents out to follow people."

"Oh God," she rubbed her forehead, "I'm sorry, I just don't know what to think. Why would anyone follow me? I don't know anything more than what I've told you. And, that's nothing! I found a letter and I don't know what it means. I was curious and then Dr. Altmeyer was dead and now I am here. You are scaring me, Mr. Griegg."

"I'm not scaring you. Your circumstances are scaring you. But you must remain calm. Look, I'm not sure if I am the one to help you or not. We'll determine that shortly. However, I can't send you back out there on your own. If you are connected to the professor's murder, then your life may be in danger; it's best to take some precautions until we know more."

In a strange way Alana felt relieved to hear him say she might be in danger. It was confirmation that what she felt was real and that perhaps she wouldn't have to face these "circumstances" alone. She fiddled nervously with her coffee cup.

Sigmund got up and refilled her cup with fresh coffee. "Would you like something stronger?" He caught a whiff of something in the coffee that he didn't recognize. His father regularly brought exotic coffees into the office.

"No, this is fine, thanks."

"Let me explain what we do, Ms. Eastwood. One might have considered my grandfather a detective, perhaps more specifically a spy, but we no longer operate at that level. Today we simply gather facts. We obtain raw information and analyze the data for those who hire us. Our clients include government entities, corporations, and universities all over the world, and every now and then, someone like your-self—an individual with a problem. I did not know Professor Altmeyer myself, though I know Tübingen University is among our clientele.

"Have you registered in a hotel here in Zurich?"

Alana listened without showing any emotion and shook her head. "No."

"Right, then my associate will take you out of our office unnoticed. He will book you into a hotel. You are not to leave the room or use the telephone. Use room service for your meal tonight. He will be back for you in the morning. In the meantime, we will conduct some preliminary research, and we can talk again in the morning. Do you understand?"

"Yes."

"Until we know who or what we're dealing with, we have to take these measures. I can't advise strongly enough the importance for you to follow my instructions."

"But Marta will expect me to call her tonight and come back to Tübingen tomorrow. What if she's in danger?"

"We will take care of your friend Marta. What is her surname?"

"Voss, Marta Voss." She gave him the telephone number and address of the cottage.

"Okay, I want you to think of anything else that might have a connection to the letter. Think about anything your grandfather may have said or done over the years. Perhaps something else you saw in his home. Anything at all that seemed out of place or unusual in any way… I want to know." Sigmund stepped back and opened the door. Ian came in promptly.

"You know what to do." Sigmund directed Ian. He then looked around at Alana. "By the way, Ms. Eastwood, our services aren't cheap. Do you have money?"

She said straight forwardly. "My grandfather left me the equivalent of 50,000 U.S. dollars in cash and equivalents and also there is his cottage."

"Are you prepared to spend it?" He locked onto her eyes.

"All of it? No. Some of it, definitely. Do I have a choice? You said yourself that my life may be in danger. I'm not prepared to die, so yes, I guess that means I'm prepared to spend what it takes to see this through."

"Is there anyone besides Marta Voss who will miss you?"

"No."

"I mean back in the States."

"No… there's no one."

"Until tomorrow then, Ms. Eastwood."

7

The Griegg Office, Zurich

"Okay people, we've got work to do." Sigmund walked into the open work area and rapped loudly on a desk to convey the urgency of the situation. Christopher and Boris turned from their computers to look at him. "Where is Ms. Bauer?" he queried.

"I'm right here Sigmund." A twenty-something petite blond-haired woman appeared in the doorway. He acknowledged her with a nod.

Sigmund had also summoned Niedermeyer from the library offices and watched as he came through the back entrance that connected the two sides of the building. They all gathered around Sigmund.

The Griegg staff was diverse: Sabine Bauer, the only local person and the only woman, had obtained a master's degree in drama from the Zurich University of the Arts; Boris Klondt came to Griegg from an elite branch of Grenzschutzgruppe 9 (GSG 9) of the German Federal Police force; Christopher Hutt was a retired inspector from Scotland Yard; and Ian

Stewart, the second Englishman in the company, had been expelled from Oxford at the age of eighteen when he was arrested in one of the most notorious computer hacking scandals in the modern era. Ian was not present as he was settling Alana at a hotel.

The two other tangential members of the team were librarian and archivist, J. Leopold Niedermeyer, of unknown background and, last but certainly not least, Andrew Griegg, Sigmund's father, who was currently in London.

"I am issuing a security alert for a special project that has fallen into our lap this afternoon. So be on notice." Sigmund had their attention with that statement.

"An American woman of German descent comes to Germany, to Tübingen in Baden-Württemberg, when her grandfather falls ill. Upon her arrival, she learns he has died. There is no reason to suspect anything other than natural causes, but his death may have accidentally put into play a chain of events that we have been asked to investigate.

"After devoting many weeks to finalizing her grandfather's affairs, our American visitor, Ms. Alana Eastwood, comes across the original of this letter." Sigmund held up the copy of the letter as he spoke and pinned it magnetically to the new whiteboard just installed at the office.

"The letter is postmarked in 1945 and had never been opened. It was addressed to Ms. Eastwood's great-uncle, Helmut Augsburg, who is believed to have died during the war." Sigmund began to write names on the whiteboard. "Kirk Augsburg is the grandfather who recently died and the younger brother of Helmut Augsburg to whom the letter in question was addressed."

Sigmund paused and looked over at Sabine, "I like this whiteboard, a nice upgrade from chalk. Thanks for bringing it in." Sabine smiled. While the others were on top of any new electronic device, she was the only one to consider something as fundamental as a whiteboard.

"Curious," Sigmund continued, "the American opens the letter to find a rather ambiguous, yet urgent, cry for help from a person named Franz, who holds a secret that must be revealed. She knows of no one by that name and found no reference to a Franz amongst her grandfather's belongings.

"There is a young Tübingen University student, Marta Voss, living in the grandfather's home as a housekeeper. Troubled by the puzzling contents of the letter, the two women decide to seek advice from one of Voss's professors, Valdemar Altmeyer.

"The professor explains that he doesn't know how he can help but asks to keep the letter overnight to discuss it with a colleague in the school's history department. The women agree to meet Altmeyer again the following morning but, when they return the next day, they find the police at the campus and learn that the professor has been stabbed to death. They are fearful that the letter may have had something to do with this tragic event.

"Later in the day they tell the story to the police. While the police showed interest in Ms. Eastwood's statement, they seemed unconvinced of a connection between Altmeyer's murder and the letter.

"Because the letter was unopened, and therefore its contents unknown, Eastwood believes the secret it refers to is still out there and may even await discovery. She drove from Tübingen to Zurich in seek of our help. It seems the professor knew of our work and gave her our card.

"I was going to send her away, but footage from our security cameras alerted Ian that she may have been followed here. If true, it gives credence to her belief that she has inadvertently stumbled upon something of great interest, which may indeed have led to the professor's death. We know nothing else, but I'm hesitant to have Ms. Eastwood leave our protection in case she is in danger.

"Therefore, I have agreed to open a preliminary investigation. Ian has taken Ms. Eastwood to a hotel for the night. We will meet with her in the morning.

"I'm not aware of any current projects that can't be put on hold for a few days, so let's all figure out what we can do to help Alana Eastwood.

"Copies of the letter and envelope, a recording of her interview with me, along with my notes will be available for each of you momentarily. I will contact the German authorities to safeguard the housekeeper, Marta Voss. And I'll see about our friend outside. If anyone has plans for this evening, they will need to be canceled."

Sigmund went to his office and called the newspaper to place a classified ad for the morning paper: *G3 would like to speak with the Gray Ghost.* The number three referred to Sigmund, who was the third generation of Grieggs to head the business. The code was

Griegg family protocol for asking an Israeli agent to contact them.

Just as he was picking up the phone again, Sabine knocked and opened the door. "Sigmund, Chris tapped into the German police wire—there may be another death connected to Ms. Eastwood."

"Marta Voss?"

"No, it's the wife of another professor at the same university. I haven't read all the details yet but wasn't the history professor named Schmidt?"

"Yes."

"Well then, his wife, Helga Schmidt, is dead. They're calling it a suicide."

"Interesting. Is this about a love triangle? Could it be that none of this is connected to the letter at all?"

"Then why would Eastwood have been followed here?" Sabine understood these were all rhetorical questions to be answered later. "And Sigmund," she added, "the German police are looking for the American. Should we tell them we have her?"

"Not yet. Thanks, I'll be downstairs in a minute. I have to make sure someone is safeguarding Marta Voss." He took a deep breath. It had been five years since any case turned dangerous, and Sigmund was beginning to worry.

The Griegg offices and library occupied the entire building at number ninety-six. In the beginning, the top two floors provided a residence for the family.

Then, in the 1920s, Sigmund's grandfather moved the family to a country estate southeast of Zurich.

Back in the day, Sigmund's grandfather still maintained rooms on the top two floors of the building, where he lived during the week. He made the trip to the "country" on weekends. Nowadays, the distance is a comfortable commute for well-heeled city workers, but life in his grandfather's time was different. Maintaining two large homes was common among his peers.

Today, the fourth floor still provides ample room for Sigmund to stay in the city. In fact, since his wife's death, Sigmund has stayed in the building most nights. The third floor is maintained to house the staff when their workload demands it, and although Sigmund was unaware of when it happened, Niedermeyer converted a small alcove off his research library into a bedroom and now lives in the building as well.

The apartments, like the Griegg family, were the epitome of traditional European style. There was a mixture of mahogany, leather, and Asian rugs in large opulent rooms. But the status reflected in the decor of their home and their affluent lifestyle came through generations of hard work and the fortitude to succeed.

The maternal line of the family migrated from Scotland in the 1850s when the Swiss textile industry called for innovation and needed workers to make it happen. Sigmund's fourth generation grandfather, Andrew Webster Gow, a menial textile weaver, moved his family to Switzerland for the chance of a better life.

THE TRAP

It was an era when a brilliant idea could move families between the "classes" and that's exactly what Andrew Webster Gow was able to do. As new forms of synthetic coloring worked through the woolen weaving process, he challenged his bosses with an alternative method. Almost overnight, the mill flourished over the competition.

The mill owners appreciated that they had hired an exceptionally innovative man. To fully utilize Gow's ideas, the small mill took him on as a partner. He purchased a home around the corner from the mill at 96 Hochbaumstrasse. The family took in lodgers on the lower floors for additional income.

When Gow's only child, a daughter, Cora, married an up-and-coming young prosecutor named Josef Griegg, the family stopped taking in boarders. Cora and Joseph lived on the second floor and Josef used the first floor, for his legal practice.

Josef's legal business prospered, and in time, their dining room became a salon for lively dinner parties; they embraced visiting dignitaries and the literati of Zurich. They instilled in each of their children the values of an honest day's work and the dignity of all people. They never allowed them to forget the meager circumstances from which they came. While the family hob-knobbed with the elites, they were just "regular folk" to their working-class friends.

When Cora's father died, they sold his stock in the mill back to the original partners. Cora's only child, Andrew Joseph, was in law school at the time and had no interest in the woolen business, other than representing them in court should they ever need his services. The Griegg lineage continued when Andrew Joseph married and had two children, a son, Wolfgang, Sigmund's grandfather, and a daughter, Corinne. It was Wolfgang who, after obtaining a law degree, formed the Griegg Research Library and then added the Information Service a few years later.

Corinne followed in the family's footsteps in studying the law and rose to be a prominent figure in the women's suffrage movement during the 1930s and 40s. Sadly, because Switzerland lagged behind the rest of Europe, Corinne passed away before seeing Swiss women receive full democratic rights. A portrait of Corinne hangs in the foyer of the Griegg building to greet everyone who enters.

Wolfgang's son, Andrew, followed his father into the Information Service business in the 1950s. By his generation, the era of posh parties and intellectual salons was long gone. The world was enduring the Cold War, and Andrew ran what was now an internationally respected research business. The technology boom after the Second World War, along with opportunities created by the space race, thrust worldwide commerce to a new level. Governments, and both public and private companies alike, needed help navigating prevailing import/export laws and customs regulations. Andrew Griegg bridged those gaps for the company's clients.

Sigmund put his stamp on the business model by expanding into academia to collaborate and provide international expertise on many research projects. While the Griegg business had its own expert staff, they had access to the best and brightest minds on almost any topic.

Sigmund was reminded of his ancestral past every time he walked through the building, but now, the present day's events and how to help the American, consumed him.

He pulled his shirt from his trousers as he walked into his bedroom. He tossed it over the chair as he passed through to the bathroom. His trousers rested on his thin, six-foot-two frame. His chest was un-tanned but had a healthy glow all the same. He splashed water over his face and dried it with a linen towel neatly folded by the sink. Looking at his face in the mirror, the thought of shaving flashed through his mind, then vanished.

This was the only life he knew: Heading up an obscure information-gathering business in one of the most vibrant cities in Europe. He had met world leaders, dined with business tycoons, and lectured at the United Nations.

His diligent work ethic had earned him these privileges, but the research/investigation business had come with a deep price. As he pulled an under-shirt over his head, he glimpsed the picture of a dark-haired woman holding a small boy smiling and waving at the camera.

He put on a clean shirt, no tie, and headed down to his office. He met Chris running up the stairs. "The German police interrupted an assailant at the home of the Voss woman earlier today. It seems she has a knife wound to her lower back. She's alive and in surgery now. Did you contact the German Police about her?"

"Yes, I stressed in no uncertain terms that the message must get to Inspector Stark immediately.

But, with what you are telling me, it was obviously too late."

"Did you tell them we have Alana Eastwood?"

"No. My message was that we had talked with her and believed the Voss woman to be in urgent need of protection."

The German police now connected the murder of Valdemar Altmeyer with the attack on Marta Voss. How the suicide of Helga Schmidt might be relevant was still an open question. They had an APB out for both Alana Eastwood and Albert Schmidt.

At nineteen, Egon was a nonperson, completely off the grid. He had never held a job other than working for his father; he had no bank accounts since his father paid him in cash; and he had no driver's license. He drove the van anyway, registering it in his mother's name. Egon had no friends and hadn't accompanied his parents outside the house in years. Nor had he been enrolled in any school for several years. A few people in the village knew his face but not his name and had no way of connecting him to either Albert or Helga. And now the Schmidt house had been cleansed of all evidence of his existence. He had an Internet presence but never used his real name online.

Brandt informed Stark that Helga Schmidt had a sister living in a town about twenty kilometers away.

It wasn't until Stark questioned the sister that they learned Albert and Helga had a son named Egon.

Helga and her sister had been estranged for years, and the sister confessed she wasn't sure of Egon's age. "About twenty," she said. "I thought he lived at home. If that's not the case, I have no idea where he might be.

"My sister was a private person Inspector. There were problems with Egon from a young age, and it put a strain on her marriage. Helga hid her problems from me, so I know little about the boy."

"When was the last time you saw your sister?"

"I'm not sure, it's been several years."

"You never talked on the phone or exchanged letters?"

"I tried to call her on her birthday last year, or perhaps it was the year before, but there was no answer. No machine picked up my call so I couldn't leave a message."

"Have you any idea where we might find Herr Schmidt?"

She shook her head, indicating no. "I'm sorry. We must appear as odd people to you. I don't know how our lives got this way. But I expected nothing like this to happen."

"In the absence of Frau Schmidt's husband," Stark said, "I must ask you to identify the body."

"Inspector, is that really necessary? I'm quite shaken by all of this. Are personal identifications even needed when you obviously know the identity of the body?"

"It is standard procedure."

"Well, I'll send my husband."

"You are the next of kin. We would prefer that it be you."

"Very well, do you have a business card? I'll call your department in the morning and, if you haven't located Albert, you can give me directions to the morgue. I will try to accommodate the police."

Stark walked back to her car knowing nothing would keep her from her parent's party that night, no matter what time she got there.

Stark did her best thinking while driving and preferably alone. She'd sent Brandt to the hospital to talk with Marta Voss as soon as possible.

She radioed in for staff to check into Egon Schmidt. She was told no update on Marta had come in. But the coroner reported that the weapon used to assault both Altmeyer and Voss was consistent—a five-inch stiletto. That probably meant one attacker.

Back at the police station Brandt reported that Marta was in the ICU. While out of immediate danger, the doctors had concern. After surgery, they were keeping her in a medically induce a coma until her vital signs stabilized.

"I'll check with them every few hours." He spoke to Marta's mother at the hospital, but she had no useful information. She had only spoken with her daughter once in recent weeks and that was the brief conversation about obtaining old marriage records. She knew that the man Marta worked for had died, but she knew nothing about the American woman.

Egon pulled his van in behind an outbuilding at the university athletic field. Although only briefly a student at the school, this place had become his refuge. The van fit in with the other utility vehicles used by the maintenance department, and no one bothered him there. He had discovered early on that he could access electricity and a phone jack from a small field house. This meant he had everything he needed to work in his van. He often slept there overnight.

After stabbing Marta Voss, Egon headed for this sanctuary. But now, sitting safely in his van, he had no recollection of the incident. Conveniently, his mental illness allowed him to block events from his mind, all the while acutely focusing on any task at hand. Earlier that day he had pulled out the letter he'd taken from Altmeyer. It was so blood soaked that he couldn't read it in its entirety. The fifty-year-old paper simply dissolved between his fingers.

Since the Augsburg name had come up during the Altmeyer telephone call to his father, finding the cottage was easy. He thought there would surely be a copy of the letter there. He stood outside the cottage watching the women through the terrace doors.

He saw Alana leave carrying a small piece of luggage. She waved goodbye to Marta and drove off. A few minutes later, when Marta also drove away, he went inside.

Once inside, Egon readily found a copy of the transcribed version of the letter lying on Kirk's desk in the study. Shelves and drawers were empty, their contents packed into boxes. He pulled open some boxes but quickly reasoned that it was doubtful that anything connected to the letter would have been packed.

Before he could slip away, Marta came back into the cottage. She had forgotten the books Alana had asked her to take to the library. When she walked into the study for the box, she glimpsed movement out of the corner of her eye. She turned to spot someone hiding behind a chair.

When she turned to run, Egon jumped out and dove for her. She tried to struggle out of her jacket, but he held her down. As he tried to think what to do, he heard a car pull up outside. Fearing that the woman could identify him or even scream out for whoever was outside, he pulled his knife from his pocket and stabbed her. Egon rushed out into the back garden as the front doorbell rang. He sprinted through the woods to where he had parked his van. The police heard Marta cry out. They rushed to her and immediately called for an ambulance.

Back in the van Egon grabbed for his medicine. He was shaking so badly that he couldn't open the container, so he bashed it hard against the dashboard spilling the pills over the floor. He didn't take his meds frequently, but he needed them—anything—now. He fumbled to pick up the pills he could see on the mat around his feet and popped one capsule into his mouth, trying to draw enough saliva to swallow it. That was when he noticed the blood covering his right hand and jacket. It wasn't his blood. He checked his pocket for his knife and, when he felt it, he drove off.

8

On the Move

Egon's value to his father's propaganda machine was, in part, his computer skills. He was the only member of the group proficient in information technology. Coincidently, the repetitive process of digitizing the library material actually diminished the manifestation of his psychological issues. He had mastered the complex database software in a short time, which enabled the group's research to be cross-referenced using various data points.

Albert didn't know the extent of his son's talent, which now included advanced use of the Internet. Everyone in academia and business was beginning to learn the capabilities of the World Wide Web, but Egon had already tapped into just how helpful the Internet could be to rally like-minded people behind any cause.

He had set up a Multi-User Dungeon (MUD) online chat room. In just a matter of days, he had acquired several hundred active followers. He boldly shared portions of his in-progress novel with them. But that was only the beginning. He now imagined thousands of followers over the next few months.

Egon considered the Internet his future. With his ability to publish online, Egon believed he would outdo anything his father's group could accomplish with their outdated methods of paper-pushing snail mailers and leaflets pinned on bulletin boards in schools and gathering places. "What a joke," Egon thought.

While it was tempting to imagine the future, the mysterious letter was in the present, and the library database had already proved useful. Connected to his database and the Internet from the university athletic field house, Egon was a self-contained research hub. He found Helmut Augsburg was a member of the Nazi Party before and during the wartime period. He cross-referenced the entire database for people with the given name Franz. There were hundreds of matches. Cleverly using such data points as age and location, three names surfaced as likely candidates to have authored the letter.

The first was Ulbrecht Brinkmann, an actor. He dropped the awkward name Ulbrecht and went by his stage name, Franz Brinkmann, to give him wide European appeal. His talent on the stage had led to several film roles, but before his career blossomed, the war brought it to an end.

Franz Brinkmann had stunned Berlin by refusing to perform before Hitler in 1940. Rumored to have stayed in Germany throughout the war, Brinkmann reportedly assumed several identities to help Jews in the underground network escape to Spain, and then ultimately travel on to America. Officially listed as a missing person, Brinkmann never surfaced after the war. If he was alive when the letter was written, his whereabouts remained unknown.

The next name was Franz Walter. His story was more thought provoking. In 1943, this Franz was an executive at Keitel-Rhine, a small but instrumental armaments company, working with Messerschmitt to design and equip new guns for the prototype Me-262 jet fighter. The SS was pursuing him on suspicion of espionage when Walter suddenly vanished.

Whether or not Walter spied for the Allies went unresolved. If true, he could have fled Germany to England. But the dates of any such an escape made little sense to Egon. He believed it more likely that Walter met his fate at the hands of the SS, but without confirmation, Franz Walter was a definite suspect as author of the mysterious letter.

The third name was Franz Ziegler, one of Hitler's architects in service to the Third Reich. Of the three, he was the most intriguing to Egon. Ziegler would have had regular access to Hitler. Although Egon had found no articles to suggest that Ziegler was a Hitler confidant, his work placed him in the right place at the right time to have had access to secret information plus the opportunity to hide it. As the letter indicated, he was working as an individual with no network to help him.

All three men were about the same age, had grown up in the same locality as Helmut Augsburg, and could have been in Berlin at the end of the war. But the third Franz, Franz Ziegler, worked and lived in Berlin. Did he have any other connections to the letter? What did the words "the trap" even mean? Or the words *I am Jew, I am German.* None of these men were Jewish. How many more men named Franz were not in the database?

Egon had become a thoughtful researcher. This was a significant start, but he couldn't wrap his head around all the possibilities that could bring meaning to the letter. Then he thought about his followers on his Internet MUD chat room. He hadn't intended people to help in his research, but why not? He opened a new thread and entered the three names: Ulbrecht (Franz) Brinkmann, Franz Walter, and Franz Ziegler asking if anyone has any information on any of these men. "Can anyone tell me what these men were doing in 1945? This is for background on a character I am developing for my novel. All information must be absolutely factual." The events that started his journey meant there was no turning back. Killing Altmeyer had put him on a path with no viable exits. Now on the run, Egon needed support from any available source.

As messy as he had made the situation, he didn't want a way out. Hearing of the mysterious letter had energized him. Within his chaotic mind, he believed solving the mystery of the trap would give him the power his father had sought but never attained. It was the power to spread the viability of Nazism to a broader audience. He laughed at the irony: At the very time his father tried to shut him out, it would be him, not his father, who would solve the mystery of the letter and claim the glory. No matter what secret he found, he had the power to reveal it or destroy it—whichever suited his purpose. To Egon that was supremacy; it was his, and he deserved it. He had killed for it.

Horst heard a knock on the door. Impatient, the caller banged again loudly before he could get there to open it. "I need your help, Horst." It was Albert, and he was at the end of his rope. "I'm in trouble." Albert walked passed his friend and went through into his kitchen. "I need to borrow your car."

"What's going on Albert?"

"I can't explain without putting you in jeopardy. Do you have any coffee brewed?"

"Sit down. I'll make you a cup. Have you eaten?"

"I can't eat. The police are most likely looking for me, so I can't continue to use my car. I hate to ask, but I need your car."

"We can talk about that, but I'm concerned about you. Is this about Valdemar Altmeyer?"

"Yes." Albert struggled with what to say. "Egon is in trouble and he's disappeared. I have to find him. I can't tell you more."

"Well, it seems obvious it's got something to do with the letter you asked me to get from Altmeyer."

"Did you go to his office?" Albert asked touching his hand to his chest.

"Yes, but he was already dead when I got to the university. I saw the police vehicles and asked some students what was going on. I turned away. I've been trying to call you ever since."

"Horst, Egon heard me talking with you about retrieving the letter. Later, I heard him leave the house. He rarely goes out, so after a few hours when he didn't return, I began to worry. It was late, but I went over to Altmeyer's office and found the body. I'm afraid Egon killed him. Oh God, I shouldn't be telling you."

"It's okay, Albert. What are you going to do?"

"I don't know. I've taken data from the library. I've got to hole up somewhere until I can figure out what's so important about that letter. I must find Egon before the police do."

"Stay here, we can work together."

"No, Horst, you don't understand. The police will come here because of your involvement in my research. The women who brought the letter to Altmeyer were coming back to see him today. Her name will most likely be in his diary. As soon as they talk to her, my name will come up.

"Your name may be in his diary, because I scheduled you to pick up the letter. Altmeyer may also have talked to others at the school; I don't know what the police will learn or how fast their investigation will proceed.

"You need to warn the others. Maybe I'm wrong, but we need to be prepared. I don't want this to turn into front-page news involving our entire group. I'm afraid the press will try to implicate you all."

"All right, I understand. I'm just concerned about you right now."

Wearily, Albert sat at the kitchen table. He sank his head into his hands, "I wish to God I had done something with Egon years ago. I should have known something like this would happen sooner or later. But his mother, and all those doctors, they said he was okay." Albert looked up, "They always acted as if there was something wrong with me!"

"You can't blame yourself for Egon's actions. The police won't blame you."

"No, you're wrong. It's that damn letter."

"What was the letter about?"

"I don't know—there was nothing more than an obscure reference to something hidden away that only this Helmut Augsburg person would know where to find it.

"It dated back to 1945, so I was interested—the writer claimed to be Jewish. A search of our database revealed that Augsburg was a medic during the war. We only had that information because he registered as a member of the Nazi Party. He died in the war. Someone named Franz signed the letter, giving no last name. You know as well as I that it would be a longshot to find further information, especially without Egon's help.

"But Egon went berserk when I asked you to get the letter instead of sending him." Albert repeated in anguish, "I tried to warn Altmeyer, but I was too late."

Albert gulped his coffee and stood up. "I've got to go." He rubbed his hand across his chest as if he was struggling to breathe.

Horst walked over to the counter and opened a drawer. "These are the keys to my son's car. He's taking a semester in England. No one is using the vehicle at the moment.

"Park your car in the garage. I'll try to keep quiet but if push comes to shove, I'll say you came by with car trouble so I lent you the car. Nothing else said, okay?"

"Thank you. You are a dear friend."

"Wait, Albert," Horst reached for his wallet, "take one of my credit cards to use for petrol, really anything you need. The police might track your cards."

Horst watched Albert fumbling to insert the card into his wallet. "Albert, I'm worried about you. I wish you would stay at least a little while to rest and eat properly."

"No, I'm fine. As I said, I can't involve any of you. That is, any more than I already have."

When Albert left, Horst called the four main members of Albert's group to schedule a meeting. He omitted the new person, Claus Richter, from the meeting. He was a student of Albert's who had just recently started work at the library. Barely acquainted with the members, there was no point to involve him. But he did call Claus to say the library would be closed while Albert was away on business. Horst then called his lawyer.

Within a few hours, the members gathered at his house. "I'm afraid something serious has happened." He explained the situation as vaguely as he could. They agreed not to meet until further notice and to "lie low" as Horst put it.

"The police may or may not want to talk to you." Horst continued, "If they do come to see you, just remember that there is nothing to hide. I need not remind you that all our work is completely legal.

While I can reassure you that there is nothing to fear, we all know that the police take sport in harassing people like us. Therefore, I wanted you to be aware of the current state of affairs and prepare for what might happen."

One by one they left, only Galiena Kaufman stayed behind. "I deserve to know everything Horst; I've got a lot at stake here."

"Calm down, Galiena, that is exactly the kind of attitude that will get you into trouble. Believe me, I have no other information."

"You're lying."

"I'm not." Horst guided her to the door with his hand behind her back.

"I can't be in the dark. If the police investigate Albert, you know they'll find out about me. If my husband learns what's been going on, I stand to lose everything!

"Galiena, the police don't care about extramarital affairs. You have nothing to do with Dr. Altmeyer. Do you even know him?"

"I know *of* him. But what if they find out about our financial transactions? Then our companies are finished as well! I can't believe this is happening."

"Galiena, Albert has done nothing wrong. He is worried about his son. Egon's gone missing and he's looking for him. That's it. If he finds Egon today, and he's done anything wrong, then all of this will be about nothing." Horst was a confident liar. "As far as those financial transactions are concerned, you can relax. Trust me. There is no way they can trace anything back to you. It's simply not possible."

"How did I ever let you involve me with those Africans? I can't be exposed," she cried.

"Do I have to remind you that your finances and probably your marriage would have been finished if I hadn't involved you? I'll use the word *sponsored* when referring our African acquaintances. All we did was provide financing, and we have complete deniability of the details. Anyway, it's over and done." Horst put his hand on Galiena's shoulder. "It's all in the past, a one-and-done deal." He repeated, "It's in the past. Our finances are now strong, and we'll never be forced into anything like that again. Just calm down and act rationally if the police come to your door."

Horst sent her away. Then he grabbed his car keys to drive over to his lawyer's office. When he had spoken with Albert, it hadn't occurred to him that a police investigation could expose the financial transactions that worried Galiena. Now he realized she might be right; they could both be in trouble.

Egon left his parking space behind the university athletic field after working and sleeping. He headed for the town he had found a few years prior, the first time he ran away from home. It was a place where he could hide in plain sight.

Egon drove for hours before he saw the bar sign and pulled in. A nondescript place on a rural road, it seemed a throwback to when the road was a truck route between the mountains. Egon walked in and sat at the bar. "Beer," he said.

"Local okay?" the barkeeper asked. He was an older man with tattoos covering his arms and neck. Egon nodded and put cash on the bar.

Egon saw a young woman at the end of the bar. She was alone, and she was looking straight at him. Regular girls never looked at him. Everything about Egon was odd.

Before long she came over and asked, "Buy me a drink?"

"I'm not a social type, so I'm not interested in talking."

"I can't talk if I'm drinking."

"Have what you like." He put more money on the bar.

She signaled the bartender to bring over a double vodka.

"I've known women like you before."

"Well, I'd say that makes it easy for me then." She'd been drinking before Egon came in and was now downing this one fast. "They have a room in the back they let me use."

Egon didn't respond. He had lied. He had never known a woman like her and didn't know how to talk to her. But the intensity of the recent events empowered him in many ways.

"Don't you like having a good time?"

Egon said nothing. He'd never had a girlfriend. There were several times at school, before his mental illness became so entrenched, when he found himself with a girl who would do more than kiss. But even then his jumbled-up mind ruined any possibility of sex. He was only ever capable of masturbation.

145

He'd been in similar places before when he'd run away from home as a teenager. There were bars where it was easy to buy drugs, weapons, or sex in any form. He had hung with skinheads for several weeks before his mother hired a detective to track him down. He came home with his head shaved and the stiletto knife he now carried. Helga convinced Albert to increase Egon's workload in the library to prevent him from running away again. Albert agreed if he grew his hair back. He couldn't have a brazen skinhead working in the group. It would draw unwanted attention if anyone connected Egon to the family or the library.

Now in the bar, this woman wasn't going to be ignored. "You're not answering me. Let's have some fun."

"I need to eat." He ordered food and ate it without talking. She ordered another vodka and hung on him while he ate. With no other prospects in the bar that night, she kept after him. "Come on, you look like you need to relieve some tension. I know exactly what you need."

He watched her pull her blouse off one shoulder to show him a lacy red bra underneath. She had lily white skin and, against the darkness of the bar, she looked beautiful and exotic. Convinced he could perform, Egon slid down off the barstool.

No one seemed to notice when they walked through the door at the far corner of the bar. The small bedroom was even darker than the barroom. A metal-framed bed was pushed up against the wall with a small table at one side. There was a lamp on the table; its shade had been pulled off and the bulb was missing. The room was illuminated by a street light a hundred feet from the bar. The light filtering through the dirty window created weird shadows across the bed. It was better not to see the filth.

The woman slid across the faded red chenille bedspread that covered a mattress without sheets. She leaned against the metal headboard and pulled open her blouse and let it fall over her arms. She then reached down and pulled her skirt up to the top of her thin white legs. She was naked underneath.

Egon stood at the edge of the bed watching her.

"Oh, come on, you're not going to cut out on me, are you? Eighty marks on the table, that's all it takes." She upped her price because he was so weird.

Egon pulled some bills out of his pocket and threw them on the table without counting. A look of relief came to her face.

Already aroused Egon dropped his pants. But when he climbed onto the bed and wedged himself between her legs, things went wrong.

"Fuck," he said.

"Hey, that's all right, you're nervous. I can get things started."

"No! You can't. I can't do things the normal way." He reached into his vest pocket and pulled out his knife, the source of all his newly found strength and power.

She didn't see it, but she heard it click open and knew she was in trouble. "Oh my God." She felt the tip of the knife prick under her chin.

His full weight was on top of her now. His left hand covered her mouth, while his right hand held the knife. He awkwardly lurched back and forth. As he did this, a single drop of blood ran down the blade of the stiletto. When he felt the blood on his fingers, he ejaculated. The strange ordeal was over in minutes.

"Keep your mouth shut, you hear me?"

She nodded.

Egon pulled up his pants and walked straight out of the bar and drove away. His goal was to continue driving to the town where he would blend in with other like-minded individuals. He detested that many of "his kind" were degenerates that lived in squalor. But he could never go back to his family's estate; living like a skinhead was his only future. The town where his mother's hired detective had found him years before was a place where he could hunker down to continue researching the letter.

The woman grabbed at the bedspread and held it to her chin. She felt her hands shaking. Prostitution was legal in Germany, but she wasn't registered. She avoided regulation by working independently. Her livelihood—the support of her child—depended on having this room; she couldn't afford to be thrown out. Going to the police meant confessing what had reluctantly become her profession… and that wasn't going to happen. He was just a whack job that she'd never see again. She grabbed the money from the table, tidied her clothes, and looking for a tissue, she returned to the bar for another drink.

9

Mossad Safe House

Early the next morning Sabine answered the door and let the visitor into the Griegg office. She notified Sigmund, and he came out to welcome the caller.

"Sigmund!" The man greeted him warmly.

"David, my God, have they got you on stakeouts these days?"

"No," he grinned, "I didn't follow the American here. But this one has a different feel to it, Sigmund. I thought I should come talk to you myself."

David Rosen was Israeli Intelligence. He and Sigmund had met professionally at times over the years, first when David worked with Shin Bet, then Mossad, the national intelligence agency of Israel. They each deemed the other a trustworthy colleague.

"Come in then, David, we'll talk."

The two men walked into the conference room, the same room where Sigmund had spoken with Alana the day before.

"What do you know, Sigmund?"

Sigmund had no qualms being entirely candid with David. First he acknowledged placing the ad in the paper. Then he recounted everything Alana had told him, adding that he knew someone had followed her to Zurich.

"Now, what can you tell me? How do you fit into the life of an American with a puzzling letter?"

"About six months ago, we caught wind of this faction of neo-Nazis headed by the man you just mentioned, Albert Schmidt. You know how it goes, Sigmund." David leaned back in the chair and glanced around the room, "We can't pay attention to all these political deviants, but we like to keep our eyes and ears open.

"But then we connected this particular group to a gun-smuggling scheme out of North Africa. That wasn't normal behavior for so-called intellectuals, so we infiltrated one of our people into the group.

"We tapped Schmidt's phone but heard only the usual academic chit chat for weeks. Then we intercepted the call from Altmeyer about the letter. It caught our attention as would any letter mailed from Berlin in 1945, where the writer cries out to be a Jew while hiding a secret that he wants revealed to the world. That rang a few bells." David chuckled. "Since the letter went unopened until a few days ago, whatever secret it was hiding could still be intact. We had our man go out to work in the Schmidt house library that day to keep an eye on things.

"During the telephone call with Altmeyer, Schmidt said he would send a colleague to pick up the letter the following day, but later that evening Schmidt suddenly grabbed his car keys and bolted from the house. Our man followed him to the university. Unfortunately, he's not trained to do anything more than observe and report, so he stayed in his car. Schmidt went into the building where the professor's office is located. He didn't stay long enough to have a conversation, in fact, there was just barely enough time to walk up the stairs to the office and back down again. Oddly, Schmidt didn't come out the way he went in. He used a different stairway and came from the back of the building to get into his car and drive away.

"Our man, as I said, was untrained for anything more than casually watching. When Schmidt drove, off it was late, so he went home. We have no idea what went on inside the professor's office or where Schmidt went after he left the university. He might have decided to pick up the letter himself. What we don't know is whether the professor was dead or alive when Schmidt got there."

"Or if he killed him." Sigmund interjected.

"I doubt that, what would be his motivation?" David said confidently. "No, Schmidt is an unlikely killer. He's vehement in his beliefs but not violent. However, my gut tells me that Ms. Eastwood's letter has opened a can of worms. How or if it plays into the gunrunning scheme we are looking into, I have no idea. But, in any event, that's how we became tuned into her activities. I put the tail on her that followed her here. Have you heard Schmidt's wife is dead, a probable suicide, and that the American's friend was attacked and is in the hospital?"

"Yes, on both counts." Sigmund stated, "I called the German police to watch Marta Voss, but she had already been attacked."

David explained, "When our young man returned to the university the morning after the killing, he saw Horst Wilhelm outside Altmeyer's office building.

"Without admitting much to the police, I had to fess up to watching 'some people' and cautioned them to guard Eastwood and Voss. Eastwood left to drive here before the police arrived at the cottage. It appears they got there in the nick of time to interrupt the attack on Voss."

"Do you think anyone else tailed Eastwood to Zurich?" Sigmund asked.

"We don't think so." David paused. "But you have me at a disadvantage my friend. May I see the letter? Altmeyer didn't read the letter in its entirety over the phone. He just paraphrased its contents, so the transcript of the telephone call that I read was incomplete."

Reaching into a stack of papers on the table, Sigmund pushed a single sheet across to David. "Obviously, the original letter has disappeared; this is the English transcript." He watched his friend's face as he read. David had aged since they met last; Sigmund hadn't seen him in glasses before. He thought the glasses suited David—they were large and brash. Sigmund lamented that the American had stumbled on a dilemma that had triggered David's presence in their office; it meant the situation could be serious.

"Who knows what it means." David pushed the letter back to Sigmund. "You know as well as I do that conundrums like this turn up now and then. Not as much now as in the '50s and '60s. That was before our time, but I fancy you've worked your share over the years. Do you mind?" David reached in his pocket for a pack of cigarettes. Sigmund wouldn't have given the nod to anyone but David. "I'm too old to quit now," David said shamelessly. Sigmund reached for a saucer from the beverage cart for him to use as an ashtray.

David opened a new pack of French Gauloises, crumpling the wrapper onto the table. "As I said, I wouldn't have thought Albert Schmidt or any of his cohorts would resort to violence like this, even if they were financing guns for other people. There's simply no reason. However, our person on the inside put us on to Albert's son, Egon Schmidt. He's one of those brilliant-minded people who may have a screw loose upstairs." David pointed to his head. "Our guy hasn't met him yet. Apparently Egon works outside the library and communicates with the group through an electronic mail system. Remember, our mission was collecting data for our files. It was just an informal look and see. The murder shocked us."

"What's your agent's name?" Sigmund asked.

"Agent is not the word I would use. I only know him by his undercover alias, Claus Richter. He is the nephew of one of our Embassy people in Berlin. I'm told he is a candidate to start at the Mossad training academy when he finishes his university studies. You know, Sigmund, getting through the *Midrasha* training is tough now, not like any training I ever received back in the day.

"Anyway, we set Claus up with a Nazi-friendly background. He transferred to study at Tübingen University this past year. You know how it works." David took a long drag on his cigarette and exhaled away from Sigmund.

"If fanatical intellectuals started killing people, we'd all be in trouble," David lamented as he took a drag on his cigarette. "Anyway, both Schmidt and his son are in the wind now, perhaps one of them did do the killing. I don't know."

Sigmund stood up and rubbed the back of his neck. He'd had little sleep, and at forty-five, he couldn't pull it off as well as he did as a younger man. "How committed are the Israelis on this?"

"Oh, I don't know," David hesitated. "Don't forget we're dealing with two issues now. We'll track down the gunrunning regardless of anything else. As far as the letter is concerned we're in long enough to see what the Jewish connection might be. The 'Jew' line in the letter is intriguing. But it's hard to say what our level of commitment is right now. I need to know more."

Sigmund started to pace. "We'd like to sort this out, but it may be out of our league without your help." He picked up the cigarette wrapper from the table and dropped it in a waste bin. "As you know, we try not to get involved in business like this any-more."

"I know that. That's why I'm here." David lit up another cigarette. "But like it or not my friend, you were in up to your neck the minute that American walked through your door."

Sigmund considered his options. Alana might well be in the office already, and he would have to talk with her soon. He wanted, he needed, David's help.

"Where's Andrew?" David asked as he stashed his cigarette pack in his pocket.

"My father's in London; I've filled him in."

David stood up to leave. "I'll get an answer from my people on how to proceed." He stopped at the door. "What's this American like? Will she hold up for us?"

"Unknown, David, unknown."

"But she's not a kook?"

"No, she's not a kook." Sigmund shook his head no as he recalled her story of psychic dreams. There was no need to concern David with that right now. "By the way, I'm not going to mention the attack on her friend just yet. She's already scared. I want to wait to hear the prognosis for Marta Voss's injuries."

David left the office and returned to the street via the back entrance. Ian had not collected Alana yet, so Sigmund drove to the hotel.

When the knock came on the door, she blurted out, "Who is it?"

"Sigmund Griegg."

Alana opened the door; she was obviously frazzled. He handed her a cup of black coffee. Sigmund looked polished in another perfectly tailored suit. "Thank you." Alana said running her hand back over her hair. She didn't even have a comb or toothbrush with her.

Once it was confirmed that the tail on Alana was a known Israeli agent, Sigmund felt safe collecting

Alana's overnight case from her car. "I brought this for you." He placed the case on the bed. "Have you had breakfast?" he asked holding up a small paper bag.

"Thanks." She took the bag and opened it to find two pastries. She removed one and offered the other to Sigmund. He waved it off.

Sigmund sat in the chair next to the bed and, in his no-nonsense style, got right to the point. "We agree with you that it is likely the letter you found is connected to Dr. Altmeyer's death. We have little information so far, but we can speculate it involves some sort of fanatical neo-Nazi group.

"We contacted Israeli Intelligence, and as long as they will provide protection, we will continue to work with you."

"Israeli Intelligence? I can't believe what you're telling me." Alana looked so vulnerable. Normally, Sigmund interacted with colleagues, not victims, so perhaps his tact could have been better. Whenever there had been danger in the past, it was between professionals who not only knew the risks but also the consequences of their line of work. Sigmund always focused on the facts at hand without regard for human emotions. That was how he believed he best served his clients.

"You said if the Israelis will help you, then you will help me. What if they won't help?

"We'll talk about that later once we know their position. But it's possible we will pass you back to the German police."

"Do you know who followed me to Zurich?"

"Yes, it was an Israeli agent. Ms. Eastwood, it may take a while to get to the bottom of this. Have you thought about what you might be getting yourself into? How will you hold up?"

"What do you mean?"

He struggled for the right words. "It's possible things could get rough."

"I'm no scatterbrain if that's what you're getting at. But I've never been in a situation like this before. I'd like to think I can handle most anything that comes my way. But honestly, I don't know. I can't really say how I'll 'hold up.' I'll try not to disappoint you or myself for that matter."

Sigmund tried to lighten things up. "Come now, you never had a robber come into your bank?"

"No, never," Alana snapped back, "but I knew the protocols and would have followed them if one had."

As they drove to the Griegg office, she dwelled on the fact that he knew she had worked at a bank, because she hadn't mentioned her employment the day before. Did he also know they fired her? Neither of them spoke until Sigmund looked over and smiled. "We're almost there."

"Yes, I recognize the area. Should I sink down in the seat so no one sees me?"

"That won't be necessary. It was the Israelis who followed you yesterday, and they're on our side." Sigmund smiled at her. But he was glad to hear she paid attention to such detail. As they turned onto Hochbaumstrasse, Alana saw a ticket on her car.

"We will let the police tow your car." Sigmund pulled into an underground parking lot behind the row houses and led her to stairs that went directly into the Griegg office. David had already returned.

David and Sigmund met privately for a few minutes, after which they called everyone into the conference room. "We will ally with the Israelis on this case," Sigmund told his staff. "You all know David Rosen; David, this is Alana Eastwood. Alana meet David Rosen, Israeli Intelligence."

"Hello, Ms. Eastwood." He glanced at her with a nod then turned his attention back to Sigmund. "I have arranged to move us to our safe house outside Zurich," he said. "That will make it possible for us all to work together in a protected environment with our full resources at hand. Do you have any problem with that, Sigmund?"

"No. We can work anywhere. I appreciate the level of support your people are willing to provide. But Niedermeyer must remain here. Can you protect him as well or should we seek private security?"

"Yes, I've been told that your Mr. Niedermeyer is even more reclusive than when I knew him years ago. I have people on their way here. Two agents will stay with Niedermeyer and the others will transfer us to the safe house."

"Well, that's good of you, David. Please pass along our gratitude." Sigmund stood up. "All right, let's pack it up people and get ready to evacuate."

Outside the room Alana approached Sigmund. "I hate to mention this, but all I brought with me is an overnight bag with a few essentials. I have no clothes with me."

Sigmund smiled. "I'll have Sabine take a look upstairs to see what she can find. We all keep clothes here." He looked at her as if checking her size. "You're too tall for Sabine's clothes, but there are other clothes that I think might fit well enough." The smile left his face, and he seemed troubled when he replied, "Not to worry."

Back in Germany, Stark and Brandt interviewed each member of Albert Schmidt's research group. The questions were general: Did they know Dr. Altmeyer? Did Albert Schmidt ever talk about him? Did they know an American woman named Alana Eastwood? They asked about Egon. They asked if they knew of a letter Albert had just been asked to research. While two of the people appeared nervous, it didn't seem they knew anything of interest about the case. It wasn't until they got to Horst Wilhelm that they learned anything.

"I understand that you spend a lot of your time at Albert's home."

"I don't know that I would call it a lot of time, but yes, I spend some time writing with him. We publish books and pamphlets. You're a police detective, you might call us history detectives," he said with a smile. "The library in his home is a convenient place for us to collaborate. We work well together."

Brandt was just itching to get into the subject of that literature, but Stark kept it simple at this stage in the investigation. "Do you know Egon Schmidt?"

"Yes, he works with us at times."

"When was the last time you were at the Schmidt house?"

"Let's see, today is Friday. Ah… I was there on Monday, I think."

"Was Egon there on Monday?"

"Yes, but I believe he was working in his flat. I received a message from him on my computer, but I didn't see him."

"Have you seen either Albert or his son since Monday?"

"No."

"Do you know where they are now?"

"No."

"Do you know that Helga Schmidt is dead?"

Horst's jaw dropped. "No… when… how?"

"Thank you for your time. Here's my card if you think of anything helpful to our investigation, we expect you to call. We also want to know if you hear from either Albert or Egon. They may be reluctant to contact us directly."

"Yes, of course. But please, I'm shocked to hear of Helga's death. How did it happen?"

"We'll be in touch." The officers walked away.

"Wait!" Horst panicked with the news of another death. "Albert did call me. He asked me to go to the university and pick up a document from Valdemar Altmeyer in the business school. When I arrived, the police were turning people away, so I left. I heard about Dr. Altmeyer's death on the news like everyone else. I've been trying to call Albert since then, but I haven't been able to get through to him."

"What else?" Stark said.

"No, that's it. I didn't tell you because, honestly, I didn't think that information was important. I had nothing to do with Altmeyer... I just knew who he was at the university."

"Mr. Wilhelm, this is a murder investigation, and you have to let us decide what is or is not important. Are you sure there's nothing else you want to tell us?"

"No, nothing else, Inspector, but please tell me what happened to Helga. I didn't know her well, but Albert is a dear friend."

"I can't give you much information, but it looks like a suicide." Stark and Brandt turned and walked away. Suddenly Brandt stopped and turned back as Horst was about to close the door. "Did you ever see the professor at Schmidt's house?"

"No, he was never there, at least not that I'm aware of." While that statement was true, Horst had proved himself a good liar in his other testimony. And he now believed he was correct in telling Galiena that the police were just interested in information about Altmeyer and no other issues. Perhaps they would be safe.

Galiena Kaufman was the last name on Stark's list. She had composed herself since leaving Horst and had practiced the answers to every question she thought the police might ask her. Finally, the doorbell rang.

"Frau Kaufman?"

"Yes."

"I'm Inspector Stark, this is Detective Brandt. We are investigating the murder of Dr. Valdemar Altmeyer, and we'd like to ask you a few questions."

"Yes, come in, but I don't understand how I can be of any help." Her first rehearsed line. "I didn't know Dr. Altmeyer. I've just heard about his death on the news."

Galiena was a heavy-set woman with a stylish hairstyle and flashy clothes. She was about the same size as the inspector, but Stark's badly wrinkled suit, purchased when she was ten or even twenty pounds lighter, made the inspector feel bedraggled walking behind her.

They went through the entranceway into a large sitting room where Galiena motioned for Stark and Brandt to sit on a gold brocade sofa.

"You work with Albert Schmidt at his home?"

"Yes I do, Inspector."

"When was the last time you saw Albert?"

"I don't really recall, a few days ago, perhaps Tuesday. None of us go to the Schmidt residence on Wednesday or Thursday because of Albert's teaching schedule at the university."

"But you were there this week, you saw him at his home?"

"Yes."

"Was Schmidt's son, Egon, there?"

"He may have been in the house, but I didn't see him."

"Do you know Egon?"

"Yes. I'm an amateur historian, Inspector. I work on research projects for Albert and sometimes Egon edits my work. He helps me when I need statistics or other data from the computer database. But Egon works alone. Our interaction consists of sending and receiving files through the computer mail system. I rarely see him face to face."

"How do you contact Albert about this work he gives you?"

"I just go out to his library when I have free time to work." She didn't expect this question and wondered if they would access her telephone records. "Sometimes I call him at his office at the university or on a private office line he has at his home."

"Do you call him on a mobile phone?"

"I'm not sure if any of the numbers I have for Albert is a mobile line. I may have inadvertently spoken to him on a mobile line, I can't say." While Galiena lied with that last statement, she was pleased with her performance over all. Horst was right, she thought, it was a murder investigation, and it didn't involve them.

But then Stark threw out the wild card. "Do you know Helga Schmidt?"

"I know her by name, of course, but I don't think we've met."

"You work in the house and never met her?"

"Yes, Inspector. She doesn't involve herself with the library."

"Do you know she is dead?"

"What?" Galiena went pale and had to steady herself. She had been standing but now sat in a chair across from the police. "No, that's terrible." Galiena tried to compose herself.

"Thank you for your time, Frau Kaufmann." They all stood. "Here's my card. If you think of anything that might be helpful to our investigation, we expect you to call."

"Yes, of course, Inspector, how did Frau Schmidt die?"

"We are treating it as a suicide."

As soon as the police left, Galiena poured herself a double whisky to stop her from shaking. What was happening, she thought. Why were people dying? She ran into her husband's study to examine his schedule. The last thing she needed was for him to show up now. Thank goodness he was away on business several more days. She immediately dialed Horst to ask him about Helga.

The Israelis transported the Griegg staff along with all their computer equipment in a utility van out to the Israeli safe house. It was a forty-five minute drive sitting on a cold bench seat against the side of the van. Everyone took the drive in stride. Sabine and Chris chatted a bit with Alana, asking her about Connecticut and other nominal topics about how she found her travels in Germany. Sigmund sat up front with David and, while they talked throughout the drive, David kept his voice uncharacteristically low so no one could overhear their conversation.

What the Israelis called their "safe house" turned out to be a three-story eighteenth-century house on a large country estate. The utility truck stopped at the security gate and was immediately cleared to enter the compound. They drove up the long, tree-lined driveway to the ivy-covered stone house.

Alana followed an Israeli agent out of the van. It was a different world from what she had left in Zurich. The property was vast. The house had been built on a ridge overlooking a mountain pass. Sheep grazed on the sloping fields. Out buildings of various sizes punctuated the landscape.

Alana supposed this was once a grand working farm. Now she wondered if the sheep served only to disguise the real purpose of the property. Beyond the fields, the woods were thick. It was both peaceful and foreboding at the same time.

"Alana," Sabine called out as she walked toward the house. "I should have mentioned this in the van. I packed some clothes for you." She handed Alana a canvas bag. "I hope you'll find something suitable. But let me know if you need anything, and we'll sort it out, somehow."

"Thank you." Alana grabbed ahold of the bag without stopping.

Inside the house, they gathered in the foyer to wait for instructions from the Israelis. Alana looked about at the people on whom so much depended.

Sabine and Christopher stood together. They gave the appearance to be more than just coworkers. Sabine was young and energetic. She was someone you immediately liked, and it comforted Alana to have a woman among the group with whom she could speak freely. Christopher and Ian were both forty-something and similar in appearance: tall, thin, spectacled Englishmen.

There was David, of course; he was rather pompous. Alana noticed that in the meeting before they left Zurich he made eye contact with everyone but her. She presumed it was because she was the outsider, but he made her uncomfortable. She wasn't sure she could trust him. The person who would keep her safe unsettled her. That couldn't be good, she thought.

And, then, there was Sigmund. Like Alana he was aloof, keeping his distance from the others. He was enigmatic, with piercing blue eyes and a smile that, when he used it, was captivating. When he looked over at Alana; she quickly looked away, embarrassed that he caught her watching him.

Alana peered around the corner to see more of the house. She saw a large sitting room with French doors overlooking a terrace. Beyond the terrace were more sheep fields. It was an idyllic setting, yet it all felt surreal. What am I doing here? Was all this really necessary?

She wanted to get in her car and drive back to Kirk's cottage. She wanted to shout: "This is all a mistake! I don't belong here! I'm going home!" Then an armed guard bumped her as he passed by, and she realized things were out of her hands. Leaving was not an option. For better or worse she would have to see this through, and these were the people to help.

David started speaking, "Here are the ground rules." He motioned to a woman walking into the room. "This is Gretchen, she runs the house. If you need anything, see her. You are all free to move about the house. Our work area, or 'war room' if you will, is to the left, dining is to the right, and the kitchen is further back, past the dining room. Unfortunately, we have to restrict outdoor access to the terrace," he pointed, "straight ahead of us. Gretchen will show us to our rooms now. We will meet in the war room in a half an hour. Gretchen, please put some food out so people can grab a bite when they come back downstairs."

Gretchen nodded in the affirmative.

"Are there any questions?" He surveyed the group. Taking a deep breath, "Right then, I'll see you shortly."

While others went upstairs, Sigmund and Ian went straight to the war room to set up computers. David came in with a bottle and a cigarette and sat down to watch. "I'm still a street man, you know." David's voice was piercing, a trait Sigmund found curious for someone in the business of surveillance.

"They've got me computer literate now, but you know me, I don't want a desk job. I still want to be out on the streets whenever I can. I bring the young guns in when needed. The higher-ups trust me to know my limits."

Sigmund walked over and poured two fingers of whisky from the bottle. "Are you giving more credit to the support staff now?"

"Oh, you know me too well." David looked into the whisky he was swirling in the glass. "When I was on the streets alone, I was a rebel, perhaps arrogant. But it may surprise you to learn that I now see the effort it takes to support agents." He stood up. "I'm going to see if Gretchen has put the food out." As he walked away, he remarked, "I'm a changed man, my friend, and all for the better, Sigmund, all for the better."

"All the computers are set up and connected into our office server. Everyone will have access when they log on," Ian reported to Sigmund. "What's your plan?"

"I want you to take point on finding the identity of this Franz person. But why don't you get your room sorted out and come back as soon as you can. And find out which room I'm in while you're up there."

"What can I do?" Alana walked in wearing a light blue jersey and navy trousers. Other than the slacks being a little long, the clothes Sabine had given her fit nicely.

Sigmund froze on her image as she stood in the doorway.

David walked by with a plate of food. "When did we last work together, Sigmund? Let's see, Evelyn died in 1990, right?"

Sigmund didn't answer. Staring at Alana, he downed his whisky then looked away.

She walked to him, "May I see the envelope?"

Sigmund turned to a stack of files and pulled out a copy of the front and back of the envelope on a single page.

"No, I need the original."

Sigmund went back to the stack and without question offered her the original envelope.

"I'll be sitting on the terrace." She passed Sabine and Christopher walking into the war room as she left.

"So Sigmund, am I right? Was it five years ago?" David repeated.

"Yes, David, five years." Sigmund turned away.

THE TRAP

Ian had seniority in terms of employment with the company. But responsibilities fell differently in each case they worked; seniority played no role. Each were masters of applied logic and critical thinking, but Sigmund knew their individual talents, and he alone assigned their workload accordingly.

Sabine might seem the odd one out with her background in theater. She had met Andrew Griegg, Sigmund's father, while researching the character of Emma in the Harold Pinter play *Betrayal* two years prior. Andrew was on the board of directors of the Theater Carmenstrasse, and they met through the play's director when Sabine stopped by his office for some guidance with her research.

Sabine was one of those people whose left and right brain functions were equally robust. She was intrigued by Andrew and the investigative work done by the Griegg company, so when the play fizzled and closed after just a few weeks, she found herself talking to him about a job.

A career as an actor proved unstable for Sabine. This was the third play she had been cast in and not one had run longer than a few weeks. While her individual reviews would have encouraged most young actors to struggle on, the uncertainty of the lifestyle was not to her liking. She wanted a regular paycheck. Andrew snapped her up on the spot, knowing how her creativity would benefit the group.

And he was right. Her resourcefulness brought a much-needed skill set to the group. Her theatrical training enabled her to go into any situation and glean information with ease. This was a role in which the senior Griegg also excelled; the others at the firm were either too technical or analytical to socialize well with strangers. Sabine's energy level was high, and she had remained composed in all the investigative cases she had been presented with so far.

Andrew had also recruited Ian. He was the son of a long-time friend and colleague. When Andrew learned of Ian's arrest for computer hacking, the young man's skills intrigued him. Ian had hacked Scotland Yard's computer system simply to see if he could. He had been in and out of the network clean on ten occasions over a three-month period. Once in the system, he did no harm. He simply read case files because they interested him.

Like most hackers, he grew overconfident and was caught breaching the MI-6 firewall on his first attempt. He thought he had gotten in unnoticed, but that wasn't the case. Their security detected the intrusion and allowed him to go far enough in to "hang" himself. Although his motivation was not sinister, the prosecutors had a clear case of a national security breach. Ian pled guilty and was sentenced to five years in prison. He was released after two years.

Of course Andrew took Ian's crime seriously, but both he and Sigmund foresaw that the nature of their information gathering and research would change. "Cyber centric" wasn't just a buzz phrase; it forecast a revolution on the horizon. Ian embodied a vital asset necessary for the Grieggs to remain at the leading edge of business technology in a changing world. Andrew recruited Ian immediately upon his release from prison. He literally walked out of prison and onto a plane to Zurich.

THE TRAP

The author of Alana's letter was the starting point of the investigation. Ian had begun his search the day before, after settling Alana at the hotel. He turned to census data first. Germany held a national census every five years between 1875 and 1910. The census enumerations thereafter did not include the full population. Church records, civil registrations, and newspapers were all valuable secondary sources to piece together the past.

Germany was behind other nations in making genealogy records available to the public. The Griegg office held licenses that allowed them to access many countries' census data, as well as birth, death, and marriage records on microfiche or microfilm. But in Germany, Ian had to resort to local genealogists for the information. The office worked regularly with members of the German Genealogic Society. Ian looked forward to the day when reports would be available over the Internet as experts were predicting.

Alana had seen Helmut's birth certificate, so Ian knew he had been born in Tübingen in 1910, and because the letters were addressed to Helmut at the Augsburg cottage, he inferred that Helmut had lived there for much, or all, of his life. Furthermore, because Franz had written, *When you saw what we used to call the trap, you reminisced how, as children, we would hide things inside.* Ian concluded that Franz and Helmut had been childhood friends. Franz was most likely born within a two-year period plus or minus from 1910. A remote date would be a four-year period, increasing the range from 1906 to 1914.

The author of the letter claimed to be Jewish. If true, Ian would look for someone Jewish or perhaps someone with one Jewish parent, who may or may not have been a practicing Jew. He would also look at school enrollments, tax registers, and military records. Surely, at least one of these accounts would reveal their Franz.

The search for Jewish records was more difficult. During the Kristallnacht—Night of Broken Glass—in 1938, many synagogues were burned throughout Germany, including the synagogue in Tübingen. If Franz was Jewish and had attended a synagogue, the official records were most likely lost.

Boris was tracking the military angle, specifically where Helmut Augsburg served during the war years. He would meet the others at the safe house later that day.

Alana sat on the terrace with the envelope in one hand and a pencil in the other. Gretchen had found a sketch pad for her. A picture, possibly connected to the mystery, was taking shape in her head. She hoped that touching the envelope again might help clarify what she was feeling. Nothing could be forced. It wasn't something she could turn on and off. It either happened, or it didn't.

But what if she did envision something that she deemed helpful? How would she even present it to the group? These people dealt in facts. That's what they were busy doing right at that moment—documenting historical facts. How could she walk into the war room and say, "I've had a vision," and expect to be taken seriously? Yet, if she was to be any use at all, she had to follow her own direction, therefore she sketched. The day drifted on. Gretchen brought out a cup of coffee saying, "You must be cold out here."

"You're right. I was just about to move inside."

Around 6:30 she heard someone enter the front hallway. David must have received a notification from the security gate because he marched out of the war room, passing Alana without a glance.

"Andrew! It's good to see you again." David's voice resonated throughout the house. "Different circumstances, of course."

"Hello, David. Good to see you. I'd rather be back in London, but duty calls."

"I'm told you are semiretired from the business." David responded.

"That's true. I have given Sigmund the reins." His voice emphasized *reins*. "Although he's been in control for many years, it was important for me to make it official."

"I hear you keep busy." David stated.

"Busier than ever! I'm on the lecture circuit, talking to young minds about how to transition Europe into the twenty-first century. We live in an interesting time, David. It's the only time in my life that no one falls asleep during one of my lectures." He chuckled.

"We are indeed in interesting times. Has Sigmund briefed you on our case?"

"I might be a little behind, but I understand we're meeting shortly. I'll get up to speed."

"Everyone's working in here," David gestured to the war room, "I'll get Gretchen to show you to your room. You know Gretchen, don't you?"

"I certainly do." Andrew came around the corner and saw Alana sitting by the door that led out to the terrace. "Are you Ms. Eastwood?" Andrew had a pleasing voice. So crisp and clean. She thought he could recite Shakespeare with ease.

"Yes, I'm afraid I've caused all this kerfuffle. That may not be the right word, but I don't know how else to describe it."

"Oh, no, my dear, you're not the cause of anything. Consider yourself a catalyst for the solution." He put his bags down. He held out his hand and gave a welcoming handshake. "I'm Andrew Griegg, Sigmund's father." Then he glanced into the war room where everyone was working. "I'm going to hunt down some coffee," he said, "would you like a cup?"

"Yes. I'll go with you." Alana picked up her cup and followed the well-dressed senior Griegg through the dining room to the kitchen. He had obviously been at the safe house before.

Without a thought, Andrew pitched the existing pot of coffee into the sink.

Alana said, "I wish everyone would stop calling me Ms. Eastwood. It's Alana," she said looking at Andrew, "I feel enough of an outsider as it is."

"Well, I'm sorry for that Alana. Sigmund will solve this mystery for you." Andrew pulled a small package of ground coffee from his jacket pocket. "You are about to have the best coffee of your life." He began making a new pot as he spoke. "I had time to pop into Harrods before leaving London. What part of the States are you from Alana?"

"I'm from Connecticut."

"Oh, you don't say. I was just in Connecticut," he said with enthusiasm. "I lecture at Yale University in New Haven from time to time."

"That's just about twenty miles from where I live."

Alana felt a friend had arrived. Once the coffee brewed, Andrew poured two cups, and they walked back to the settee where Alana had been sketching. "You're right, this coffee is very nice." She said with a smile.

"I told you so… didn't I? Best in your life! Where is Sigmund? I better check in with him before Gretchen tracks me down."

"Everyone is through that door." She raised her chin toward the war room.

Andrew was charismatic and energetic. He must be mid-sixties or older to be Sigmund's father but, like Kirk in his healthy days, Andrew seemed to transcend the aging process. He was a vibrant person for any age.

Andrew entered the war room with continued gusto. "Where's Ian? Come here, Sigmund, I want both of you to see what I have for you." Andrew said hello to Sabine as he passed. He removed a computer chip out of his briefcase and handed it to Ian, "The latest in encryption, Ian; this little beauty will scramble or unscramble whatever you have. Well, that's what they tell me anyway. I have no idea what you do with it."

"Thanks." Ian accepted the chip.

"The developer told me to 'drop it on you' and say 'booyah.' There was some sort of complicated hand gesture involved as well, but I can't remember all that. He looked about fourteen years old and had a nose ring. I didn't understand a word he said, but the kid is brilliant and that's all that matters."

Just then Boris Klondt entered the safe house; he lacked Andrew's bravado, but flashed a broad smile as he greeted his coworkers. They were all together now. Sigmund called for the briefing to start; he stepped out into the hallway to look for David.

When David entered through the terrace door, Alana followed him into the war room and took a seat at the table, placing her sketch pad face down in front of her. Gretchen came in with a pot of coffee. As she passed Andrew, she bent down and whispered, "Hello Andrew. See me when you are done. I will show you to your room."

Andrew nodded with a smile.

Sigmund walked in. "Here's what we have so far," he said as he took his seat. "Ian, start us out with what you have found on our Franz person."

"I identified several candidates for our mystery author but strongly believe we are looking for Franz Ziegler. He was born in the town of Tübingen in 1910. While the family is listed as Catholic, we believe them to be of Jewish ancestry. The family descended from Ashkenazi Jews who have lived in southern Germany for centuries. While curious, that wouldn't be our concern, except it appears some of the family members may have died in the Hep-Hep riots of 1819. History tells us that many Jews made a choice to keep their faith quiet after that terrible

THE TRAP

event. This may tie into that curious line in the letter that says, *I am Jew and I am German*. As we all know, Jewish people changed their names *en masse* during that time period. Chris will report more on that aspect in a minute, but we now know that at some point the family became known as Ziegler and lived down the road from the Augsburg's home. Franz went to school with Helmut. This is the only person who matched every data point of our research criteria. But there's additional data that strengthens the case even more.

"Franz attended the Institute of Technology in Berlin-Charlottenburg, graduating in 1936 with an honors degree in architecture. He was a student of Albert Speer.

"Franz was a member of the National Socialist Party. Based on photographs in which Ziegler is seen posing with Speer at the Nuremberg parade grounds, we believe he joined Speer in the construction of Zeppelin Field in late 1936.

"It seems Ziegler was a bit of a prodigy. While still in university and under the tutelage of Speer, he developed a new method of subterranean support for large buildings. At the time Ziegler didn't garner much credit for his work; but apparently, Speer took notice and continued to mentor him over the years. Together they revolutionized the construction of subterranean structures, a method that would be utilized up to the final days of the war.

"Franz Ziegler took over the construction of the Führerbunker system in 1940. He was still building tunnels as the war ended. But his bunkers didn't

177

hold up as well as those constructed with earlier methods. Whether that was due to design defects, faulty construction materials during the difficulties of war, or intensive bombing by the allies, I can't say for sure.

"Anyway, it's an interesting connection. This guy worked in Berlin at the end of the war. He had easy access to sensitive information and had any number places in which to hide it. We know Hitler's bunkers had storage vaults, but we also know the SS gave orders to destroy documents when the war effort was believed to be lost.

"The letter asks that a secret be revealed, but we can't be certain that any physical item would have survived the war. I just put out the possibility that we may be searching for something that no longer exists. I'll continue background research on another person of interest, but I am 99 percent certain Franz Ziegler is our man."

"Christopher, what do you have on the family?" Sigmund was a master at painting a picture with his team's research. He called on each member to add their color in exactly the right order.

"Okay. I believe Zimmermann was the original family name. It's a fairly common Jewish name. It comes from the German word for 'carpenter,' derived from the word *zimber,* which means timber or wood, and *mann* obviously meaning 'man.' The double 'n' indicates a Jewish surname. As Jewish names were historically replaced in Germany, I found many families simply shortened their name to Zimmer.

"I did, however, find one family that took the wife's surname of Ziegler, and that's the family line from which I believe our Franz Ziegler descended. But I acknowledge Ian's interest in keeping at least one other name open. We've all been down the wrong rabbit hole in the past.

"During Franz Ziegler's adult life, he lived outside Berlin with his wife, Monica, and their three children. I located death records for the family. All but one of them died 29 March 1945. It appears a daughter, named Dagmar, survived the incident that killed the others. There is no death record for her to date.

"I found the nursing facility where she lived after the war and spoke with the nurse who cared for Dagmar. The woman is elderly now but remembered her young patient well. She told me she had no children of her own and had taken pity on the child. She offered to adopt her, but the surviving grandmother wouldn't allow it.

Anyway, according to the nurse, Dagmar arrived at the nursing home the winter after the war ended. Scars indicated she had endured severe trauma to the head. Her motor skills were impaired, and she suffered short seizures, which left her unresponsive for several minutes. Severe head pain would follow. She needed medication daily to reduce the frequency of the attacks. Her cognitive abilities were compromised to a degree, but it was primarily the seizures that prevented her from living outside of nursing care. It was customary, in those days, to hospitalize patients with Dagmar's condition, which never improved throughout her tenure at the home.

Dagmar never attended school, but the woman I spoke with taught her to read and write, saying she was a delightful child—but one who never grew up. She was always childlike. The nurse suffered a mild stroke just before the nursing home closed in 1980, causing her to lose contact with Dagmar. She begged me to find Dagmar so they might meet again.

"I haven't found her yet, but I will, provided she is still alive."

"Good work, Christopher. If this Dagmar can communicate at all, we'll need to make plans to visit her. Do you have anything for us, David?"

"Well, I've distributed bios on all the members of the neo-Nazi group headed by Albert Schmidt. I know the police are talking with them, but so far no one has seen Schmidt. They're tracing his car and credit cards, but nothing has surfaced.

"Basically, the police have zilch. We've agreed to share information with them, but I'm not sure how much they will share with us as we move forward. We have a somewhat turbulent relationship with the German police; therefore, our level of cooperation depends on the individual officers involved.

"Inspector Stark and Detective Brandt are the two assigned to this case. They know we have Ms. Eastwood; they want her back. I've told them that wouldn't happen at this time. They are also looking for Albert Schmidt's son, Egon.

"I will reiterate what I told Sigmund earlier. We have been watching Albert's group for some time. We managed to plant a civilian operative into the group, because we suspected some involvement in a gun smuggling scheme out of North Africa.

"Keep your eyes open for that angle. Prior to Altmeyer's murder, we didn't think the group was violent. We think the guns might have been a way to finance their other political activities. I still have a problem believing Albert is our killer, but we can place him at the university the night Altmeyer was killed. I have just typed out my report, and it will be distributed to each of you shortly.

"Egon is the twenty-year-old son of Albert and Helga Schmidt. He works with his father and is a member of the neo-Nazi group. He is a person of high intelligence but appears to have substantial emotional baggage. Father and son may be traveling together or separately. The son may be our killer. We have nothing of real substance at this point, just speculation."

Boris had traced Helmut to the medical corps during the war. For the time being, Sigmund skipped reports from Boris and Sabine. Their research would be pertinent at the next briefing.

"David, we need to interview Dagmar Ziegler, whatever her condition. I'd like the two of us to go together. Can you make the arrangements?"

"Certainly, we have a helicopter at our disposal."

"I'd like to go with you." Alana said firmly.

"That's out of the question." Sigmund stacked up his papers and tapped them on the table in preparation to stand and leave.

"Wait a minute. I have something to contribute, and I think I should go to the nursing home with you." Alana said.

David interjected, "We have two dead and one person in a coma; our focus must be on safety. Please leave this to us."

"Who's in a coma?" Alana questioned nervously. "Who?"

The room turned quiet until Sigmund broke the silence. "Marta Voss was attacked soon after you left for Zurich. After you went to the hotel, I notified the local police in Tübingen and requested they put her under protection, but I was too late. Luckily for her, David's people had already alerted the police and officers were dispatched to the Augsburg home. When they arrived, they interrupted an attacker. Ms. Voss had been stabbed, but all indications are that she will survive her injures."

"Why didn't you tell me?"

"Look," Sigmund responded begrudgingly, "you came to my door with a story of what you did on your summer vacation. I know little about you, but I'm trying to help you in the best way I know how." He slowed his voice. "It seemed pointless to burden you with any more distress until we knew more about her recovery. As I said, for you to leave the safe house now is out of the question. We simply can't guaranty your safety."

Alana stood up. "You think I'm on vacation?" She put both hands on the table and leaned toward him. "You want me to sit around here until you tell me to go home and say, guess what happened to me this summer!

"Well, let me tell you something," her voice was forceful and deliberate, "this is no fucking vacation. I didn't ask to be part of it, but it's my life, and it's happening to me. You can't exclude me."

"The attack on your friend is the very reason we can't include you. Even with efforts to protect Ms.

Voss, the police couldn't get there in time. I have no obligation to tell you anything, but this meeting should demonstrate that we are willing to share all our research with you.

"I chose not to tell you about Marta Voss because it would make you feel even more vulnerable. I couldn't risk having you fall apart. There was just no need for that. It's the way we operate. I'm sorry David let it slip."

Alana tossed her sketch pad across the table to Sabine. "That's what you're looking for. That's 'the trap.' I'm sure Sigmund will explain it to you if he thinks you have a right to know." She slammed the chair against the table and walked out.

Andrew followed her out of the room. She picked up a phone off the table in the foyer. There was no dial tone.

"I'm afraid you'll need an access code to make a call." Andrew said quietly.

"I don't know why I picked it up. I have no one to call." She threw the phone at Andrew pulling the cord from the wall as she turned to run up the stairs.

Andrew went back into the war room.

Half listening to the commotion in the foyer, Sabine turned the pad to face her. It was a sketch of a dragon-like creature. A serpent of sorts with one leg clamped within an iron shackle and chain.

The creature looked foreboding with a long outstretched tongue. Sabine glanced at Sigmund as she pushed the pad across the table toward him.

Sigmund informed the group, "Ms. Eastwood tells me that she has experienced psychic episodes at times in her life. I do not believe that information relevant to our investigation. Let's get back to work."

"Wait a minute, Sigmund," Sabine interrupted. "You told me to look into the Zimmermann family. As we just heard, the name literally means carpenter. I've learned that they were, in fact, cabinetmakers, master woodcarvers to be precise; they passed their skills along from generation to generation.

"Their furniture is much sought after to this day. They were famous for carving mythical creatures into their designs." She continued, "I didn't share this information because it didn't seem relevant, until now. Seeing this sketch makes it all fit together.

"While I haven't seen this particular motif, it is similar to the carvings I've seen in photos of their furniture. It seems too much of a coincidence that Alana drew this figure when she knew nothing about the presumed ancestors of the Ziegler family as wood carvers and cabinetmakers. Don't you tell us there's no such thing as a coincidence?"

Sigmund picked up the pad and looked at the creature. "I concede your interest. We should all keep it in mind. Now let's get back to work."

Andrew stood up and walked over to his son. "Come now, Sigmund, you didn't think we needed to know about Alana's psychic ability?" He left the room. In the foyer, he poured a scotch whisky and a glass of wine and asked Gretchen to show him to Alana's room.

He knocked on the door. "Alana, it's Andrew. May I come in?"

"Yes, of course."

"I didn't know if you were a scotch drinker, so I also brought a glass of wine. You can choose."

Alana took the wine. "Will Marta be okay?"

"Yes. There's no reason to believe otherwise; I'm told the doctors are optimistic."

"All of this is happening because I found that stupid letter. People are dead and now Marta has been injured... it's my fault. Why couldn't I have just let it go?

"In my first meeting with Sigmund, he suggested that I go back to Connecticut, just forget about the letter." She continued, "But I can't leave now, can I? I mean this place. I can't go home now, can I?"

"No, I don't believe David would allow it," he said quietly.

"I feel I'm the one in 'the trap.' How can I help if I'm not even given information? You should have seen the way Sigmund looked at me when I appeared in the war room earlier. It was outright disdain. I don't belong here with you people."

Andrew took a deep breath while he chose his words. "It was not disdain, Alana. Sabine told me that the only clothes she could bring for you came from Sigmund's flat in our Zurich office. She brought clothes that had belonged to his wife. Her name was Evelyn, and she was killed five years ago.

"Sabine told him she needed to give you Evelyn's clothes and he approved, but I'm sure seeing you dressed in them for the first time was unsettling." Andrew had a way of defusing heated emotions, just as Kirk had done throughout the years. "Sigmund can be difficult for an outsider to understand. Please

185

know that he wants to help you in every way he knows how."

"I'm sorry." Alana looked down into her glass. "I wish I'd known that before."

They sat quietly for a moment.

"Any idea what the serpent means?"

"No, I've been trying to sort it out."

Andrew walked to the window and spoke as he gazed into the darkness. "I knew a psychic once." He turned to look at Alana. "He saved my life and I'll be forever grateful. I haven't thought about him in years, but it's good to be reminded, because I truly believe that not all things in life can be explained by conventional reasoning. Sigmund likes things cut and dry. As an investigator, he sees black and white, but that is not always the way life is."

He turned around, "It was in the aftermath of the war when a psychic saved me from assured death. I had been too young to serve, but it was soon after the war when I started working with my father. The details aren't important. Perhaps it's a story for another time." He cleared his throat and sat down beside her. "Sigmund is not your enemy, my dear. It will just take a little time for you to see him as your friend.

"He tries to protect people, and sometimes he tries too hard. It's nothing to do with you personally. It's just who he is, and he's very good at his job." He touched her arm. "I'm asking you to trust him."

"I'm sorry I caused a scene; that's not like me."

"When you're ready, I want you to come back downstairs. You are important to the investigation. I think everyone knows that now. Sabine explained to us that the Zimmermanns and then Zieglers were cabinetmakers, and it appears that carving images of mythical creatures was their trademark."

Alana's face lit up, "Really?"

"Yes, really. Do you see now how you add value to this investigation?"

"The sideboard in Kirk's cottage, where I found the letter, the Zieglers must have carved it. There was a signature inside one of the doors, but I couldn't decipher the name." She closed her eyes tightly to see if she could recapture the image of the signature in her mind. She couldn't.

"There was no dragon carved on the sideboard, not like the one I sketched, anyway. The sideboard was carved with trees and blossoms, and if you looked closely, there was a little gargoyle figure perched in the tree on each door. Marta called them Wasserspeiers."

"This is exactly why you are needed downstairs. So come down when you are ready. There's no rush." Andrew left her room.

Back downstairs, Andrew asked Sigmund to take a break. They sat on the terrace with a drink. "I saw William while I was in England. He sends his love, as always. He looks more like you every time I see him, although he's wearing his hair long now."

"I will go see him after we wrap up this case."

"You should. Philip is retiring soon. Daria's health isn't what it used to be. They want to move to Malta when William finishes school. They feel that since he will be off to college next year, this is the right time to start planning some changes. Who knows, William may want to come home to Zurich and go to college here. He might even want to join the company."

"I understand he's getting older. You act like I've abandoned him. You know that's not true. He's here every summer and school holidays. At least he was until going off with his friends became more fun. But still, either one of us is in London to visit him every month. Forgetting the distance between us, I think we have a normal relationship."

"Sigmund," Christopher shouted out from the war room.

"What have you got?" Sigmund asked as he stood up.

"Sigmund," Andrew grabbed his son's arm, "Don't discount Alana."

"I won't, Dad. Let's go see what Chris has for us."

"I've found the nursing home where Dagmar Ziegler lives," he said. "David's preparing a cover for you to get in and visit with her. But the weather might be a problem."

Sigmund looked at his watch, "Well, it's too late to move on it now; let's hope the weather cooperates so we can take the chopper up in the morning."

The door was open, but little daylight filtered into the room. Albert's eyes strained under the light of a single bare bulb strung from the ceiling. Horst had called on his mobile to tell him that Helga had committed suicide. It threw him into shock; it was the only thing that had interrupted his self-centered pity since finding Altmeyer's body.

A chill ran down his spine when he thought of Helga. None of this was supposed to happen. The smell of mold in the room suddenly became unbearable. He walked outside to be sick.

Albert didn't think he could go on. It was as if his body was attacking him from the inside out. Back indoors, he sat on the floor resting his head against the damp wall. He wanted all the events of the last days to go away. He wished his mind to go blank, for even a moment. Every bone in his body ached. Just when he thought he might rest, he heard a noise coming from outside.

"Albert, it's me."

"Go away."

"I brought you some food."

"Just leave it."

"I can't, Albert, we need to talk."

"I've already said too much to people. I'm telling you," he raised his voice, "Go away. NOW!"

There was a long silence before he sensed he was alone again. He thought, "How did I think I could do any research on the letter or track Egon." The notion seems utterly ridiculous now. He had found Helmut Augsburg in their database, but that was it. There was electricity in the hut but no telephone line for his modem. Now, with the knowledge of his wife's death, he faced the fact that he was completely dysfunctional in mind and body. He resigned himself to surrendering to the police and telling them about Egon. But he couldn't gather the strength to do it. First, he needed to rest.

He awoke, letting out a long painful moan and walked to the door. He saw the food tray. The thought of eating made him nauseous. Sweat beaded up on his forehead, and he felt an immediate need for air. Just a few steps out into the grassy field, he doubled over, heaving with pain in his chest. He stumbled to the ground and vomited. "Pull yourself together!" he thought aloud.

Albert opened his eyes. He didn't know where he was. His cheek was lying in his vomit, and his vision was shrouded in a haze. But how could it be? Why couldn't he move? All he could do was stare out into the blades of grass in front of his face. He couldn't feel anything.

Alana came downstairs reluctant to face everyone after her outburst. She went into the kitchen for a cup of coffee. Her heart sank when she opened the door to see David's face. Then she saw Andrew. "Come in, I'm making fresh coffee, would you like some? David is having tea, so you have your choice."

"I'll have a cup of your great coffee. Thanks."

"David just reminded me that his father was one of the original members of Mossad." For Alana's benefit, he added, "Israeli Intelligence. It was at the end of the Second World War, an unlikely assortment of Jewish survivors united to form a quasi-underground organization. They called themselves the Avengers. I'm afraid we have to call them what they were David—vigilantes."

"No objection, they had the right." David said in confirmation.

"This home belonged to one of those original members." David added, "It wasn't long before those people disbanded; some of them were killed, but the survivors drifted off in different directions. My father stayed on, and this is where I grew up. When my father died in 1971, my mother had nowhere else to go, so she stayed here to take care of the place. I was here on and off throughout the years, but I moved to Israel after I finished my schooling.

"We've come a long way together, Andrew." He put his hand on Andrew's back. "In those early days for my father, life was cheap and many died on both sides. Thank goodness it's not that way anymore. Not usually, anyway. We just keep working toward better days.

"People kill for many reasons, Ms. Eastwood, reasons you might consider insignificant, but to them, they're quite rational. It could be religion, politics, money, or power."

Andrew interrupted, "Power is a subjective force. It has different meanings for different people. But greed and power can cause even a man like Albert Schmidt to kill."

David said, "Don't underestimate what we have to do to keep people safe. We know our job Ms. Eastwood."

"I realize that," she said, "I am sorry for what I said earlier."

Without any conciliation to Alana, David excused himself and went back to the war room.

Andrew invited her to sit with him. "Tell me, Eastwood is not a German name, so what is your background?"

"My mother was German, my father American. They married when my father was in the army and stationed in Germany. I was born on the Bayern-Kaserne army base."

"You're an army brat!"

"Well, my father served just four years, and I don't remember any of those army years. We moved to Connecticut when I was a baby. Does that qualify me as a brat?"

"Still, do you know the origin of the colloquial term BRAT?"

"I'm embarrassed to say no."

"It's an acronym for British Regiment Attached Traveler." Andrew spoke with authority even with a bit of fun trivia. "That's the official answer. There are other unofficial answers."

"From what I understood, my mother was a bit of a rebel in her youth. To be honest with you, I think marrying my father meant a one-way ticket out of Germany. It's funny how close I became to my grandfather, when she wasn't close to him at all. She landed in America and never looked back.

"I don't know where my family name Eastwood comes from. Obviously, his roots go back to Africa at some point—no Eastwoods there I should think, except possibly a throwback to the colonial era." Alana shrugged, "I don't mean to make light of it. I'm not naïve; I know the origins of many African-American surnames. That's a dark spot in history, and not just in America. It's just that I haven't looked into my heritage on either side of my family. I don't know when my father's ancestors came, or were brought, to America.

"I believe Eastwood is an English name; how I came to have it could be an interesting story. I know no one in my father's family. He was born in the south, in Mississippi. As I got older, I sensed that his family disapproved of his marriage. I didn't infer that from any psychic ability, just intuition. They weren't a part of my life."

Alana felt comfortable talking to Andrew.

"I thought I might discover something about my German ancestors in my grandfather's house, but I found nothing. That was disappointing, especially now, after watching how Christopher and Ian have uncovered the history of our Franz character. It's intriguing and makes me want to investigate my roots when I return home.

My family was limited to my mother and father and Kirk because I never met anyone else. Ian actually found a Family History Center close to where I live. I had no idea that the Mormon Church has been microfilming church and civil records all over the world. The fact that they make them available to the general public might just have me hooked into investigating. It seems quite fascinating.

America is called a melting pot, and I am a good example of that—for all the good and bad of what that means. Perhaps it's time I should know more about the ingredients of my genealogical pot."

"Alana, I've found studying genealogy can deepen ones sense of belonging to history, being part of something bigger than yourself and the trials and tribulations of each day, especially in light of what you face now. Why are you, of all people, burdened with solving the mystery of the trap? Knowing more about your family history could be cathartic. For you to unravel the mystery of the trap is not an accident, it's your destiny."

"Thank you for that Andrew. I've been asking myself, why me, since this ordeal began."

"Enough philosophy." Andrew poured another cup of coffee, "Tell me about your psychic visions."

"I can't explain it. It just is. Ninety-nine percent of the time I'm just like everyone else. Once in a while, however, it seems that some cosmic forces align, and I somehow connect with events from the past in a way I can't explain. Every time I've had a vision, it has proved true. That's all I can say.

"But, Andrew, something is bothering me. I feel terrible about wearing Sigmund's wife's clothes. Should I talk to him?"

"Oh no, please don't be concerned. I told you so you would understand Sigmund a little better. You were right, you needed to have more information to function as a member of our team. I told you about Evelyn because it was something you needed to know. You're an interesting woman, Alana Eastwood, but right now we need to get back to the war room to see what's happening."

When they walked in, Sigmund was speaking with Niedermeyer on speaker phone. They saw two computers scanning sequences of letters and numbers across each screen. Alana didn't recognize the significance, but Andrew knew them to be automobile registration plates.

Niedermeyer's distinct voice filled the room, "I have uncovered some interesting information for you, Sigmund."

"Go on, you have our attention."

"Not permitted any official role in your soiree in the country, I decided to familiarize myself with the so-called research group attached to Albert Schmidt. With some information that Boris shared, I enlisted an old acquaintance in Tübingen. He informs me the young Egon Schmidt drives an old van with the German registration plate: MUB RT364. This van has been spotted near the German-Czech border. "He could not give me any new information on the father, Albert Schmidt, but curiously a car belonging to a member of Schmidt's, let's use the word 'club,' filled up with petrol yesterday not far the university where he works and the professor was killed. The car belongs to a Horst Wilhelm and is normally driven by his son, whom I'm told is at school out of the country. That plate number is: RUB ZK295."

"How did you get that information before we did or the police for that matter?"

"I have my secrets, Sigmund."

"Is everything quiet at the office?"

"Serene," Sigmund, "it is simply serene. I am functioning under the full lockdown protocol that I established with the assistance of Andrew's father, Wolf, many years ago. There's a man with a large gun in our lobby and another man with a gun is on constant patrol. I am very safe."

"Thank you, Niedermeyer."

"Should I acquire anything else of interest, I will call again. Good-bye to all."

Of all the people involved, Niedermeyer was certainly the most unusual. He had spent his entire adult life working in the library for the Griegg family. They believed him to be seventy-four, but no one could be 100 percent sure, because no official record of his birth was ever found. He had been conducting intelligence gathering since its infancy in the modern era.

Niedermeyer still used the old cataloging system of index cards that he had begun as a young man. It didn't bother him that many cards were now marked with the word "deceased." No card would ever be purged from his records. He now had five trays containing hundreds, perhaps thousands of cards.

Everyone referred to Niedermeyer by his surname. If they needed a history lesson, they went to him. His photographic memory never failed him. When Boris joined the firm, he surreptitiously attempted to profile J. Leopold Niedermeyer. He later confessed his undertaking to Sigmund, saying that Niedermeyer didn't exist.

Sigmund laughed, "Yes, it appears our eccentric friend has managed to have all details of his life expunged from the records. Not even my father knows anything, and they have worked together their entire adult lives.

"We don't know where he was born, what family he is from, or where he was educated. We don't know what the J stands for. We think he was self-educated. My grandfather, Wolfgang, hired him at a young age despite no claim of prior work experience. Niedermeyer tells a bizarre story of being lifted from an opium den in Indonesia by my grandfather, but that is sheer fantasy, because I know my grandfather was never in Indonesia and I doubt Niedermeyer was either. We trust everything Niedermeyer says without question, except for that story. The way he grins while recounting it makes clear it's his quirky way to keep us guessing about his life."

As the world changed, Niedermeyer stayed the same. His word-of-mouth method of obtaining his intelligence, once commonplace with everyone in the industry, was still as integral to the organization as all the state-of-the-art automation the others used. No one ever doubted Niedermeyer.

His nonconformity showed in the suits he wore. Some were fifty years old. He once told Sabine that by never changing his wardrobe, he was assured never to put on weight, which he explained was important because his only exercise was "of the mind."

When he took up residence in his office, he scheduled time in the Griegg apartment twice a week to bathe and take care of his laundry. When Sigmund assured him, he could use the facilities at any time, Niedermeyer responded: "I couldn't possibly intrude without a reservation."

Someone in the group was always bringing food for him. He slept in a tiny room off his library and rarely needed to leave the building. No one knew where the bed came from; it simply appeared one day.

He worked the phone for his information. Sometimes his contacts came to him. But that wouldn't be the case during lockdown. Niedermeyer was a loner and never worked one-on-one with the others. His pride and amusement came from contributing vital nuggets of valued and targeted intelligence at just the right moment. Everyone loved him.

Egon pulled into a gas station and went inside. He put cash down on the counter for petrol. "Where can I get something to eat around here? Some place quiet." He asked the young boy behind the counter.

"Don't know, it's late."

"Can I park my van here and get a few hours sleep?"

"I'm closing up in an hour. Do what you want."

"Can I plug my computer into an electric outlet? I have a long extension cord. Maybe I could plug my modem into your phone line? I've got a splitter. Just till you close?"

"No, the owner would go crazy if I let you do that."

"I'll pay you."

"That's not the point. I can't let you do that."

Egon grabbed a bunch of snacks and went back to the van. He wanted to dial into the Internet to see if anyone had responded to the thread he started in his MUD room. In addition, he wanted another file from the library server, but he now realized that wasn't going to happen. Truth be told he was too tired to work, anyway. He ate chips, drank a soda, and fell asleep in the back of the van.

10

High Over Germany

Up early the next morning, Sigmund and David left the compound by helicopter from the sheep field. The sound of the whirling rotors woke Alana. She lay still, allowing herself to fall asleep again as soon as the noise faded in the distance.

The helicopter left Swiss airspace heading east-northeast into Germany toward the Lusatian Mountain range. Staying south of Munich, their destination was just shy of the Czech Republic. The weather had cleared from the night before, and the autumn morning offered CAVU flight conditions (ceiling and visibility unlimited). As they flew farther up the mountain range, signs of civilization became sparse. Sigmund saw an occasional group of farm buildings surrounded by grazing fields that led to deep forests. Periodically a road would show itself through an opening in the tree canopy. Suddenly, the temperature inside the cockpit dropped; Sigmund reached for his gloves. They would arrive at their destination before needing to refuel. He figured that would be another hour.

The time passed quickly. They landed at an airport roughly twenty kilometers from the nursing home. David's people had a car and driver waiting. Inside the car, they gave Sigmund documents that would establish him as Henri, Dagmar's cousin.

There was nothing special or unusual about the nursing home. It was a nice enough place although not lavish in any way. The head nurse in charge was skeptical about a visitor for Dagmar, because she had lived there so many years with no callers.

"You can imagine I was overjoyed to discover a living relative." Sigmund spoke as Henri in German.

"We found no evidence of relatives," the nurse exclaimed. "She was a complete orphan, a ward of the state, since her paternal grandmother died."

"No, I assure you your records are incomplete. My connection to Dagmar is through a half sister." Sigmund held out his papers for the nurse to inspect. "Otto von Rutler fathered a child a year before his marriage to Dagmar's maternal grandmother. You can see for yourself. These papers are all certified genealogical records. The child was my mother. It was an out-of-wedlock birth. You must appreciate that this was commonplace during that time period. I also have a letter from von Rutler acknowledging the child and the agreement to keep it secret." The Israelis had totally fabricated this claim.

"Wait here a minute, please." The nurse walked through a door marked *PRIVATE* and didn't return for several minutes. When she reappeared, she stood behind the protection of the nurse's counter.

"I'm afraid your cousin suffered brain trauma from a childhood injury. She is now a woman in her mid-fifties with the mental acuity of an adolescent. She can appear functional one minute and then have a seizure and debilitating head pain the next. Are you sure you want to meet her? It would seem cruel to explain your ancestral connection. I don't want her upset in any way."

"I assure you that I will say nothing to distress her. I knew before I set out on this journey that she had an injury that meant she could not mature normally. I will just say I am a cousin. Perhaps in some way I can bring comfort to her and make her life a little happier. I should like to let her know she is not alone and that she has someone who cares. What is the harm? Surely you can understand."

Sigmund reached out for the nurse's hand and pressed it down onto his paperwork on the counter. The act was totally out of character for him, but he played it naturally. Her hand braced against his, then relaxed as he squeezed lightly. "Just for a few minutes, I've come so far. Please," he smiled, "sit with us."

"No, that won't be necessary. She is recovering from a cold, so we confined to her room today. You must leave the door open while you are in there. We'll take notice."

They walked down the hallway to room number seventeen. "Dagmar we've got a surprise for you, my dear. This is Henri; he is here to visit with you. He is your cousin."

Sigmund looked at the woman sitting in a chair playing cards on a small tray balanced on her lap. She was a handsome woman despite a glaring scar across her forehead. The hairline behind the scar was thin, exposing a slightly recessed area down to her ear.

"Hello Dagmar, I'm Henri."

"Hello, I don't know you."

"No, you don't know me. I have only recently discovered that we are cousins. Do you know what a cousin is?"

"It means you are a member of my family."

"Yes, we are family. I am related to your grand-father, Otto von Rutler. Do you remember him?"

"No, my family is dead."

"Mine as well, that's why it was so important for me to come and see you. I brought something for you." He pulled a small parcel from his pocket and handed it to Dagmar. She had never been given a present like this before. Every patient at the home received a gift at Christmastime, but this was totally different. The parcel was expertly wrapped and held together with red ribbon. Gretchen had done this at Sigmund's request. Dagmar opened it carefully so as not to rip the paper. Inside the box was a colorful scarf. She immediately tied it around her neck. "I like this. It's very pretty."

Satisfied that he was harmless, the nurse quietly left the room.

"Do you remember your mother and father?"

"That's Mama and Papa," she said, pointing to a photograph on her bureau. Sigmund looked over his shoulder. His eyes glanced over the photo to focus on a small wooden box. He fixated on the carving on the top of the box—it was the dragon, the one Alana had sketched the day before.

"What a lovely picture, may I look at it?"

"Yes, I am the baby in the picture."

Sigmund walked to the bureau. "What a beautiful baby you were." He said as he looked at the box. "This is beautiful."

"That is my box. I keep my things inside."

"May I look at it? I have never seen a box like this before."

"Yes." She got up quickly and protectively took the box from him. "I will show you what's inside." She brought it back to the bed and sat down.

"I like you, Henri. I've never had someone come to see me before."

"I like you too, Dagmar. Show me what's inside. I would like to see."

"Sometimes the top gets stuck." She strained and made a face as children do when they struggle; then the top came free. She pulled out a photo. "This is my father." The picture was creased and frayed around the edges. "He was an important man."

"Yes, I know he was smart. His job was to design buildings. Did you know that?"

"Maybe, I just know he was smart. The nurses tell me how important my family was. It makes me feel good that everyone cares about them, but they all died a long time ago, that's why I live here."

Dagmar explained each one of the half-dozen pictures kept in the box. But, to Sigmund, nothing seemed as important as the box itself. Was the box the trap?

Sigmund held the pictures one by one after Dagmar explained their significance. Positioning himself behind her sightline, he could use the tiny Minox "spy" camera that one of David's men had given him to capture an image of each photograph and item in the box. Everything would need scrutiny back at the safe house. When the box was empty, Sigmund assured himself that there was no hidden compartment. Then he photographed the box as well.

One photograph of her father showed him at a construction site. The others were all of her family. "Dagmar, do you know where these pictures of your family were taken?"

"Yes, that was our house. We lived in Berlin. But now I live here. Let me show you the one of my grandmother. Her name is Gertrude. She used to come here to see me, but now she has died." It was the most recent photograph in the box. It depicted Dagmar and Gertrude in the garden at the nursing home.

A bell rang three times.

"That bell means you have to leave." Dagmar slipped off the bed and began placing everything back into the box. There was a definite order that she had remembered. She placed the box back on the bureau and sat back on the bed.

"They are serving lunch now and visitors can't stay. Most days I work in the kitchen, but I have a cold, so I can't work today. I usually wash all the dirty dishes, but today I must eat in my room, and I can't wash dishes afterward.

"Some people are coming to read to us after lunch. I hope someone will read to me in my room. When will you come back and see me again?"

"I don't know because I live very far away. But I will send you another gift, so you remember me. Would you like that?"

"What will you send me?"

"Oh, I don't know. What would you like?"

"I would like a red sweater. Like the ones the nurses wear. I wish I was a nurse so I could take care of the people who live here."

"All right, I will send you a red sweater." He bent down and kissed the top of her head as she sat on the bed.

"Thank you for this scarf." Dagmar reached with her hand to touch the tip of the scarf tied under her chin. I don't remember your name."

"Henri. My name is Henri."

Sigmund collected a calling card as he passed the nurses' station on his way out.

It surprised David to see Sigmund walking down to the car so soon. "They let me in to see her, and I managed to photograph pictures of the family in their Berlin house." David's profession made him expert at reading people, so he knew Sigmund was hiding something.

Once they were back on the road to the airport, Sigmund said, "She had a wooden box, which held family keepsakes. The image of a dragon was carved on the top... the figure looked just like the one that Alana sketched yesterday. I examined the box. There was no secret compartment. It contained several photos, some buttons, and costume jewelry. I took photos of everything."

"Curious." David muttered.

"Yes. Curious, indeed."

"Did the woman remember anything?"

"Not anything of value. Perhaps an examination of the pictures will prove useful. She took some sort of blow to the head. She has a scar along one side of her skull. I've seen similar scars from gunshot wounds where the bullet just grazed the surface.

"She did say something of interesting though. The nurses tell her she is from an important family. I don't think it's a coincidence that she is being cared for here. I suspect the place has had its share of Nazi families over the years."

They flew back to the safe house without exchanging many words. Sigmund's mind was in overdrive after seeing the carving on the box.

Meanwhile, trouble was brewing in Zurich between the German police and Israeli Intelligence. Each side was independently looking for Albert and Egon, and the police weren't happy that Mossad still had Alana in their custody. Inspector Stark had learned who Sigmund Griegg was from her captain and how Griegg was involved in her investigation. Stark was trying to negotiate another interview with Alana. The territorial conflicts were unmistakable, and now that Alana was out of Germany, the inspector had limited authority. It was difficult for Stark to grasp that something that had happened fifty years prior could have triggered the events of the past days. This case didn't fit the model for modern policing protocols, even for Stark, who was quite capable of thinking out of the box.

Egon's psychiatrist was also unwilling to discuss her patient with the police.

"I just want to know if he is capable of violence." Stark asked.

"We're all capable of violence, Inspector," replied Dr. Erma Haase.

"Would you like more people to die?"

"Don't be dramatic, Inspector." The doctor was undaunted. "I can tell you that my patient is a highly intelligent young man. He loves his job. Social skills are difficult for him, but he's made real progress in navigating a path through what he finds difficult. His work in the library provides an intellectual challenge, and I believe this work has stabilized him. Writing is another outlet for him. Did you know he is writing a novel?"

"And you don't care what he writes about?"

"I don't know what he writes about. It's not my concern."

"He's a fucking Nazi." Stark fired back.

The doctor didn't answer.

"What about medication? Is he taking any?"

"You know I can't tell you that."

"Do you know his mother committed suicide?"

"Yes, it's terrible. Helga had her own problems, but she wasn't my patient. Other than what Egon mentioned, I didn't know her at all."

"Has Egon tried to contact you in the past few days?"

"No, he hasn't. I will give you that."

"Where did he live?"

"At the Schmidt home; I understand he had his own flat above the garage."

"Well, those rooms have been cleaned out. Do you know where he moved to or when he moved?"

"No." The doctor took offense. "I told you, to my knowledge he lived at the family home."

"Did his mother drive him to his appointments?"

"I don't think so. She did when he was younger, but I believe he's been driving himself for many years now. He's nineteen or twenty years of age. He functions as any young man."

"He doesn't have a driver's license."

"I don't know specifics like that. He was driving. Anyone would assume he had a license."

"Do you know what type of car he drove?"

"No."

"Here's my card. I'll expect a call if you hear from him." Stark started to walk away but then turned to the doctor and said, "We found no recent pictures of Egon at the Schmidt home, so I will need to send a police sketch artist over here. I expect you to help her with a likeness of Egon."

"Of course."

"And Doctor, it better be a spitting image, or I'll be back to arrest you."

The doctor walked away.

Stark had issues with doctors like Haase. Twice in her career she had been assigned mandatory counseling. Both instances concerned the use of force.

208

THE TRAP

The first incident occurred when Stark was a rookie. A woman fired at a police officer during a robbery. The woman had then pointed her gun at Stark, who fired immediately. The robber was badly wounded but survived. Her male accomplice surrendered without further violence. The second time was a few years later when she wounded a teen gang member. It was during a summer filled with gang violence. The boy had threatened her with a knife. She shot him in the leg.

Both incidents drew countrywide scrutiny. A mandatory police review confirmed that they were cases of authorized use of force, so the counselling assignment didn't sit well with Stark. She had done her job. She had dealt with the shootings. She had no need to "talk" about them. After the second incident, she transferred out of Munich to the regional force in Baden-Württemberg where she now worked.

When Stark returned to the station, Brandt told her that the Griegg office had given them two auto registration plate numbers of concern. They also made them aware of the gunrunning investigation being conducted by the Israelis, which as Brandt told her "is connected to at least two members of the Schmidt research group."

It outraged Stark to be hand-fed evidence from either Griegg or the Israelis. She told Brandt to get the car; they were going back to talk to Horst.

As they were leaving, a call came from Galiena Kaufman. She reported that she had found Albert Schmidt—dead.

Following Galiena's directions, they left for an abandoned property owned by Galiena's husband. When they arrived, they found Galiena sitting in her car at the side of the road. She got out and hurried toward them. "I did not know he was here when we talked at my house. I swear it.

"He called me later in the day to say he was in this old cottage. It's just behind this group of trees." She pointed. "He didn't ask for anything, but I brought him some food. When I got here, he wouldn't speak to me. He screamed for me to go away. I left the food outside the cottage. Later, when I got home, I thought he had sounded so strange that I came back to check on him. I found him dead and called you right away." Galiena was frantic.

They walked across the sheep field to a derelict building. Galiena showed them the body lying in the grass, then asked if she could leave.

"I don't think so." Stark turned to face Galiena. "My detective has some questions about guns that he'd like to ask you." Then she called the medical examiner.

Andrew entered the war room, asking for an update. "What have you got, Chris?" Alana had seen Andrew drive off in his car early in the morning but hadn't seen him return to the safe house.

Chris looked up, "I've discovered that Horst Wilhelm lost his shirt in the stock market over the last few years. At a time when the DAX had healthy gains, Horst was taking enormous risk speculating with venture capital companies. When it all went bust, he got involved in the derivatives market. I guess he was desperate to recoup his money, but again, he lost big time.

"Then I found an interesting sequence of bank transfers. Listen to this, because it directly ties into the Israeli's charge of arms dealings in North Africa. It all starts with this shell corporation called HMP Intermediaries. Money from HMP goes to Wil-Vest, another Wilhelm Industry subsidiary. Soon after that the money is sent back to the clearing house and is divided up between a half-a-dozen accounts all belonging to Galiena Kaufman and Horst Wilhelm, both members of Albert Schmidt's neo-Nazi group. Kaufman and her husband have several business connections with Wilhelm. The husband is on the board of Wilhelm's parent company." He looked up with a smile, "They are an incestuous little group.

"Comparable patterns of money laundering have occurred three different times this year alone. The transfers originate in different companies and use different banks and clearing houses. I ran this by David's people, and the timing is consistent with the gunrunning transactions. The outcome is clear: I've found the money the Israelis have been looking for.

"Kaufman and Wilhelm were financing and profiting from trading guns in order to save their companies from certain collapse. David requested that I turn what information I had on their scheme over to the German police in Baden-Württemberg to sooth the tension between them and us. I'll stay in the loop but, honestly, I don't think it has anything to do with our 'trap' puzzle."

Alana spent the day combing through intelligence evidence as it was being gathered. Most of what the team uncovered would prove unrelated to the case. But she hoped that scanning the data herself might trigger a vision about the letter. This was the tedious task of investigative work: sifting through volumes of information to find an obscure fact that might solve the case. Establishing an accurate depiction of the past was always a difficult, albeit an interesting assignment.

Alana was astonished at how easily Ian and Boris could access digital information. They told her that all the municipal computer systems operated with first-generation firewalls, which meant, for someone with advanced training, they had no firewalls at all.

"Do you know what a firewall is, Alana?" Boris thought he should ask because Ian often talked over people's heads.

"I know a firewall provides security by filtering the traffic on a computer network. I worked at a bank so we were well aware of the importance of our firewall."

"That's good. But the firewalls put into place when the Internet was in its infancy were primitive. Few people envisioned how online activity would mushroom in such a short period of time. Older software systems were never intended to 'talk' to each other, so there was no reason to keep people out. Now it's 1995 and these legacy systems are out-dated, yet still in use. Security is a joke, and people are just waking up to that realization." Ian explained.

"Anyone with a telephone line and a little bit of determination can penetrate another network. The operating systems used by all the police departments are no exception." Ian told her. "Once you're logged in on one system, there's a domino effect that leads to other interconnected government offices—they're all using the same class of systems. Most of the time nobody knows we've ever entered their network. We're not out to do harm... but we could."

Sabine came over to Alana with the sketch of the dragon and asked, "May I interrupt?"

"Sure."

"So what do you think this could be?"

"I don't know." Alana shrugged. "I could be wrong, and it means nothing."

"Sigmund told us about your ability to see things in a way we can't."

"Well, no one has ever depended on me like this before. I don't honestly know if I am psychic or clairvoyant. I just know that at certain times in my life I've felt things and dreamed things that turned out to be true."

"Well, let's advance the discussion by assuming you are right and that the creature in the sketch has meaning. Sigmund asked me to compile options for what the words 'the trap' could mean and how it may be connected to your dragon."

Alana mused, "I've seen so many symbols like it on buildings all over Germany."

"Yes, I thought along those lines too. I've also checked for a coat of arms that contained a dragon and found nothing useful for our situation." Sabine said "But I think we are past that now. The letter says: *When you saw what we used to call the trap, we reminisced how, as children, we would hide things inside.* Since we've learned that the Ziegler family were cabinetmakers, I think it has to refer to a piece of furniture with a hidden compartment.

"So," Sabine added, "let's go back to the letter. Remember, he implies in the letter that his death was looming. He was in or near Berlin, so this hiding place had to be at his disposal. Therefore, whatever he wants to hide must be easily transported, right? It must be something small that could be carried around, perhaps even concealed in a pocket or bag."

"That could be a lot of things," Alana said in frustration.

"True," Sabine replied. "But that the hiding place was familiar to Helmut is also clear from the letter." Sabine became animated. "Stay with me on this. We have no evidence that Helmut ever lived in Berlin. So 'the trap' had to be in the village where they grew up and then also in Berlin in 1945. It was in the Ziegler home—that's seems clear now reading the letter.

"So, it seems likely we're looking for a cabinet, or maybe a storage trunk? Sigmund mentioned this in passing, and now I think he's right… we're looking for a piece of furniture with a secret hiding place."

Sabine looked back at the sketch. "Look at the dragon's leg, Alana. You sketched this band around what would be the creature's ankle."

"It's just what I saw."

"Alana… the creature's leg is shackled… it could be construed that the creature is caught in a trap!"

"Yes, oh my God, it's the trap!"

They heard the drone of the helicopter, first at a distance, then closer, until it landed in the sheep field behind the house. The commotion of its arrival was in sharp contrast to the peaceful hum of their day. Alana walked out to the foyer and watched through the terrace door as the sheep scattered to lower ground. She couldn't take her eyes off Sigmund as he jumped from the helicopter, lowering his head to run under the rotor blades. It was important to her that he accept her as part of the team. This whole ordeal originated because of her, and she wanted to be part of the solution.

"Gretchen!" David howled, "I'm starving." He hurriedly went through to the kitchen passing Alana, who was just a few feet away.

Andrew appeared in the foyer and came to stand next to Alana. Sigmund had called from his mobile but hadn't provided all the details over the phone. He wanted to reveal his findings with everyone present. Within minutes, the group gathered around the table in the war room.

Sigmund began, "The trip turned out to be more than I expected." He looked at Alana. "I found your dragon."

"What?" Sabine seemed more interested in the news than Alana. "What is it?"

"Although Dagmar knows nothing of value to us, she had a small wooden box that caught my eye. It had Alana's dragon carved on the top."

"What was inside?" Sabine asked excitedly.

"A half-dozen family photographs along with a few bits and bobs of costume jewelry. I have photos of everything." He handed the tiny Minox spy camera over to Boris. "Do you mind?"

"I'll develop the film right away."

Gretchen announced that she had put food out in the dining room.

By the time they had finished eating, Boris had multiple copies of the photographs ready. He passed them around as the group had coffee.

"Franz was a handsome man," Sabine remarked with a smile.

"Yes," David piped in, "a handsome man or a Jewish bastard building Hitler's bunkers!"

"But David, he repented." Sigmund gave a sly smile. "That's why we're here."

"Well, he might have left additional clues in that enigmatic letter of his," David quipped.

"Hansel and Gretel did a better job dropping bread crumbs," Ian chimed in. "Oh, scratch that. Those bread crumbs got eaten... so they weren't any good at all. Gosh, I guess I'm tired."

"Stop complaining. Come on, Ian, solving these mysteries is what we live for." Sigmund smiled, "Unless you're no good at your job, in which case I'll have to sack you!"

"I hack computers, people are not my thing. And these people make my skin crawl."

Alana tuned out all the chatter, picked up the photos, examining the face of the man who had upended her life. She had seen his face before in the old newspapers the group had uncovered, but these family photos were private moments captured in time. The others could joke to let off steam, but this was personal for Alana.

She picked up each photograph one by one. First, for a quick look, then she went back to scrutinize every detail. With each examination, her focus became more acute. The photograph of Dagmar's box gave her pause. It resembled the box that contained the Franz letter, but that box had minimal embellishment. The carving on this box was a work of art. "Does anyone have a magnifying glass?" she asked.

"I'll get one for you." Boris stood up and left the dining room.

Sigmund came over to Alana, "I'm getting a cup of coffee, would you like one?" Deeply engrossed in the photos, she didn't respond. He leaned over her shoulder and whispered, "I want you to know that I think it's amazing that your sketch was identical to the carving on the box."

Again, Alana didn't acknowledge his words. Boris interrupted when he handed her a magnifying glass. "Thank you." She held it over the picture in her hand.

"Look at this, Sigmund." She looked up at him.

Sigmund looked through the glass and saw the family posing in what appeared to be the dining room of their home. "What am I looking for?"

"Just look. If *you're* any good at your job, you'll see it." Alana whispered, "… or I'll have to sack you."

Sigmund took the magnifying glass from Alana's hand. The seconds ticked away with each beat of Alana's heart until she could stand it no longer. "Look between the children," she insisted.

And there it was… in the narrow space between the two older children, Sigmund spotted the image of the dragon. It was barely visible, but under magnification it was unmistakable—it was the same image as carved on Dagmar's box and in Alana's sketch. Sigmund turned his eyes from the magnifying glass, "You've done it again."

All eyes around the table were on Sigmund and Alana, waiting for their private exchange to be shared with the group. Alana knew when Sigmund saw it; he didn't have to say a word. In fact, his acknowledgement, when he gave it, didn't register with her.

"I'm sorry, you must excuse me." She stood up and rushed away.

"Alana, are you okay?" Sabine ran after her. At the bottom of the staircase, she grabbed Alana's arm. "Wait, talk to me."

"I'm all right. I just need to lie down. Go back to the others. Sigmund will show you 'the trap.' Tell him I'm sure that what we're looking for is hidden inside that cabinet."

Sigmund disclosed to everyone what Alana had discovered.

Up in her room, Alana fell onto the bed. The second she closed her eyes she saw the face of Franz Ziegler. He appeared to be standing in a cave. The image was transparent; she could see through his body.

Alana just wanted to rest. She tried to erase the image of Franz from her mind, but she couldn't. Such images were never in her control. She heard the distant sounds of explosions. Suddenly the image of Franz became clear; he was running through fog. Wait, was he in a tunnel? Was it a bombing raid?

Wherever he was, the space was collapsing, spewing dust into the air.

Alana then realized Franz wasn't in fog at all; he was in a tunnel, and bombs were exploding overhead. Was this the bunker he had been constructing outside of Berlin? Yes, he was running through the network of interconnected tunnels that stretched deep into the hilly terrain on the outskirts of Berlin. But the project wasn't finished. A direct hit could be catastrophic.

The faces of two SS officers appeared across her mindscape. Their faces were grotesquely distorted as if she was looking through a fisheye lens. Then, they came into focus. "What are you doing?" Franz's voice shouted. "We have to get out of here. These tunnels are caving in around us! We'll all be buried."

"We have orders to destroy the vault."

"Why? The bombs will do the job for you! Aren't you listening to me? We will die if we don't leave now." Franz was frantic.

"Shut up and take us to the vault."

"You're crazy." Franz tried to push his way passed the men.

One man lifted his gun. "Take us to the vault."

Franz turned. Their lights made the dust in the air appear as a solid wall before him. He could hardly breathe. Moving in the darkness was disorienting. Franz kept his bearings by running his hand along the wall. As they reached the vault, the air cleared.

"Open it."

Franz said nothing.

"Open it or we'll blow the door with you standing next to it."

There should have been a guard at the vault, but when the outer tunnels started to collapse, he must have fled for his own safety.

Franz fumbled with the vault combination until he heard the dial click on the last number. He pulled at the massive door. It was so heavy. He had learned to pull the door open just enough to allow him to squeeze through and then push the door open from the inside. It was the easiest way to do it. But just as he got in position to push, another explosion hit. The pressure wave of the explosion blew the vault door off its hinges, slamming Franz's body into the back wall of the vault. He dropped motionless onto the floor.

The contents of the vault swirled about in the thick air as Franz regained consciousness. The reinforced construction of the vault had saved his life. The SS men lay dead, crushed by the massive door that the hinges had failed to hold in place.

Confused, Franz pulled himself up to his knees and wiped blood from his forehead. He couldn't muster the strength to stand. He just balanced there on his hands and knees for what seemed the longest time. His vision was cloudy and nothing seemed real. Covered in gray dust, his arms looked like those of a stone statue.

Half buried in a pile of books and papers, his thoughts turned to his children; he could envision them in his mind but couldn't hold on to the image of their faces for more than a second. He longed to see their faces again. As his sight returned, he focused on the wreckage inside the vault. Photographs were scattered around him; the faces of emaciated men, women, and children stared up at him. He fixated on a photograph depicting a sign that read AR-BEIT MACHT FREI, a German phrase meaning "Work sets you free." It was the gate at Auschwitz.

Franz lifted his right hand and peeled away a photo stuck to his palm. It showed piles of dead bodies with SS men standing casually nearby. He picked up a paper and saw body counts listed by month and by location—victims enumerated in some sort of deranged inventory. He felt complete and utter horror.

There was a painful ringing in his ears. He rolled off his knees to lean against the wall. Rubble from another explosion now covered the bodies of the SS men. Franz picked up another photograph and stared again at what he could not comprehend. But the truth was spread across the floor. He couldn't take his eyes away. Yes, he had heard stories of death camps and, like others, he had ignored them.

Monica forbade him to listen to rumors. Before the war, she would say, "We need not concern ourselves with the Jews. They will be better off somewhere else, not in Germany." During the war, they never spoke of the troubling rumors. But now, faced with the knowledge that the truth was even more horrific than the rumors, Franz was overcome. He leaned against the wall of Hitler's vault and wished to die.

Alana's eyes fluttered. Her dream had not disclosed that in reality, Franz suspected that his father-in-law, Otto von Rutler, had learned of his Jewish parentage. Otto had called him early in the morning; their conversation was disquieting.

Otto wanted to know what time Franz planned to be back at his home. He asked about his itinerary for the day, saying he might want to meet for coffee. This was most unusual. Otto had never called him before, nor had he ever suggested they meet. Also, Otto's call came just after Franz had received a coded letter from his Austrian cousin and former benefactor, saying that several members of his family, in his words, "had been taken away." Fearful that their letters would be intercepted by the gestapo, Franz and his cousin had developed a code to write about such things during the war. Now Franz wondered if someone from his mother's past had betrayed him. Was the secret of their Jewishness exposed? He wasn't sure.

Suspicious, Franz lied to his father-in-law about his schedule and said he wouldn't be home until late in the day. He was actually scheduled to be in Berlin, but he had gone to the new bunker site outside the city instead.

Franz had turned a blind eye to so much, not just now, not just in the midst of war, but throughout his life. After the death of his father, his mother had abandoned their Jewish faith and moved to a place where no one knew them. Religion wasn't part of his upbringing. He didn't think it mattered. He was a good person, what else counted?

He became an architect because he wanted to design buildings that would enhance the lives of the German people. But the war had come so early in his career that he never accomplished any of that. Instead, he built bunkers for the Nazis, those who destroyed the very lives he had sought to help. By the time he realized what it had meant to abandon his faith, it was too late.

Alana's eyes fluttered again; the vision of Franz in the vault returned. He looked upon the bodies of the dead SS men. Numb to his surroundings, Franz wondered if he could wish himself dead. Then he speculated he might, in fact, be dead. Perhaps he had died when the explosion blew his body against the wall. He looked again at the debris on the floor. His eyes now fixed on a small black-and-white notebook labeled *Der Goldzug*. He had seen it before.

Franz had heard rumors of a gold train, a Nazi train loaded with gold and stolen treasure hidden somewhere in the German hinterland. The story had spread through Berlin as the war effort declined.

Alongside the notebook was a bundle of letters bound by a red cord. He had seen that before as well. When he reached out to grasp them, he knew he wasn't dead. As he released the cord, the letters fell across his lap. The ground continued to shake beneath him but he didn't notice.

Alana saw Franz raise his light, shining it onto the paper. She watched as he read a hand-written communication between Heinrich Himmler and Adolf Hitler. A photograph fell from between the pages. It showed the two men standing above a trench filled with dead bodies. He turned the photo over to read *Secretly photographed at Auschwitz in 1944.*

Franz simply couldn't process all that he saw. Another explosion hit closer to the vault; he felt the wall crack behind his back. He heard more cave-ins as dust clouded the air again. He rubbed his burning eyes. Surprisingly, Franz now felt strong enough to move. He shoved the whole stack of letters and the photo into his pocket and grabbed the *Der Goldzug* notebook as he stood. He knew the bunker could collapse at any moment.

Franz staggered out of the vault and made his way down the bunker tunnel that he knew led to an exit. He saw the body of the guard who had been stationed at the vault. He pulled the gun from the corpse and shoved it into his belt. Unlike the SS men, both Franz and the guard knew another way out. The guard didn't make it, but Franz, now more than ever, was desperate to reach the exit. He had to redeem his disgraceful life.

Another few meters down the tunnel, Franz reached through the dust and found the trapdoor leading to a tunnel below. He climbed down a ladder and doubled back to the exit. A massive detonation rocked the ground beneath his feet, and he knew the vault had collapsed. Its contents surely lost forever.

What Franz perceived as running was merely shuffling his feet forward. He reached the end of the tunnel where a small segment of wall concealed a sliding door. It was the perfect camouflage to hide the tunnel system. He was now in what had been a cold-storage room that could have been part of any farm for hundreds of years. He pushed at the door leading to the outside, but it wouldn't open. He pushed again with no results; he couldn't get out!

Franz pulled the gun from his belt and blasted the lock mechanism. He pushed again and this time there was movement. He stood back and fired again. He was free. Alana felt the night air against his face.

THE TRAP

The exit from the bunker had been obscured in a natural rock wall along the side of a hill. If anyone had broken through the door from the outside, they would have found the storage room and nothing more—just the remnants of a long-gone farm. There was no indication that the cold storage room led to the elaborate SS-inspired Führerbunker system a mere 25 kilometers from Berlin. The complex had been Franz's project for the past year, and it was almost complete.

The SS had acknowledged that, while Germany would be victorious, they could not guarantee that the Berlin Führerbunker would survive. They had to consider that with constant bombing Berlin might fall. An alternate Führerbunker was essential. It would also serve as a viable evacuation route for people and documents vital to the war effort should the unthinkable happen—defeat. The plan provided for Hitler's escape at any cost. The location of this new bunker outside Berlin, including the tunnel system, afforded easy access to both the rail system and air passage to many destinations.

The SS were charged with safeguarding various documents of the Third Reich in the newly constructed bunker outside of Berlin. Franz had been at the collection center the week prior, when the archives were being boxed and logged for transport to the new bunker. Something odd occurred. An SS-Hauptsturmführer, whom he didn't recognize, placed a handful of items tied with a red cord into one of the boxes, then made note of the box number on a scrap of paper he put into his pocket.

This action had been notable because the officer hadn't just placed the items on top of the contents already catalogued; he had actually pushed items down to the bottom of the box. Franz also saw the officer jam the black and white notebook down the side of the same box. While it seemed strange at the time, Franz didn't react to this covert act. People just didn't question the SS.

Officials could freely enter the archive area, but everyone was searched on their way out. This system was clearly not foolproof. As Franz had witnessed, anyone with access could easily conceal information in a box destined for transport. It was what made Franz now choose the letters bound in red cord and the tiny notebook to take with him. Someone had risked much to smuggle these items out of Berlin, and possibly away from the Nazis as well, and now by default, that someone would be Franz Ziegler.

In Alana's vision, Franz was now standing outside the disguised exit from the tunnel system. He took time to orient himself to his surroundings. He then made his way into the woods, shuffling his feet forward until he collapsed. It startled Alana when she felt his face hit the cold ground. Restless, she turned on her bed and then fell back into her dream. She saw that Franz was now in his house on the outskirts of Berlin. He finished his letter to Helmut and sealed the envelope just as the housekeeper came screaming into the room.

"Herr Ziegler, thank goodness you are home. Come quickly! It's Frau Monica, she has gone insane. She has locked herself in the bomb shelter with the children. She won't let me in."

"Olga, what are you talking about?"

"Herr Ziegler, you are injured!"

"Never mind about me. What has happened with Monica?"

"Her mother and father were here. They told her they were leaving the country, and they wanted her and the children to come with them. Herr von Rutler said the most awful things about you. He wanted Monica to leave you to rot with the Jews. He called you a traitor!"

"Olga, calm down, pay no attention to Monica's father. Where are they going?"

"To Spain tonight, then they say to Argentina with others from the military. Herr von Rutler told her the Führer has gone mad, and the war is lost. Monica said she will never leave Germany and told them to leave her house. Her mother begged her to let them take the children. She said they could all be reunited after the war. Monica slapped her mother in the face!" Olga was so upset her whole body was shaking.

"When did this happen?"

"Just an hour ago. I didn't know what to do. I called your mother and she is coming here now. The entire world has gone crazy." Olga cried openly.

"I will handle Monica, Olga." Franz said calmly. "Otto knows more about the war effort than any of us, but I agree that the war is lost. I wish Monica and the children had gone with them. They are right to get away. Olga, I want you to leave as well."

"No, I'm staying here with your family. This is my home, too. I have nowhere else to go."

"No, Olga, you can't stay. There are people on the south road getting away. I want you to go with them. Do not go in any other direction. No one is safe this close to Berlin."

"How can you say this?"

"Olga, you have been a trusted employee for many years."

"Yes, sir."

"This is the most important thing of my life." Franz held up the letter. "You must post this letter as soon as possible, whenever it is safe, no matter how long it takes."

"But sir, we are safe here, all together."

"No!" he shouted in a manner that startled her. "You must leave now." He pulled money from his desk. "This is enough money for your journey. Don't let anyone know you have money. Hide it, do you hear me?"

"No! No!"

"Listen to me." He grabbed her by the arm. "Go upstairs and take all of Monica's jewelry."

"But sir, she has taken all her jewelry with her to the shelter."

"Then take my watch." He pulled it from his wrist. "Sell it and keep the money. Olga, you must believe how important it is to mail this letter. Say it to me. Promise me that you will mail this letter."

"I will, sir." Olga cried.

"Now get out. Go while there is still time!"

Olga took the letter and put on her coat. With one last glance at Franz, she turned and ran from the house, fearing she would never see the family again.

Franz grabbed a small tubular container from his desk and pulled the letters and the notebook from his pocket. How many cabinets had his ancestors made that contained a concealed compartment, he wondered. To Franz and Helmut, the hidey-hole was just a childhood amusement, but now, he reflected on the desperate conditions his people had endured to warrant creating such a unique feature. In his heart he thanked them.

Franz acknowledged his weakness of character. Through all the difficulties his family had faced, they had not done what he and his mother had done. They had not abandoned their Jewish faith.

Shoving the items into the tube, Franz then snapped the cap on tight. He walked through to the dining room and looked at the cabinet, the one he and Helmut had dubbed "the trap." The house was quiet and Franz heard himself murmur, "For the last time, my friend, we play our game," as he pushed the tube into the secret compartment. "I pray you find it." He then took an agonizing walk through his home and out into the backyard.

Franz pulled on the door that led down into the shelter. It was locked from the inside. He walked to the garden shed for a pickaxe. He reflected on his surprise in learning that the Germans didn't believe in underground shelters like the one he had built for Monica. Such shelters were prevalent throughout Europe but rare for homes in Germany. Monica had insisted they have an underground shelter in their yard; after all, it was her husband's area of expertise. In Monica's mind, the shelter would keep them out of harm's way. It was why, while other families sent their children away from Berlin, she kept her children with her. There was never any doubt in her mind that Hitler would prevail and that they would be safe.

The axe broke through the door in one strike. As Franz climbed down into the shelter, his world was again shattered by the sound of three gunshots. He looked at his wife standing over his children, gun in hand.

"What have you done?" he cried!

"Our marriage is a fraud." Monica cried. "I know you are Jewish. I couldn't let my children grow up knowing they were Jews. My mother wanted to take them away, but that wouldn't change the facts. We are not leaving our home, none of us." She raised the gun.

"You're insane!" Franz pulled the gun from his belt and shot his wife in the head. He hated her and he hated himself. He pushed the gun up under his chin.

Sigmund was about to knock on Alana's door when he heard her voice.

"Forgive O Lord thy people Israel whom thou hast redeemed. I ask not that thou forgive me, I only pray that they who were slain should rise again. Lord bless my children, cleanse them; bestow upon them forever Your merciful righteousness..."

Sigmund gently opened the door a few inches and saw Alana lying on the bed. Her hands clenched the bed cover.

"I welcome hell, for I am too weak in faith to face what life would bring me now. O Lord, praise and resurrect the innocent... "

The words were coming from Alana's mouth, yet she was neither awake nor asleep.

At that very moment, Alana felt Franz experience what she could only describe as a passion of faith. In this bizarre event, kneeling in the blood of those he loved, Franz prayed as a Jew. He hadn't done so in so long he didn't know if he got the words right. It didn't matter. He freed himself from his surroundings, from his body and from his mind, unable to face the burden of reality.

Alana felt a fleeting sense of euphoria within her body, seemingly coming from Franz. It was a feeling that transcended space and time... and within that transitory moment Franz pulled the trigger.

She opened her eyes wide and saw Sigmund standing beside the bed. "Franz killed himself," she whispered.

"Yes, we were just discussing that possibility downstairs. It appears that Franz shot the entire family. Only the youngest child, Dagmar, survived."

"No, you're wrong. Monica shot the children."

"What?"

"Trust me." Alana asked, "How long have you been standing there?"

"Not long. I came to see if you were ready to come downstairs. I heard you speaking and came in."

Alana sat up on the bed. Sigmund saw blood in her palms. She had clenched her fists so tightly that her fingernails had punctured her skin.

Sigmund remembered how he had consoled his son after a bad dream. But he didn't know what to say in this situation. He opened her hand. "Let me get something for this." He walked toward the door.

"I know what happened and what we're looking for." Alana spoke quietly.

"Collect your thoughts. We'll talk downstairs."

Sigmund sent Sabine to tend to Alana's wounds. He thought Sabine would be a greater comfort to Alana than he.

"Sigmund tells me you know what happened," Sabine said quietly as she wiped Alana's palms with antiseptic cream and wrapped them with gauze.

Alana nodded her head yes with a painful smile.

"When you're ready, we're in the dining room."

Alana touched Sabine's hand. "I don't want you to leave."

Sabine smiled at her.

"When I was in college, I received a letter from a high school friend. I remember I fell asleep holding the letter. That night I had a dream in which Sara was crying out for help.

"When I awoke, I wasn't sure what to do because I often had weird dreams." Alana wiped her nose. "I have experienced peculiar dreams since childhood but, as I got older, I came to understand that they were more visions than dreams and that they would turn out to be true.

"Before I had chance to contact my friend, my mother called to say Sara had died. I later learned that she had been ignoring abdominal pain for days before her appendix burst. She was alone when it happened. Someone drove her to the hospital the following morning, but it was too late to save her.

Her appendix had turned gangrenous and finally it ruptured. She died after the surgery.

"She was already dead when I had my dream. I couldn't have saved her. Each time it happens I seem to receive more and more information... but today, this was something I never expected. I experienced the deaths of the Ziegler family. I had the strangest sensation at the moment Franz killed himself. I felt myself enveloped by what seemed to be a ball of intense energy and then poof... gone... I felt nothing." Alana's hands were shaking. "How long have I been up here?"

"Several hours."

"I can't explain it." She picked at the bandages on her hands. "I'll come downstairs with you. Would you wait while I freshen up?"

"Of course, take your time."

When Alana came out of the bathroom, Sabine said, "I wish I knew what to say to you. They hired me because I would be the one who could connect with people in any circumstance. Yet I find myself speechless."

"No worries. I have yet to figure out what to say to myself."

Alana walked down with Sabine. Her shirt and trousers were stained with spots of blood from the wounds to her palms. She took a seat at the table in the war room.

"First of all, I'd like to tell you that when I have a vision, it leaves me feeling disoriented and tired. Please don't think that I have come unhinged. I'm fine. I'm going to recount for you everything as I saw it in my mind."

Alana recalled all the events perfectly. When she finished, she said, "I am an observer in these visions, just watching. It is as if I were somehow hovering over Franz. But I wasn't seeing events through his eyes. I know he saw photographs and read letters, but I don't know what was depicted in those photographs or written in those letters. I appreciate that it may be difficult for you to grasp, but it is all I can say." Alana looked and spoke as if she had been through the war herself. Her voice was monotone, her face expressionless.

"You don't know what Franz hid in the cabinet?" Sigmund asked.

"No. But I saw papers and something with a black and white cover. I don't blame you if you don't believe me. I know I am not part of your group. But I know myself, and I believe you will discover that what I have told you is factual. I just come to facts a little differently than you."

The room was quiet. Everyone fixated on Alana's obvious pain from the ordeal.

Alana staggered up the staircase. She fell asleep, wondering what they all thought of her now.

Elsa's Story

Elsa Bauman's family owned a dairy farm not far from where Kirk and Helmut grew up. She was

Kirk's age and had known both brothers since they were all at school together.

Elsa fell in love with Helmut as a teenager. Just when she expected a proposal of marriage, her much older brother and only sibling contracted polio. It devastated her family, of course, but because they owned a working farm, the loss of an able body put their livelihood at risk. Farm work had already taken a toll on her parents, now in their fifties and not in good health. Elsa put her life on hold for the sake of her family. She took over running the farm.

This happened just as Helmut had enrolled in Tübingen University. He split his time helping with special chores on the farm and taking classes. He was there for things Elsa couldn't handle with the limited help her mother and father could offer. The fact that Helmut never proposed was lost in the drudgery of Elsa's life.

Helmut knew Elsa awaited a proposal, and it weighed heavily on his mind. He had expected they would go their separate ways when he went to university. But her brother's illness changed everything. It made it impossible for him to stay away. He cared for Elsa and felt obligated to help. But as he grew into manhood, he knew that he didn't love her.

One day, while hoisting hay into the loft with a grapple, Helmut slipped on the loose hay in the wagon, landing on the spiked end of the grapple's sharp claw. The blade sliced through his thigh, causing excruciating pain.

In the hospital, the liberal use of morphine during his lengthy recovery left him addicted to opioids. Drug addiction was not uncommon in those days because so many users were soldiers who had been seriously wounded or crippled in First World War. When the Nazis gained power, drugs were plentiful and easily found. But truth be told, Helmut had experimented with drugs even before his accident. Thereafter, his on-again off-again battle with drugs was heart wrenching for everyone around him.

Elsa's brother endured the debilitating effects of polio. In time, he resumed minor duties intended more to keep him busy than to relieve Elsa's burden. Her brother did the best he could, and everyone was grateful that he had regained a degree of purpose in his life. Elsa's parents talked of selling the farm, but Elsa would have nothing of it. In good times, the farm produced adequate income and a comfortable lifestyle. Farming was Elsa's heritage; she believed she had to carry on.

While Elsa struggled to maintain the family business, she never lost hope that Helmut would conquer his addiction and that they would marry and work the farm together. Sadly, Elsa never understood that Helmut wanted no part of that life.

Over the years, even after lengthy stretches of sobriety, Helmut would inevitably relapse into his old ways. In the late 1930s, he ended up in prison after breaking into a doctor's office for drugs when he didn't have the money to buy them on the street. To secure a shorter sentence, Helmut went into the military. He joined the medical corps and found it satisfying to serve his country in that way. Then, within a few years the war broke out.

During the war, he learned that using opioids and amphetamines was not only accepted, it was often encouraged within reason. Helmut was careful to stay below the limit.

The Augsburg brothers had grown up in the shadow of the First World War. Their father was conscripted into the army in the early days of the fighting. The family existed on funds from a relative on their mother's side. It wasn't much, but they got by and better than most. Their village didn't suffer the same food shortages as many urban areas, but everyone's rations were reduced and a close eye was kept on supplies to make sure they would last until the next bit of money arrived.

The fighting, with few exceptions, occurred outside of Germany. While the loss of men disrupted everyone's lives, the villages, shops, and schools still functioned. Kirk and Helmut started elementary school during the war years. They were instructed on "the Three Rs" as usual. In addition to their studies, they were compelled to sing patriotic songs. Propaganda within the German school system was heavy and influential.

Too young to comprehend either the reality or the consequences of war, they played soldier games in their yard. During each imaginary battle, one or the other brother would be declared dead, and he would drop to the ground. When the war ended, Helmut was eight and Kirk was six.

They had no lasting memories of their cheerful and loving father before the war, except for a couple of photographs showing his obvious affection. He fought in northern France and Belgium under what was later called the Schlieffen Plan. In mid-1917, he wrote his wife to say that his infantry unit would be repositioned to the Eastern Front. She heard no more until he was on his way home in 1918. He came home without physical, injury but as his wife told her sister soon after, "the war has stolen his very soul. He won't talk of his experience, but he wakes in the night with the bedsheets drenched in sweat. He pushes me away if I try to console him. We barely speak without arguing, as he interprets my every word as a criticism."

Like most boys of the time, seeing their father in uniform was exciting. They had family pictures taken with their father in all his military gear before he stowed it away in a trunk in the attic. Occasionally, the boys would sneak up and try on the jacket, pinning the badges on their chest. When their father caught them, a lock appeared on the attic door.

Their father returned to the factory on the Tübingen road and to the same job he had left four years prior. He gave the appearance that nothing had changed, yet in private nothing was the same, and as his wife had foretold, their lives would never return to normal. They did, in time, come to terms with a new normal that was comfortable enough.

There was no rivalry between the boys when they were young. But as they grew into their teenage years and entered secondary school, they made other friends and grew apart. It was neither unusual nor did it warrant any explanation. It was so subtle that even their parents didn't see it for the longest time. One day they just realized their children were vastly different people with different visions for their lives.

Kirk went to medical school. After graduating, he joined a small surgery in Tübingen as an assistant doctor. During the war he, like many others, was designated a surgeon and compelled to take training in internal wound care and amputation.

Kirk served at several field hospitals along the frontline. Because Helmut was in the medical corps, their paths crossed from time to time. In 1944, Helmut received orders to stockpile medical supplies near Tübingen. He found an opportunity to visit his parents and stopped to see Elsa. He arrived at the farm to find Elsa in the barn checking on an older cow about to calve. Earlier, the cow had moved slowly, dragging her hind legs as she walked in from the pasture. Elsa knew calving would occur within forty-eight hours... but it wouldn't be that night. When Helmut's face appeared in the doorway, she was overcome with emotion. It had been three years since they said goodbye. She fell into his arms, and they retreated to the house where everyone was asleep.

By chance, Helmut's next assignment was to deliver medical supplies to the hospital where Kirk was stationed. It was a stormy day with cold, heavy rain. A welcomed side effect was a lull in the fighting. The radios were quiet as Helmut pulled the ambulance up to the hospital. He hoped it would stay that way long enough to talk with his brother.

Dr. Augsburg was finishing surgery on an officer who had been too unstable for the procedure when he arrived from the battlefield the day before. When Kirk exited the operating theater, he found Helmut sitting on a bench. They had not seen each other in over a year.

Kirk's face lit up. Ignoring the sounds of disorder outside, he walked toward his brother. But before they could even greet each other, an SS officer barged through the door, dripping water from his slicker and tracking in mud from his boots. "Doctor!" he snarled. "Come out here immediately!"

"I cannot leave the hospital," Kirk gestured to his surroundings. "We must have some level of sterility. A triage medic will assist you."

"He says he cannot help. I want you out there—NOW!"

Kirk stood back, thinking how to respond.

"Do not make me unholster my revolver."

At that moment a medic appeared at the door. "Doctor Augsburg, the man is dead." He added nervously, "It is Obergruppenführer Baumgärtner."

The commotion in triage escalated. Kirk felt the need to break protocol and leave the tent to restore order. He turned to his brother and said, "Can you stay so we can talk?"

"Not if the fighting has resumed. I will have to go with the ambulance. But if there are casualties, I will be back."

"Helmut," Kirk put his hand on his brother's shoulder, "it's good to see you. Stay safe."

Kirk looked at the body of the now-dead general. His name was one everyone recognized. He was a Nazi war hero. He had been shot in the left chest. The injury was 100 percent lethal. It surprised Kirk that he hadn't died instantly. Turning to the SS officer, he said, "There was nothing that could have been done to save him. He was a dead man the moment the bullet hit. He just continued to breathe for a short time while blood filled his chest cavity." Kirk walked away expecting a backlash but none came.

Within minutes of leaving the hospital, Helmut was back. His ambulance never made it to the battle site. Mortar fire hit the caravan of medical vehicles, injuring Helmut along with several other men. Kirk watched anxiously as the body of his injured brother arrived. He saw one leg crushed and mangled. But as the doctor gazed over his patient, he assessed a wound that would likely be fatal.

"They tell me my leg is gone, is it true? I cannot feel anything." Helmut struggled to talk.

"Your leg is injured Helmut, we shall have to take a look at it." Kirk said calmly.

"Kirk," Helmut used every ounce of strength to raise his head. "Don't try so hard." He gasped for breath, "Let me go." Kirk didn't have to agonize over his brother's final wish. Helmut's head fell back onto the stretcher; he was dead.

This was the fate of millions of men, women, and children all over Europe, as in other parts of the world. Millions upon millions snatched from their unfinished lives. Kirk held the pain of his patients inside him. Now his brother was added to the list.

But Kirk didn't let bitterness destroy him; instead, he looked upon the memories as inspiration to live a life that respected those denied their future.

Unlike most who lost a family member in the war, Kirk took his brother's body home. His mother and father fought back tears as the body arrived. They believed that Helmut had turned his life around and that to die now was even more tragic. It devastated Elsa. She had tried to prepare herself for what might happen, but seeing Helmut's body over-whelmed her.

"Helmut asked me not to write to him during the war," she told Kirk. "So, I never did, though I spoke to him every day as I did the chores; talking to the cows made me believe that I was not alone."

Kirk watched her as she talked.

"I had no illusion that he would turn his life around. Did you know he came home last week? I know he was still on drugs. I would never tell your mother and father; they thought he had conquered his demons. When I saw him at your house early in the day he looked good and acted himself. But when he came to the farm that evening I know he was high on something. I could see it in his eyes." She turned away from the body, "Who could blame him. I fear that all our lives are now doomed to sadness. It would have been no different if we had married, probably worse."

Elsa continued, "My brother is sick again." She took a deep breath as if to clear Helmut from her mind. "I think he has pneumonia. Each morning I expect to find he has died in his sleep. Perhaps Helmut is the lucky one."

Kirk heard Elsa's melancholy words. He picked up her hand. "Please don't think like that. We must believe there will be happiness after this horrible war is over. You must give yourself a reason to live." Kirk looked in her eyes, "Elsa, I want to live. I won't let Hitler rob me of my life."

"What if he already has?"

"I don't believe that. Let's go back to the farm; I will look in on your brother."

Kirk hadn't been on the Bauman's farm since he had followed his brother around after school. It was sad to see how much it had deteriorated, but the animals were alive and supporting many families with milk and cheese and occasionally meat.

Elsa's brother did not have pneumonia *per se,* but prior bouts of the disease had brought on a condition referred to as "wasting away." It was a vicious cycle; his wasting could lead to pneumonia at any time. Kirk explained to Elsa what she could do to help her brother maintain better health.

Elsa made coffee; they sat and talked long into the night. In difficult times, friends often reminisced about better days, and that is what they did. For a few hours, they seemed just two ordinary people, laughing over the trials and tribulations of coming of age in a small village. Kirk stayed the night with Elsa before starting the journey back to the hospital the next day. Amongst all the sorrow, the warmth and comfort of another human being made it bearable to get through the night.

In the morning, when Kirk came out to the kitchen, Elsa handed him a cup of coffee while shielding her eyes from his view. "I am embarrassed about what happened last night," she said. "My parents are out with the cows. Would you leave before they come in?"

"Elsa, don't you know how much I have cared for you since we were at school together?"

Elsa didn't answer his question. She simply said, "Please come home. I can't bear to lose anyone else."

"I will."

Back in 1986, Alana was still grappling with her visions. They seemed generally true to real life events, but she struggled to fully grasp their meaning. Even now, years later, interpretation could be elusive. But back then, she knew nothing of the love triangle that existed between the Augsburg brothers and Elsa—if only in Kirk's mind. When she dreamed of him coming home from the war to discover his wife pregnant, Alana inferred that the child couldn't possibly be his. From family photos in Kirk's cottage, Alana recognized the woman in the dream as his wife, Elsa. But Kirk had shared little personal information about his wife who had died so young.

That brief dream in 1986 didn't help Alana piece together her family's unspoken past. In reality, Elsa was pregnant when Kirk returned to Tübingen after the war, but they didn't marry until weeks after his homecoming. Had Elsa taken a lover or been raped by a soldier as so many women were?

Then in 1995, after reading the affectionate letters Elsa had written to Helmut, Alana surmised Helmut to be the father—but was that even possible if he also served in the war. Were Kirk and Elsa even a couple prior to marrying? Unaware that both brothers had spent time with Elsa just months before the end of the fighting, made anything Alana might imagine just speculation. She had no proof the Elsa who signed the letters was the same Elsa that Kirk married... but it was. And it seemed unlikely for Elsa to have been intimate with anyone other than Kirk and Helmut in that short window of time, so who was the father? In truth, Elsa did not know. Kirk never asked.

Kirk's income as a doctor provided money to hire a farmhand for Elsa's family. As German society stabilized after the war, the farm became self-sustaining again. Under Kirk's care, Elsa's brother's condition improved. He lived at the farm for the rest of his life.

Elsa experienced long periods of happiness with Kirk, but the troubling times in which she mourned Helmut came far too often. She continually wrestled with the question of which brother was the father of her child. She had buried the brother she loved and married the brother who loved her. Elsa tried to live with her past, but time did little to relieve her grief.

When she died, Kirk found two bottles of army-issued opioids in her dresser. He suspected she may have taken them from Helmut, with or without his knowledge, and kept them hidden through the years. Kirk chose to believe her death was an accidental overdose. Anything else was just too painful. Alana's mother was ten years old when they buried Elsa.

11

Convergence

Alana was the last to enter the war room, again wearing clothes from Sigmund's wife's closet.

"Let's kick the morning off with good news. Marta Voss is out of her coma, she's alert and talking," Sigmund announced with an uplifting voice. "The doctors have upgraded her condition to fair and indicate another upgrade may come soon.

"Marta is aware of what happened to her but cannot identify her assailant. I think it is now safe to say it was Egon Schmidt.

"The police have found Albert Schmidt dead. He was hiding out in a shed on property belonging to a member of his group. All indications are he died from a stroke or heart attack with no sign of foul play.

"It appears he took documents from his library in an effort to track down his son. The police are scouring those files now, but I doubt they will find anything that we don't already know.

"Based on our supposition that Egon murdered Dr. Altmeyer and stabbed Marta Voss, we have to assume he is searching for what the letter calls 'the trap' as we are. We believe Egon has been acting alone, and as I said, Albert was trying to find his son when he died."

Sigmund continued, "Before we had the photograph of the cabinet—aka 'the trap'—Sabine used the Internet to search for clues to Alana's dragon sketch and remarkably she found an obscure volume on German furniture listed on the website of an American Internet bookseller called Amazon—I think we've all heard the news about this Amazon company over the past year.

"Anyway, the book seems promising, and Sabine has contacted the publisher in Germany; more information should be forthcoming.

"The book documents the history of Germany furniture. The ancestors of Franz Ziegler, identified under the surnames we have already discussed, are well known in the industry and are listed in the book. The book may not be helpful to us now, but it is certainly easy to imagine how the Internet might change our business model in the future." Sigmund asked Ian to speak next.

"I discovered an obituary for Franz's mother, Gertrude Ziegler, later Gertrude Neuchatel. It said that she was survived by her granddaughter, Dagmar Ziegler. It described how Gertrude Ziegler saved the life of the child during the war by delivering her into the hands of the Swiss Red Cross. Sadly, the child did not receive medical attention soon enough to make a full recovery, if that was ever possible.

"Gertrude took Dagmar to Switzerland for long-term medical care where she met and married Liam Neuchatel, a Swiss industrialist and philanthropist. Within a short period of time, the child was sent to a nursing home in Germany. When Liam died in 1949, Gertrude lived alone in their home in Switzerland until her death in 1959.

"Neuchatel was an interesting man, and under the guise of writing a book on the most influential Swiss businessmen of the twentieth century, I asked Sabine to make contact with Neuchatel's surviving daughter, Lara. I'll let Sabine tell you what she found."

"Thanks, Ian. I explained to Lara that we had her father's well-documented business records already in hand and that I was looking for the personal story of the man behind the accomplishments. Thrilled to have her father included in such a book, she spoke openly. Surprisingly, her long account of her father's life excluded Gertrude. When I asked about his second wife, I hit a raw nerve.

"Lara almost hung up on me but then unleashed a tirade on Gertrude. She said that Gertrude's marriage to her father had appalled the family, in part, because they understood her to be sympathetic to the Nazis well after the war. They all felt Gertrude had cast some sort of spell over their father, because he hated Hitler and all that had happened.

"Lara told me her father was in poor health when he met Gertrude. And, when he announced just weeks later that they would wed, the family insisted that he rewrite his will: If Gertrude survived Liam, she could live in the house for the remainder of her life, but she would receive none of his wealth, just a modest allowance for living expenses.

"Lara was adamant that I understood that the family had no connection with Gertrude at all. After Gertrude's death, the family found their father's home in disrepair because Gertrude had used her stipend to pay for Dagmar's nursing care.

"Of interest is that, in a roundabout way, Lara confirmed what we've already pieced together. She didn't know the cause of Dagmar's injury, but she knew Gertrude's son, his wife, and the other children were all dead. She let slip that they nicknamed her 'Rude.' She said Rude had shipped her son's family furniture from Germany to Switzerland when she married Liam. Then, after Rude's death, Lara supposed Dagmar must have become a ward of the state. Under the terms of Gertrude's will, all of the furniture she brought from Germany went to a Catholic church associated with the nursing home where Dagmar lived.

"Lara was certain the nursing home was one of 'those places' friendly to Nazis and their families. She was horrified to think people might connect the Neuchatel name to such a scandalous place."

Boris took over from there. "The Catholic church and an associated school are located in the town of Mechlenburg, which as we know, is the same town where the nursing home is located. They are just a few kilometers apart.

"We have to consider that the furniture would have been valuable so they may have sold some or all of what they received. But I found brochures for the school that show furniture similar to what we saw in the photographs Sigmund brought back from visiting Dagmar Ziegler. It appears likely that they kept at least some pieces. There are seven or more buildings in the church and school complex, which is a lot of area to cover if we want to find the cabinet in the photo. I'm not sure how we do that without drawing attention."

An urgent call from Niedermeyer interrupted Sigmund. "Hold the line a moment, Niedermeyer. Boris, get us a map of all the buildings."

"Sigmund, my information is such that I implore you to put Boris on hold before myself."

"Go ahead, Niedermeyer, you're on speaker now. Talk to the group."

"A man with, what I shall refer to as, a depraved nature has surfaced in a town called Neufeld driving the van you are looking for. This town is a distance from where he was last spotted and is about twenty-five kilometers away from Dagmar Ziegler's nursing home. It appears he has found the same connections as you have."

"Thank you, Niedermeyer." Sigmund hung up and turned to David, "Is the copter still here? We need to get Boris to Neufeld."

David nodded, "I'll notify the pilot and arrange for departure as soon as possible."

"Can you get a second copter? I'd like to get into the church and school buildings."

"Yes, but I may need an hour or more." David left the room.

Sigmund turned to Boris, "Arm yourself, Egon is a bad actor."

Ian walked over, "I'm finally getting the police sketch of Egon Schmidt. It's coming in on the fax machine now."

Alana spoke up, "I want to go this time. I believe I can help find what we're looking for. I understand the risk."

Before Sigmund could react, Andrew interjected, "We must split up to cover all the ground. I'll partner with Alana."

Sigmund vacillated, and then said, "Dad, you're putting me in a difficult position. I agree that Alana could prove helpful in a way we can't fully understand. But I don't think either of you comprehend the danger. This Egon Schmidt fellow could be there."

"Give me a gun. My father was ex-military. He taught me to shoot when I was a teenager. I've never had to defend myself, but I can handle a gun; I'm an excellent shot." Alana claimed.

Sigmund half-heartedly complied, "Get ready. We have to leave as soon as David can get a helicopter here." The tension in Sigmund's voice was something the rest of the staff rarely heard.

Exiting the war room, Sigmund sought out Gretchen. He handed her the calling card he had taken from the nurse's station at the convalescent home. He gave Gretchen some money and asked her to purchase a red sweater and mail it to Dagmar Ziegler at the address on the card. "She is about your size. Pick one of simple design that buttons up the front. Sign the card, *Your cousin, Henri.*"

THE TRAP

It was late the previous night when Egon pulled into Neufeld. As he suspected, it was a place where he could hide in plain sight without raising suspicion. He backed his van into an alley next to a twenty-four-hour laundry, where a few Deutsche Marks to the attendant gave him access to electric power and a telephone line for his computer modem.

When Egon logged into his MUD room, it amazed him to find so many responses to his thread. He spent the next hour reading the posts. Most of it was useless crap from wannabe researchers, but two people donated interesting information that would prove valuable.

One responder copied a news article, dated 31 March 1945, about the deaths in the Ziegler home. Reading this, Egon ascertained that one child was still alive. Another follower posted the names of several nursing homes known to be Nazi sympathizers after the war. Like Dagmar, many people entering nursing homes in the 1940s needed care for the rest of their lives.

Hours later, while Egon was still online linking Franz Ziegler to Helmut Augsburg, one of his new followers posted the name of the nursing home where Dagmar Ziegler lived. Egon realized he had unwittingly created his own research team. It was worth the effort to separate the wheat from the chaff. Egon rarely displayed emotion, but he was elated to find Dagmar was within an easy drive.

Egon needed to take a break. He went into the laundry to use the bathroom. The attendant told him he was going off duty, so Egon had to disconnect the wires he was using for his computer. "No problem," he replied. "Danke schön."

"I'm back on duty tonight if you want the same deal," the attendant told him, looking for more cash.

Out on the street, Egon picked up a newspaper and read that both his parents were dead and that the Voss woman was alive. He felt nothing. That life was behind him. When the article recounted Dr. Altmeyer's murder, it bored him, and he moved on. No photograph of him accompanied the article.

Opposite the laundry was a rundown bar featuring punk rock bands popular with skinheads. Punk bands had lost popularity throughout Europe by 1995, so dingy subculture bars were the only places most could get gigs.

Egon saw the sign plugging a British group called Nasty Business. He knew of the band. He wanted a gun badly, but he really didn't know how to buy one without drawing attention to himself and getting caught. He believed he could find a connection in the bar.

A German band called Unser Krieg also played at the bar, and by mid-afternoon, their thunderous beat blasted out into the street. Egon rounded the corner and walked in. He took a seat at the bar next to a coarse-looking guy about his age who looked like he knew what was happening. Egon nodded at him and said, "Guten tag." The guy called himself Gerhardt, and said that he had just been kicked out of Unser Krieg because he hadn't shown up to play for three days. The band had replaced him. Gerhardt was at the bar to bad mouth the band and seek revenge.

Before long Egon was sitting in Gerhardt's car watching him get high. Egon never smoked dope. Gerhardt appeared to be living rough in his car. "You know where I can get a gun?" Egon asked.

"I have one." Gerhardt volunteered that he had a military-issued luger that he had stolen from his grandfather. Gerhardt had what Egon was looked for, a car and a gun, and Egon had the one thing Gerhardt needed—cash.

Egon wasn't sure about Gerhardt long term, but he could be useful right now. The police would be tracking his van, so he had to ditch it fast. He had used his knife twice; now he needed a gun.

Gerhardt and Egon got out of the car. Gerhardt was high and wanted to go back into the bar to hear the other band. They stood in the alley. Gerhardt spoke up, "You said you were on a mission of some kind. I could go with you, help you."

"Yeah, what else did I say?" Egon didn't recall saying he was on a mission.

Gerhardt flicked his cigarette up against the brick wall of the alley. "You're a writer. Maybe you could write lyrics cuz I can make good music. Unser Krieg is a crap band. I'm too good for them. They sacked me because I intimidate them. If you write for me, I could attract good band members."

"I am a historian and political writer not a song-writer."

"Man, I sing about the same stuff you write about—Hitler's Generalplan Ost, and all that crap. Everyone likes my music. Maybe we get famous."

"I don't want to be that kind of famous," groaned Egon.

To Egon, Unser Krieg was just a loud pounding beat; they weren't good musicians. But being at the bar and getting caught up in the trashy atmosphere made Egon remember he liked the club scene. He hated regular people, but the types of people in these clubs were more like him. Of course, they weren't as smart as he, but he could relate to them. He had been shut up with old people like his father far too long.

Gerhardt was certainly not, in Egon's mind, an equal, but he could help Egon meet other like-minded people. And he could help him finish his current mission. "I have to check out a person in a hospital up in the Lusatian Mountains. You want to drive me there?"

"Drive yourself."

"The police may be looking for my van. I need to dump it."

"What did you do?"

"Nothing. You know what it's like for people like us. They just make stuff up to pull you in. I just can't let anything interrupt me getting to that hospital. It's important."

Gerhardt was in. He had nothing better to do. They would get rid of the van first.

Starting the motor, Egon looked out the open window. "Maybe tomorrow you can help me buy new transportation." Then he followed Gerhardt out of town to a remote dirt road. When it dead-ended in thick woods, they packed Egon's belongings into Gerhardt's sedan and then pushed the van into a ravine, covering it with branches.

In packing his things into Gerhardt's car, Egon saw an American-style hand grenade in an open box beneath the rear seat. There were also bullets, which he assumed were for the gun Gerhardt spoke of, but he didn't see the gun.

They drove back to Neufeld as the sun went down. That night Egon shaved his head, and they both got tattoos. To distract his mind from the pain of the needle, Gerhardt contemplated just how much cash Egon might have in his pockets.

Alana went out on the terrace, staring out over the sheep field to collect her thoughts before the helicopter arrived.

Andrew walked out and looked at the sheep, "Do you know why there is one black sheep out there?"

She turned to look at him. "Yes, actually I do. It's a method of counting. One black sheep per hundred, right? So the shepherds could know the approximate number of sheep at a glance."

"Very good, few people know that bit of trivia." He smiled. "Of course when William was a child, we lowered that number to one for five because that was all we had room for. We just thought it would be fun for him to have one black sheep.

"When we bought him a pony, we had a hard time getting him to come into the house, even for meals. He spent all his time with the animals."

Alana asked cautiously, "How did Sigmund's wife die? David said something. I think it was before you arrived. He said it was five years ago and implied you were working together at the time."

Andrew cleared his throat. "Yes, Sigmund told me David brought that up in such a casual manner. Sigmund could have choked him for his insolence." He looked away from Alana and over the sheep fields before continuing. "I believe I told you her name was Evelyn. She died in a car bomb attack that we believe was meant for Sigmund. That is the torment that he carries with him. He blames himself for his wife's death. But it was just as much my fault. You see, I was the one who had involved us in the project.

"In the days of my father, his name was Wolf, Wolfgang Griegg," Andrew said proudly. "He had no fear of violence—and, believe me, he got himself in some dodgy situations. Wolf's clients ran the gamut from politicians to business titans, perhaps a criminal enterprise from time to time. They all understood that he was exclusively a researcher. He harbored no harm toward anyone—but that was in a different era, and I'm afraid I didn't comprehend how the rules had changed by the 1980s.

"When a friend asked for help reopening the Camp David Accords, what became known as the Oslo Accords, we had no idea what we were getting into. Norway was brokering the deal and my friend was an attaché with the Norwegian government collecting background data for politicians from several countries. We never thought we were in any danger just by compiling historical data.

"The terrorism that surfaced at that time didn't prepare us for people willing to kill over the use of a phrase or even a single word. We inadvertently upset some folks with ties to terrorism, and they took it out on Sigmund. Evelyn was in the wrong place at the wrong time. To this day, we have no specifics as to who did it, or why they targeted Sigmund. Terrorists have no ethics." Andrew turned to Alana, "It's possible they targeted Evelyn to punish Sigmund. I learned a long time ago that trying to rationalize something so evil will eat you alive.

"We thought reopening the Camp David Accords was an honorable cause. We let our guard down, thinking we were a small cog in a very large wheel—insignificant, really." Andrew coughed. "Our business has changed since then. We take on much less risk now. Our clients are mostly academics, still some intelligence gathering, but nothing like back then.

"But when you came to us, Alana, you were in clear danger. Sigmund couldn't turn you away. He tries to protect people, and it affects him deeply."

"I don't know what to say. My problem seems so small compared to what you've just said, but I guess no problem is small when violence is involved. I'm sorry I brought this on you and your son, on everyone."

"No, you can't look at it that way. What might have happened if you hadn't come to us? Everything happens for a reason. Sigmund will get you through this."

They sat quietly on the terrace bench.

"Are you frightened about today?"

"No. It's only been a few days, but it feels like a lifetime. I'm certain that I have to go," she said. "Don't worry. I can defend myself if necessary."

"Just let David's men do their job and everything will be fine. Have you been in a helicopter before?"

"No." She made a grimacing smile. I'm more worried about the flight than what will happen when we get there."

"You'll be just fine." Andrew patted her back in a fatherly way. He reached into his pocket. "Would you like something to settle your stomach for the flight?"

"Thank you for offering, but I don't experience any type of travel sickness, on the water or in the air, so I'll be okay. It's just wrapping my head around going up in the helicopter... my stomach isn't the problem."

"I went out to get these gingerroot tablets in case we went up. I always take one or two because I find the motion of a helicopter is unlike that of an airplane. I also dislike the din of the rotors. Even with the headset on, the constant droning gets to me." Andrew turned to leave the terrace, "I'm just going for a glass of water. I'll be back in a second."

"Andrew, wait, you've convinced me to take the gingerroot, too. Would you please bring me a glass of water as well?"

"I will... and Alana, I hope you will come out to our country home when this business is sorted out. I enjoy our conversations; I'd like to continue them, convince you we're nice people."

"I think I know that already."

Alana was alone on the terrace when she heard the drone of the helicopter drawing closer and closer until it popped up over the top of the hill and angled down into the field.

Before she knew it, she was running toward the helicopter with Andrew's hand on the back of her neck, keeping her head low as they bent beneath the rotors. Sigmund and David were close behind them.

When the copter took off, Alana felt nauseated, but the feeling subsided as they leveled out and moved forward. She was determined that nothing would make any of the others regret having her with them.

About an hour into the flight, Sigmund opened his gun case. He handed a gun to his father first. Andrew wore a shoulder holster under his coat. He immediately loaded an ammo cartridge and holstered the gun. Sigmund handed him several more ammo clips.

Sigmund then looked at Alana. "This is a Walther PPKS380 double-action semi-automatic. It's easy to conceal and yet the barrel is adequate to give you good aim."

Alana took the gun in her hand.

"It's good for a woman's grip. These are the ammo clips. Let me show you how to load and discharge them."

Alana said confidently. "This is similar to the gun I used for target practice with my father."

"Don't let the size of this gun fool you. This is a 9mm; it's a powerful gun. While I don't expect you to use it, should it become necessary, aim for the chest and tap twice." He showed her. As he touched her hand, he remembered teaching Evelyn for the first time. "There are eight rounds in each clip. You have to apply pressure to fire each bullet, but it will fire fast. You can pulse your finger on the trigger. Do you understand? That's what I meant by tap twice."

"Yes. I have used a semi-automatic."

"Here are extra clips. This holster fits like a belt around your waist. It lets you holster the gun in the small of your back."

Alana put it on and felt the gun at her back for the rest of the trip. She wasn't worried about using it. She believed she could handle the gun.

The copter set down at the same airport as the day before. They consulted with David's agents on the ground. The nursing home had already been under surveillance for any signs of Egon—there were none so far. Two new agents drove off to relieve the two on duty.

Sigmund heard from Boris that Egon was nowhere to be found in the town of Neufeld. He had confirmation from several people that he had been there the day before, but Boris found no evidence he was still there.

The plan was that Sigmund, David, and two agents would go to the school. That was where most of the buildings were located. Andrew and Alana would head to the church, then they would all meet up at the school complex. As soon as the pilot checked in at the small airport office, he would follow Andrew out to the church. Andrew promised they would not get out of the car until he arrived. As Sigmund and David had discovered the day before, mobile phone service was spotty in the mountainous area. This concerned everyone.

"There's no turning back now," Andrew said to Alana as they got into the car.

"I wouldn't want to."

Their cover was to take water samples from each building. They were well documented, and since it was nearing the end of the workday, it was doubtful that anyone would call to check on them. If they did, the Israelis would intercept the call.

In a few miles, Sigmund's car turned off toward the school campus. Andrew continued the straight climb toward the church and presbytery. The mountain roads were narrow with numerous sharp switchbacks; an earlier rain had made the road slick. Andrew proceeded with caution.

Egon and Gerhardt pulled into the nursing home parking lot, stopping in the corner farthest from the walkway to the building. This caught the attention of the Israeli agents watching the area, but they couldn't get a clear view inside Gerhardt's car.

Egon pondered what he would say to get inside. He wished he hadn't shaved his head. When he looked over his clothes, he realized they were dirty and wrinkled; even he knew it would be difficult to pass as a routine visitor inquiring about a patient.

This lack of a plan hadn't seemed an issue until they arrived. But that fact wasn't lost on Gerhardt, and he started poking fun at Egon. In turn, Egon

smashed his head against the side window in frustration.

"I thought you had it all together, man. Some big
intellectual you are. You don't even have a plan. I
hooked up with a loser!"

"Shut up!" Egon snarled.

"No, I came with you to advance some cause that
you won't share with me. Now I find out that you
don't even know what you're friggin' doing. What's
the plan—friggin' nothing!"

"Drive back to the town," Egon retorted. "I need
to change clothes and buy a cap to get in there.
That's my plan."

Gerhardt was pissed and drove off fast, almost
hitting the Israeli's car as it pulled into the parking
lot. One agent thought he recognized Egon, but
wasn't sure. Egon had shaved his head since the
police sketch had come through, and the agent had
caught only a fleeting glance as the car passed. The
driver let his partner out to team up with the other
agents and then turned to follow the suspicious car.

In less than a quarter of a mile, Egon announced
they had a tail, but Gerhardt was unconvinced. "This
is the only road out of the parking lot; you don't
know the car is following us... what, are you James
Bond now?"

"Go faster and see if he keeps up."

Gerhardt accelerated down the hill, barely able to
navigate the first intersection. The Israeli car closed
the gap, but not enough to convince Gerhardt that
they were being followed. The road curved sharply
left and then back to the right. Gerhardt continued
to make fun of Egon. "You're not James Bond,

maybe Austin Powers… no wait, who's that guy? I know, you're Dr. Evil's skinny son. He was all screwed up… just like you!" This infuriated Egon, but Gerhardt didn't stop. "What was that kid's name?" Snickering, Gerhardt looked over at Egon.

Egon screamed out, "Watch the road you fucking idiot!"

As Gerhardt's eyes turned back to the road, he saw a caution sign signaling a sharp bend in the road. His speed was now much too fast. He hit the brake and pulled the wheel hard to the right, causing the back end of the car to fishtail left on the slick road. The car spun 180 degrees just as the Israeli's car rounded the corner.

At that same moment, Andrew's car entered the curve from the other direction. He swerved to avoid the vehicles, but it was impossible. All three cars collided and shot off the road in different directions, landing in the woods on both sides of the road.

The airbags in Andrew's car deployed upon impact with Gerhardt's car. Before Andrew could brake, his car was off the road, down a ravine, and up against a tree. Luckily, the thick brush slowed their descent. Andrew looked at Alana. "Are you okay?"

"I think so." Blood trickled from under her hairline. "My ankle hurts."

Andrew had hit his head against the roof as the car dropped down off the road. His mobile phone was smashed on the floor.

Andrew got out, struggled up the ravine, and went to the car on the other side of the road. That car's airbags had deployed as well, but there had been no brush to soften the blow of the secondary crash into the woods. The car was wrapped around a tree. Looking through the windshield at the driver, Andrew recognized him as the Israeli agent who had left the airport to relieve the agents stationed at the nursing home. He was unconscious, maybe dead.

Questions flooded Andrew's mind. Why was he coming back down the road? Why didn't he go on duty at the nursing home? Where was the other agent who had been in the car? Andrew heard groaning from inside the car; the agent was alive. Andrew caught a whiff of petrol, but he knew he couldn't get into the car or lift the Israeli out on his own. "Stay calm. I'll be right back."

Alana went to the third car. No airbags in this one. Gerhardt was dead behind the wheel. His head had smashed through the windshield and was then thrown back against the headrest. Andrew came over to the car. Neither Andrew nor Alana had seen a passenger in that car before the accident. It had all happened too fast.

Andrew questioned why the accident occurred at all. Was the Israeli agent chasing this car? Gerhardt didn't match their description of Egon. Nothing made sense. As Andrew stretched into the car for the driver's identification, they saw a light coming through the woods. A voice called out, "Hello there, are you all right?"

"We need help," Andrew shouted in the direction of the light as he pulled his gun out of its holster. Alana did the same.

As the man came closer, they saw his white robes and hid their firearms from view. Clad in his High

Mass vestments, the priest appeared a ghostly vision. "It's lucky I heard the commotion. I was just leaving. There would have been no one around for miles." He paused to assess the situation.

Andrew said, "There are three vehicles involved. This one has a fatality. That's our car down there." Pointing to the left, "There is an injured man in the car on the other side of the road."

"How badly is he injured?"

"It could be bad. There's a lot of blood. I need help to get him out of the car. I can't see a petrol leak, but I can smell it, and I'm afraid it will overwhelm him inside the car."

"The church is just through the woods behind me." The cleric looked at Alana, "Can you walk to the church and call 112? I will help your friend with the injured man."

"Yes."

"Where is the phone?"

"Walk straight through the front of the church, down the nave, and turn right at the altar and through the door." The priest gestured with his hands, straight and then right as he spoke, "You can't go wrong."

Andrew said, "No, I don't want her going alone. I must go with her."

"The church is just over the ridge here; you can't see it because of the thick foliage, but it's very close. She will be fine. The two of us must help the other man."

"I'll be fine, Andrew, I'll be back before you know it." Alana couldn't admit to the throbbing pain in her ankle or that her sock felt drenched with blood. There was no time to look at the wound; she started toward the church, determined not to let Andrew see her limp.

Andrew and the priest struggled to get the Israeli out of the car, but they had trouble. The car had lodged against the limb of a tree. Taking off his robes, the priest climbed onto the car and rocked back and forth until the car broke free, bringing the car down to a better angle. Being a younger man, the priest could squeeze into the car and with Andrew's help, ease the agent out.

The man was in and out of consciousness. The priest could see the Israeli's gun holstered under his open coat but said nothing. He pulled a cord from his robes and applied it as a tourniquet around the man's arm. They rested him on the ground to wait for the ambulance.

"I looked at his identification," Andrew told the priest. "He's some sort of police officer," to allay any fear from seeing the gun.

Alana made her way up the hill. When she reached the top, she saw the church. It was a small old church of Gothic design like so many she had seen in villages throughout Germany when touring with Kirk in 1986. The presbytery was so close that it seemed to be attached.

She walked into the church and stood on the stone floor in the vestibule, unaware her hand was still clamped on her gun. Dim lights allowed her to see into the nave. The light created eerie shadows across the pews. Although Alana had been baptized a Catholic and guided her life with a strong sense of spiritual ethics, she had never been a practicing

Catholic. She usually felt solace in holy places, but the sensation she had now was quite different. No comfort awaited her inside this church.

Suddenly she found herself repeating the words Franz had spoken before taking his life. The words got louder and louder in her head until she couldn't help but whisper them aloud. "O Lord, forgive the innocent thou hast redeemed." Some force was pulling her into the church. She walked down the aisle, allowing herself to limp for the first time. Then, as the priest had told her, she turned right at the altar. A chill penetrated her body as she pulled open the door to the room with the telephone.

And there…, positioned between centuries-old church icons, Alana saw the trap. It loomed large in front of her, nearly eight-feet tall, perhaps six-feet long. Centered on each of its lower doors were the carved figures of dragons that had been barely visible between the children in Dagmar's photograph. She saw the complete carving now, eerily like what she had drawn at the safe house. The intricate carving depicted each creature with one leg shackled in a metal cuff with a dangling chain as though caught in a trap.

The cabinet was a work of art, completely at home in the majesty of the church. She froze momentarily, taking it all in. Her mesmerized gaze was only disturbed by the pulsing pain in her ankle. Then she remembered 112. Hobbling to the phone, Alana keyed in the numbers for the ambulance.

Returning to the cabinet, she searched for a location that might conceal a secret compartment. She grabbed the doors and drawers, spilling the contents across the floor. She found nothing. Raising her head to view the cabinet in its entirety made her dizzy. For the first time, she became aware of the wound on her forehead; she lifted her fingers, gently touching the area and felt the blood. She was so close to the truth, she had to concentrate.

That's when she fixated on the two fluted columns on either side of the structure. She ran her hands up and down each column, feeling for a latch that would lead to a hollow hiding place. Nothing! She tugged on both columns to no avail; they were solidly attached to the cabinet.

Standing back, she began to panic. "Focus," she told herself, taking a deep breath. She thought back to her vision. Franz had rolled items together and inserted them into a tube. She never saw what he did with the tube, but it made sense that the tube would fit nicely inside one of those columns. She examined each column again. Again, nothing.

Alana looked around for a makeshift tool she could use to force one of the columns away from the cabinet; she saw nothing that would be helpful.

But, in casting her eyes about the room, Alana caught a glimpse of her shoe now dark with blood. Looking down, she spotted a round molding that ran horizontally along the base of the cabinet. In her preoccupation with the columns, she hadn't noticed this other place that could hide a tube.

She knelt down to examine the molding, feeling for a lever that might open a compartment. Expanding her reach, she slipped her fingers behind one of the ball and claw feet that supported the huge cabinet. She felt a metal button and pushed it. Nothing moved. It had to be the answer! Frustrated, she pushed it again with all her might. Finally, a piece of the rounded trim swung away from the base. She had found the secret of the trap. Reaching inside, she pulled out the tube Franz Ziegler had hidden years ago.

"I'll take that." Alana swung around to face Egon's eerie image in the doorway. She looked over to her gun on the desk by the phone.

"I said, give it to me." He had something in his hand, but there wasn't enough light for her to see what it was. It didn't look like a gun. He was bent over, leaning against the doorjamb for support. Blood had congealed on the top of his head and one eye was swollen shut.

Alana's mind froze; she couldn't think what to do. She couldn't lose the secret now. Then she saw a figure appear in the nave behind Egon's shoulder. It was Andrew. He stood ten or more feet behind him. Alana wanted to keep Egon distracted so he wouldn't hear Andrew.

"Who are you?"

"Give me the tube." Egon reached down to pull the pin from the grenade in his hand.

Alana now realized what he had and quickly asked, for Andrew's benefit, "Did you just pull a pin from a hand grenade?"

"Yes, damn it! I'm serious."

"Here, you can have it." She hobbled toward him. After several seconds, she threw the tube over his head. Andrew grabbed it. Egon tried to run at him, but his legs were too weak. Andrew kept stepping backward.

"Give me the tube or we'll all die."

"Hold on, hold on," Andrew said, "nobody has to die." He motioned to Alana.

"Let her get out of the way, and I'll give you the tube."

"Shut up!" Egon snapped.

"Son, you've come all this way for what's in this tube. Do you really want to blow it up? I don't think so." Andrew stalled for time in the darkened church. "Just let her come out, behind me, that's all I want and then you can have the tube." He spoke calmly. "You might be willing to die for it, but we are not. You can have it. Understand?"

Egon's mind jumbled his thoughts, and he was too weak to bang his head back to reality. "Fine." He motioned to Alana to go over to Andrew.

Andrew put his arm out to move her behind him. He whispered, "Prepare to run," as she passed.

"Now give me the tube," Egon shouted.

"Will you tell me what's inside?"

Egon raised the hand grenade. "I'm done talking to you, give me the tube."

"Okay, okay son, here you are." Andrew threw it directly at him, hard. He turned, Alana had already moved back, and now they both ran as fast as they could.

Pulling the pin from the grenade was stupid, but Egon's sick mind had become even more delusional since the car accident. He fumbled with the tube, and it fell to the floor, rolling under a pew. Egon jumped for it just as the grenade exploded. It blew Egon apart.

The concussion wave threw Alana and Andrew across the floor. An eight-foot crucifix at the altar fell across Alana's legs. Andrew couldn't catch his breath; his body lay flat on the floor next to her, gasping for air.

Small fires broke out surrounding the blast site as the heat ignited hymnals and pew cushions. Several rows of pews were on fire.

Sigmund and David ran into the church and down the aisle. The upper torso of a body lay in their path.

"Dad?" Sigmund cried into the darkness. There was only silence.

Then he heard Alana say, "He's here."

As Sigmund ran toward the sound of Alana's voice, he yelled to David, "Get that copter here."

David's eyes caught sight of the mangled tube, "Is it gone, Sigmund? Has what we've been searching for been blown up?" He looked down at the smoldering remains.

"Forget it, get the copter! We've got to get them to a hospital."

"I've already called for the ambulance. That's why I was here, to get help after the car accident." Alana told him.

Andrew moaned and tried to get up.

"Don't try to move. Just stay still." He pulled the crucifix off Alana. Shrapnel had punctured her upper body when the grenade exploded. There were spots of blood all over her back and arms. A wooden spike protruded from the back of her shoulder.

"What's wrong with my back?" she asked.

"It's a splinter of wood."

"Please pull it out," she cried, "it hurts."

"I don't want to touch it. Let's leave it for the med techs." Sigmund now saw the blood on her forehead.

Andrew was wearing a heavy coat, which had protected him from the flying debris. Sigmund's mind raced. His father was older now, well into his sixties. How would he survive this, first an auto crash, then this? Good god. He chastised himself for letting them come on the mission.

"How is your dad?" Alana asked.

"I'm not sure. He can't breathe!"

"Yes, I can. Help me up." Andrew's voice was barely audible, but it made Sigmund exhale in relief.

"No, Dad, I want you to stay put until the ambulance arrives."

"It was all for nothing," Alana lamented, "all for nothing."

Just then Stark and Brandt walked into the church. David told them Egon was dead. They looked at the rubble around his bloody torso.

Stark walked over to Alana. "I'm sorry it turned out this way. Are you okay?"

"I will be."

Stark looked at Sigmund. "She shouldn't have been involved in this. You're not the police."

"This was never a police issue. This was an extension of the war, Inspector Stark, and civilians are always victims in war."

12

The Reckoning

The next morning Sigmund was back in Zurich at the Griegg offices continuing the investigation.

Andrew's difficulty breathing was the result of five cracked ribs. Fortunately, his lungs were not punctured. He had sustained a concussion in the car crash, but the MRI showed no bleeding in his brain. Once his vital signs returned to normal, the doctors saw no need to hospitalize him and agreed to let him leave the emergency room the following morning. Instead of returning to Zurich, he chose to stay at the hotel next to the hospital until the doctors discharged Alana.

Alana's injuries were more serious. By the time she reached the hospital, she was dizzy and vomiting from pain. Her right ankle had a laceration and the ligament that was sprained in the auto crash was now completely torn from the bone. The left leg had a compound fracture from the crucifix falling on her in the explosion at the church. The chunk of flying wood that had penetrated her shoulder came from the pews closest to the point of explosion and contained a nail that sliced into the deep muscles of her back. It required deep dermal sutures to close the wound. The gash along her hairline needed nine stitches. Other lacerations, while numerous, were minor. She would be released from the hospital once the swelling in her legs diminished, but because both legs were injured, she would be confined to a wheelchair for a month or longer.

As the medic wheeled Andrew to the ambulance, he slipped something to Sigmund saying, "Do nothing until we talk. I don't want to discuss it until we are both back in Zurich. Don't tell David."

When Sigmund had a quiet moment away from David, he peaked at what his father had handed him. It was a small pocket notebook with the words *Der Goldzug* on the cover. Sigmund whispered to himself the Gold Train and tucked it away unopened.

Sigmund took the helicopter back to Zurich with David, but instead of going to the safe house, he asked to be dropped at a heliport near the Griegg office. He wanted to access their safe as soon as possible.

As expected, the doctors released Andrew, and as planned, he stayed in the adjacent hotel to assist Alana in any way he could. Sigmund had hired a nurse to stay with Andrew around the clock. Both Andrew and his nurse spent the next day at Alana's bedside. He was able to tell her that Marta's health continued to improve. She planned to go to her mother's house when she was released from the hospital.

Pain permeated Alana's entire body. She resisted medication, but it became too much to bear. Andrew and his nurse talked her into taking the opioid the doctor recommended. Later, the normally restrained Alana spoke openly to Andrew. She told him about her dream that led her to believe that Kirk was not her biological grandfather and about reading letters that someone named Elsa had sent to Helmut before the war. She shared her suspicion that it was the same Elsa who married Kirk.

Finding Franz's letter about the secret hidden in the trap had pushed everything else into the background. And now, lying in her hospital bed, there was nothing left but to relive all the events in her mind. She told Andrew she now believed that Helmut was her grandfather, not Kirk. "I'm not sure if my mother knew it or not."

Alana had never told anyone that she once overheard her mother saying that she wanted desperately to leave Germany and that marrying Alana's father gave her a one-way ticket to America. Alana was about five years of age at the time. It was one of her earliest childhood memories, and it stuck with her for life. "I never understood how a mother could say such a thing with her child in such close proximity. She had to know I would hear her talking. She said nothing of love, just a ticket to America.

"I always loved Kirk for the man he was, so does it matter if he was or wasn't my biological grandfather? It's something I will never know. I know they talk of DNA testing these days, but I'm inclined to just let it be. It doesn't make any difference to me."

The medication made Alana ramble. "I wish the people at the bank would have let me complete the work on my desk before dismissing me. I had known my clients for years," she said with a sigh. She would then doze off, just to start talking again when she woke. "I loved my father so much… Andrew, I keep seeing this word in my head, Goldzug, and I don't know what it means.

"My dad instilled in me the necessity of being aware of my gun 100 percent of the time. He would tell me before every practice that holding a gun comes with immense responsibility." She woke an hour later and found Andrew sleeping in the chair next to her bed. His private nurse wasn't in the room. He woke up when a hospital nurse entered the room on her regular rounds.

"Andrew, I left the gun Sigmund gave me on the desk when I called 112 in the church. My father would be so disappointed with me. I let everyone down."

"No, Alana, you didn't let anyone down. Please don't think that way."

"How can I think any other way? I should have killed the man. I was so sure you could trust me to defend myself. Did they say his name was Egon? So we were on the right track?"

"Yes, we were on the right track. And it's a good thing you didn't kill him. He had a hand grenade, and if it had gone off with you in that small room, you would have killed been too. I don't want to hear anything about blame."

"I didn't know what he had in his hand when he first came to the door," she admitted. "It wasn't until he pulled the pin that I realized what it was."

"But Alana, you had the gun after the explosion," Andrew recalled.

"I reached over and grabbed the gun while you were asking him to let me out of the room. But by then I knew he had a grenade, so I couldn't use it."

"Alana, forget it. It's all over now. Hindsight is always clear. You will be fine. Marta will be fine. I've been in this business long enough to tell you there's no way to predict the ending of any investigation.

"Finding the letter put you on an unavoidable path. But it's over and we go on. I'm not diminishing what you've been through, just keep it in perceptive. I think that is what Kirk would have told you. If you ever feel you are responsible for any of this, I want you to call me immediately, whenever or wherever you are, because I won't let you think that way."

The hospital nurse rushed into the room. Alana's heart rate monitor had triggered an alert. Andrew reassured the nurse that Alana had momentarily talked about the accident but that she was okay now. The nurse watched her heart rate come down. "That's all right," the nurse said, "But it would be best not to dwell on the accident."

Inspector Stark suddenly appeared in the door-way. Andrew stood up, "Inspector," he said sternly, "The nurse has told us that Alana shouldn't think about the events of the past days. Do you really need to talk to her now? Surely it can wait."

"I'm not here to cause Ms. Eastwood any stress, Mr. Griegg. As I said in the church the other night, perhaps that's something you and your son should have considered."

Alana spoke up, "Please, Inspector, I'll tell you anything you want to know."

"I don't have questions. I came to see how you are doing and tell you that Marta Voss was released sooner than the doctors expected; she is home with her mother today. She knows that the person who attacked her is dead and there is no further danger. I'm going back to Tübingen later this afternoon."

"Inspector, does Marta know the whole story?" asked Alana.

"Oh, come now," Stark said in disbelief, "*I* don't know the whole story, do I?"

"I meant does she know what happened at the church? Does she know I am in the hospital?"

"Not entirely. She knows you broke your leg. She knows that whatever you people were searching for has been destroyed. I had our local police tell her, because I wanted her to know the danger was over and that she could go home in peace. News of the deaths and the investigation is being reported in the newspapers. Her learning anything more than that is up to you. Would you contact me when you are back in Germany? There may be some loose ends to close out our file."

"I will." Alana said wearily. With that, Stark left the hospital room without looking back at Andrew.

Andrew asked Alana to continue telling him about her father. She was now able to stay on topic for increased periods of time.

"Well, his army training enabled him to get a job, and he became a skilled tool and die maker. It was a career that lasted his whole life. He worked for the same company, and he provided well for our family. In the 1970s and '80s, as manufacturing headed overseas, his company economized and kept the business profitable in America.

"But the conditions surrounding his marriage were always a source of friction. Just as I knew my mother wanted out of Germany at any cost, he knew it too. That weighed heavily on their relationship. An interracial marriage, as they called it back then, had obstacles for even the most loving of couples, so they struggled at times. Remember, that was a time when their marriage would have been illegal in many states. Movies like *Guess Who's Coming to Dinner* were considered groundbreaking. It was just the beginning of social change on both sides of the Atlantic. But they stayed together, and I never noticed tension.

"I really had few issues growing up. Connecticut was a good place to live and go to school. I knew I was different and introverted, but I think I grew up well balanced. I would have been the same person no matter what my ethnic makeup. I've always been comfortable with who I am."

Andrew found her both easy to listen to and easy to talk to. He hadn't had private conversations like this with anyone in a long time. It made him reflect on how much he missed Evelyn.

Andrew went on to talk about losing his wife when Sigmund was young. "She died of cancer at a time when almost everyone diagnosed with cancer died quickly. We barely had time to come to terms with her disease when she had to be confined to the hospital. She passed away soon after that." Andrew believed that when Evelyn died and Sigmund sent William to England to live with her parents, it was because it was so difficult for Sigmund when he lost his own mother at a young age.

"It was supposed to be temporary, perhaps a year or two. But William thrived at school in England and made so many friends that he wanted to stay. But to tell you the truth, I think Sigmund was happy to have William in England so he could bury himself in his work. That's what I did when I lost my wife."

Andrew continued to reminisce, "Sigmund has allowed himself casual relationships over the years, and by that I mean, just a dinner date now and again when someone he knew was in town." He went on, "There was one woman who lasted longer, but I don't know if Sigmund will ever be able to have a real relationship. I wish he could, because he's a good man with a lot to offer."

"How did Sigmund meet Evelyn?"

"She was the daughter of a Welsh couple working in Zurich. Her parents were both born and raised in Wales, then lived in Oxford before relocating to Zurich on business. They returned to Oxford after a few years." Andrew's eyes twinkled as he talked about Evelyn. "She had studied languages and was working as an interpreter in Oxford at the time we met her. She had that Basque look, as so many of the Welsh people do. She was dark in complexion with startling blue eyes. She had the most beautiful black hair. But to all who knew her, her real beauty was on the inside.

"Oddly enough, we had a young woman from Wales working for us at the time. She had been friends with Evelyn at college. One day Evelyn just walked into our office and into our lives. Sigmund married her within the year. The wedding was at our country home. Those were the days." Andrew paused, remembering.

"William is dark like his mother. I have a new picture of him." Andrew reached for his wallet; he winced, momentarily forgetting how painful it was for him to move. "William has her black hair. He has Sigmund's eyes." In her pain, Alana found herself mesmerized by Andrew's gentle voice. He pulled out a picture of William with his parents and handed it to Alana. "It's funny, sometimes I look at William, and I see Sigmund as plain as day, then other times I see him as all Evelyn. But here's a recent photo of him at the stable where he goes to school. He's quite the equestrian. He loves jumping over fences."

"I hear so much love in your voice when you talk of your family." Alana fought back fatigue. "You talk about Sigmund, but you never remarried?"

"That wasn't for the lack of trying, my dear." His voice picked up. "I played around back in the day."

Alana joked back, "If I had known you back then, I think I might have wanted to marry you. You know what they say, if I were twenty years older…"

"Yes." Andrew laughed, "You know very well that the saying is: if I were twenty years younger." He raised his eyebrows, "Perhaps if I were twenty years younger!" As difficult as it was with their pain, those words made them laugh. Andrew wrapped his arm around his ribs as he chuckled.

"But Andrew," Alana said wearily, "you haven't told me how a psychic once saved your life. I want to hear the story."

"You're tired, dear. I want you to rest; we'll talk about that later." Both Alana's legs were elevated to reduce swelling, one by a wedged pillow, the other by a sling held by a pulley contraption. "Can I adjust anything to make you more comfortable?" he asked.

"No, I doubt that is possible. I'm okay."

Alana and Andrew became friends that day. When Alana was released, they planned to take the train to Zurich, but Sigmund insisted on picking them up with his car. Alana rested her legs comfortably in the back seat. Andrew was semi-content in the front. He didn't let on that his whole body still ached. The pain around his ribs was unbearable, even with medication.

They both slept on and off during the drive. Few words were spoken. Sigmund woke them as they turned off the main road and started up the driveway to their country home. Alana saw the gate through the car's side window. She turned her head to keep it in view as they passed through and drove up to the house.

Sigmund made every effort to make Alana comfortable, including providing a room for her on the first floor. The home wasn't as luxurious as might be expected from a family of their stature. Alana loved it immediately because its "lived in" quality was warm and inviting. She knew she would be happy there until she was able to travel.

Andrew walked into the kitchen where Sigmund was cooking dinner for everyone. "You know, the old man isn't washed up yet, my son," he said grinning from ear to ear.

"How did you do it? Dad, I can hardly believe it! How did you get a hold of the notebook?"

"It was dark and I distracted the fool as long as I could," Andrew said in his matter-of-fact manner. "He wasn't in good shape following the car accident. He was hunched over and unable to stand without support. One eye was swollen shut, so I knew his vision was limited."

"Does Alana know that we have the notebook?" Sigmund asked.

"I don't think so. She mumbled something in the hospital while medicated, but it didn't go anywhere. But who knows what she's capable of remembering, now or in the future. We can handle it if it comes up."

"Do you know what this means? Of course you do, it's just so unbelievable!"

"Son, I know I gave you a little notebook marked *Der Goldzug*. I have speculated about what's inside but I don't actually know… so, tell me."

"Goldzug… It's the Gold Train, Dad."

"Well I'll be. So it's real?"

"According to the notebook, yes. But there's a twist."

"Where is the notebook now?"

"It's in the safe at our office."

"We have to get the handwriting authenticated. I don't know who wrote it, though with just a cursory read through, I have an idea how to find out. But Dad, if the notebook is correct, the legend has it wrong. Yes, items were gathered and transported by train. But, as you know, the legend claims the train car itself was buried. Treasure hunters relentlessly followed railroad tracks to places where a train could be buried. The notebook says that they never buried the train at all, just its contents. If the Nazis purposefully rumored that the train was buried, it was brilliant, an inspired red herring if there ever was one!"

"Does the notebook tell where the treasure is buried?"

"If true, it's near Książ Castle in Poland."

"Near?"

"Yes, near. We know about that castle because the Nazis built a complex of tunnels beneath it. It was intended as some sort of multiplex to function as both a military redoubt and a residence for Hitler after the war. But the treasure is not actually under the castle—that's another ruse. The notebook tells where the treasure is, and Dad, it gives a complete inventory."

"That's incredible. Son, I say again, I was not quite myself that night in the church. So it came as a surprise when I got dressed to leave the hospital and found this..." Andrew pulled loose papers from his pocket. "These will need authentication as well." He handed letters to Sigmund.

"There are two letters between Adolf Hitler and Heinrich Himmler. One outlines an escape to the new bunker system outside Berlin that we now know Franz Ziegler was building. Those plans could have been implemented at a moment's notice if Berlin fell. They planned to get Hitler out of the country if they determined the war was lost. "

"Dad, this is all so amazing. I don't know what to say. We know that bunker collapsed. You don't think it's possible Hitler escaped, do you?"

"That would be extraordinary," Andrew replied. "Though people do question whether the burned remains outside the Berlin bunker are his. It may be proven someday, but with 1995 technology, there's enough doubt to fuel all sorts of conspiracy theories. You know full well that many historians vehemently believe that Russia lied about what they found when they went into the Berlin bunker.

"In the second letter to Himmler, Hitler writes about Auschwitz. There is also a photo of Hitler at Auschwitz." He handed Sigmund the photo that showed Hitler and Himmler standing next to dead bodies. "The back notes in pencil *Secretly photographed at Auschwitz in January 1944.*"

"One has such a strange feeling touching this photograph... no photo like this has ever been seen."

"Tell me about it. I've been walking around with it in my pocket for days." Andrew sat down; standing for long periods aggravated his pain. "It makes me wonder what else could have been inside the tube. What else had Franz found that made him write that letter?"

"The Amber Room comes to mind, another unsolved mystery from the war. Who knows? There are so many possibilities."

"But Sigmund, this is too big for us. Having this discovery connected to us would change the way we operate."

"So? What's your concern?"

"Sigmund, I want us to turn everything over to the Israelis for them to handle. Let this be their gift to the world. We research and broker information for other people; we don't do it for ourselves.

"Think about it." Andrew stood up holding his ribs. I'm going to go take my medicine.

"What about Alana?" Sigmund questioned.

"Keep her in the dark. Let her go home and live the life she had before all this," Andrew said.

"With her special abilities, one could say finding what was hidden in the trap *is* the life she was meant to live," Sigmund replied.

"Yes, that may be true," Andrew claimed. "But there are two parts to this puzzle as I see it: Allow the Israelis to reveal the letters for the historic value. Then, regarding the Gold Train notebook, shouldn't the goal be to return the treasure to the rightful owners? I believe we can set up an agreement with the Israelis to assure that outcome. We can take care of Alana in our own ways. Remember, she told us all along that she didn't want her visions to define her life." Andrew left the room.

The next day, Sigmund summoned David to the Griegg's Zurich office.

"I need to talk to you, please have a seat." Rarely at a loss for words, Sigmund faltered. "David, it seems our adventure has something for you after all."

Sigmund placed the letters and the photograph on the table. "My father managed to retrieve these documents from the tube before throwing it to the killer. He didn't manage to get everything, but these letters are, pun intended, explosive." He smiled as he pushed the letters to David. "The old man pulled through on this one. It's a pity we'll never know all that the tube contained."

"And what is in here?" David pulled his glasses from his breast pocket. He opened the first letter and looked at the photograph. He glanced over his glasses at Sigmund, and then continued reading. "This is stunning. We owe you for this Sigmund."

"Yes, well, we'll talk about that in a minute. My father wants the Israelis to decide what to do with the letters, and I agree. We want to be kept out of it."

"You've got to indulge me again." David reached for a cigarette and fumbled with his lighter. "I must discuss that with my superiors. This will go directly to the top. But I have to say I don't understand your need for detachment."

"We have our reasons. We'd also like to delay the release of the letters as long as possible. We'd like some space between the conclusion of this case and the announcement, perhaps a year." Sigmund walked over to David and placed a saucer on the table for his cigarette ash. He then looked down onto the street where a car was being ticketed.

"Are you driving a black sedan?"

"No, a blue one, why do you ask."

"No reason."

"This is big, Sigmund." He examined the photo again. "Really big."

"That's not all we have." Sigmund turned to face David.

"There's more?"

Sigmund placed the pocket notebook in front of David.

"Der Goldzug." David picked it up. "Interesting," he said several times over as he flipped through the pages. "What is the meaning of the codes?"

"They refer to the location of the treasure."

"You have me speechless. And you don't want involvement with this either?"

"We don't, and we're quite sure." Sigmund poured himself a cup of coffee. "The letters and the photograph are free for the Israelis." He sat at the table. "The notebook is a different story. We'd like your people to deposit one million Deutsche Marks into an account for us before we turn it over. That converts to about 720,000 USD at the current rate. We'd take dollars if that's how you wanted to pay." Sigmund took the notebook off the table. "We'd like another one million when you use the material in the notebook in any way. Again, you'll have to wait at least a year."

"You can't be serious."

"I am."

"That's steep. This was a joint operation."

"Still," Sigmund put the notebook in his pocket, "the letters and photo are yours, no charge. You pay for the notebook and nothing gets released for at least a year. We remain anonymous. We want the contents of the Gold Train treasure to be returned to those who have rightful ownership. We believe the Israelis are the appropriate people to do that job.

These are our terms. The treasure is worth an enormous amount of money. I couldn't even estimate its value. Whenever confiscated art surfaces, it brings millions at auction."

"But Sigmund, assuming I can get my people to agree with your stated goal, and we can find the rightful heirs for each piece of the treasure, Israel would not benefit. What if the notebook is wrong about the treasure or the treasure is nonexistent or already gone?"

Sigmund responded, "We stipulate that any payment depends on the validation of the notebook and that Israel can take possession of the treasure. The notebook details the location of the treasure and gives a rough inventory of the contents. You will have the information you need. We both know that Israel will benefit in all sorts of ways.

"Think about the alternatives David. Allow other government bureaucrats to intervene and have the wealth end up who knows where? We believe this can be handled clandestinely, so no one knows the Gold Train treasure was ever found, and that the Israelis are the right people to handle it. The Israelis can go public down the road if they want to, once as much of the treasure as possible has been distributed."

"I don't like this one bit, Sigmund. Israel has always done right by you and your father. I see this as holding Jewish property for ransom. It's just not right."

"That's not the way we see it. My father almost died. Talk to your people."

David picked up the letters and photo and turned to leave. Sigmund stepped toward him, putting his hand on David's arm. "There are three people who know about what was found, David. You, me, and my father."

"And the American?"

"We don't believe she knows."

"That's a big assumption given what I've seen over the course of this case."

"We'll take care of Alana Eastwood properly, have no worries about that."

"I don't worry about that at all. But you're making a mistake to profit like this Sigmund."

"David, ours is a dangerous business from time to time; we have to secure our future. We'll need a formal agreement that your people will guarantee our anonymity and spell out exactly how the treasure will be handled. We don't look at this as profiting."

"Still, you're changing the rules," David snarled.

"What rules David? Since when do you talk of rules? Don't blow this out of proportion. You know the value here. We trust the Israelis over everyone else. How else will the treasure be handled fairly?"

"I hope you know what you're doing." David walked over to the door. "I doubt we will meet again, Sigmund, but if we do, it will not be as friends. I'll be sending an emissary for any future contact." David walked away.

When he saw David leave, Andrew came into the room, "How did it go?"

"I shocked the hell out of him, Dad."

"Over the material or the money?"

"Both. David says our friendship is over."

"He'll get over it when he sees the reception he gets at home." Andrew poured two cups of coffee and sat down at the table with his son.

"Still, I'm surprised by his animus."

"As I said, he'll get over it." Andrew responded.

Sigmund proposed, "I think we should ask Alana to extend her stay with us until she has fully convalesced. We could take care of her rental car and get her back to Germany when the time comes. I don't want her traveling in a wheelchair."

"That would be wonderful, but I'm not sure she'll agree to prolong her stay more than a week or so."

"Perhaps if you're the one to ask her," Sigmund smiled. "How could she refuse? Besides, I already ordered a motorized golf cart so she can mosey about the property."

"We'll use the cart after she leaves. William has notified me he is coming back to Zurich and shipping three horses to us. Are you ready to care for horses again?"

"Always. It will be a pleasure. He implied something like that when I talked to him. But surely he needs to finish the school term?"

"Apparently he made a deal with his professors to finish school early by submitting final papers by mail. One of his horses is jumping better than anyone expected; he wants to take him on the European circuit. The Zurich show is scheduled for next month.

"I am as surprised as you are. When he asked to be picked up at the airport today, I thought he was coming alone and staying for a week or so, but he's actually here for an indefinite time. In fact, I need to be at the airport soon. His flight arrives in two hours. The horses will arrive next week."

"I'll do my best to persuade Alana to stay. But don't leave yet, Sigmund. I have something I want you to see." Andrew walked to the door. "I'll be back in a moment."

"Please, Dad, no more surprises."

"Oh, you'll like this one." Andrew came back with Alana's sketchbook. "David's man dropped off the personal items we left behind at the Israeli's safe house. Alana's sketchbook was amongst the items," He flipped to a specific page. "Take a look." He handed the book to Sigmund.

"It's impossible to explain," Sigmund smiled. He put the sketchbook on the table. It was a drawing of the gate and entrance to their country home.

Epilogue, 1996

Alana's recovery was slower and more challenging than she had imagined when she left the hospital. She didn't immediately commit to an extended stay with the Grieggs, but within a few days, reality set in, and she agreed. She called the law office handling Kirk's will to say they would have to work long distance. A moment later a gentleman was on the line.

"Ms. Eastwood, I am Rechtsanwalt Böhm, I'm sorry, Attorney Werner Böhm. I worked with your grandfather for many years, and I've been handling his estate. I have been told that you are recuperating in Zurich from a most horrific ordeal. Our local newspapers have reported on it in connection with the murder of Professor Altmeyer at the university. I am so glad to hear you are all right."

"Thank you. It's going to be some time before I'm back in Germany so will it be a problem settling the estate without my being in Tübingen?"

"No, not at all. But, I was more than your grandfather's attorney, I was his friend. I know that he planned to talk to you about something personal. He never got to do that. I would like to come to Zurich to speak with you on his behalf. We can close the will in an afternoon. Would that be okay?"

"Certainly." This aroused Alana's curiosity.

A few days later, Werner Böhm knocked on the door. They settled the terms of the will first. A real estate agent would be hired to sell the cottage, and most likely, close the sale in Alana's absence. The attorney opened a bank account for Alana in Zurich in order to provide for her extended stay. Andrew had already recovered her car from the police impound and returned it to the rental agency. Once the papers were signed, she asked Attorney Böhm to wheel her into the kitchen. She wished to offer him coffee while they continued to visit.

"I'm afraid I'm still too sore in my upper arms to navigate this wheelchair on my own." Alana's entire body needed time to heal. The pain in her legs was under control, but removing the fragment of wood from the back of her shoulder required a surgical procedure, and her every movement was painful.

When they entered the kitchen, they found that coffee and pastries had been left for them. Böhm pushed Alana up to the table and poured the coffee.

"As I said on the telephone, Kirk and I were friends. I was out of the country when he passed, therefore I didn't meet you at his funeral." Werner collected his thoughts. "A few months before he died, we had dinner together. He told me he wanted to travel to see you in America. He felt he was up to the trip. That was before he fell in the garden, of course. He had to abandon those plans, whether he was actually fit to travel or not.

"It was important to him that you know that your grandmother was the love of his life. I knew both of them, so I can attest to that. My wife and I always enjoyed their company."

"But I know that." Alana stated. "I don't understand why he thought he needed to reassure me?"

"He wanted you to know more about Elsa." Your grandmother had demons that would call on her from time to time. She went through periods of severe depression. Kirk always supported her, but for the most part, he could only watch her struggle.

"Alana, I wanted to speak with you in person because there is even more delicate information that Kirk wanted you to know. I don't understand why he didn't tell you years ago. I suppose he put it off until he felt his own mortality. Your grandmother died from an overdose of opiates. He wanted you to know exactly how she died. Anyway, the fact of the matter is that Kirk was never sure that Elsa's death was accidental.

"Furthermore, Kirk knew that Elsa had been in love with his brother, Helmut, making no secret of wanting to marry him. But, whether or not Helmut would have committed to marriage, the war intervened. Then, as fate would have it, Helmut visited Elsa just a week before his death. When Kirk brought Helmut's body home, he and Elsa found sanctuary with each other, if I might put it in those terms.

"He told Elsa that he was the brother who had always loved her. Needless to say, Kirk told me he wasn't sure if he was the father of Elsa's child, your mother. He knew Helmut had stayed with her the week prior. He said he never discussed it with Elsa, because he doubted even she knew the truth.

"As DNA testing has become available, he looked into grandparent testing, but it happens that, without comparable samples from Elsa or Helmut, any test would be inconclusive. He just wanted you to know that he loved Elsa with all his heart. And that no matter what any testing might or might not have been able to prove, he loved your mother and you with the same conviction. I hope I did the right thing to tell you."

"Yes, of course you did. I admit I suspected something. It was kind for you to come all this way to talk with me. I'm so glad to know that Kirk had a friend like you. This is a great comfort to me as well. Thank you."

Alana stayed at the Griegg's country home until the end of 1995. She made a good recovery, but her ankle never regained its full range of motion, causing her to walk with a slight limp. Sigmund had refused to take money from her for either the investigation or her stay with them. Their generosity left her speechless.

While recuperating in Zurich, she decided she would take nothing from Kirk's cottage home to America, not even the sideboard. She wanted a clean break from the past. Everything went to the Catholic Charity Services, except for a few things Marta kept for herself, including the sideboard, expecting that Alana would change her mind in the future.

Kirk's cottage sold while Alana was in Zurich. When she flew to Germany on her way home, she booked into a hotel in Tübingen. As promised, she met with Inspector Stark to find the case had been closed with nothing else needed. Alana gave Marta a sizable amount of money to help with her recovery and to get started in a job when she graduated from university. She also gave her Kirk's car the day she left for the U.S.

It was four months after the night in the church when Alana boarded a flight for home. And, like her mother, when she stepped foot onto the plane, she never wanted to return to Germany.

Alana never sought another job in the banking industry. She used her inheritance from Kirk to open an art gallery in New Haven. She found exhibition space in an artsy district adjacent to Yale University referred to as "Little Bohemia."

The gallery exhibited both award-winning and emerging artists, as well as historical paintings and small sculptures that she purchased at the New York auction houses. Frequently, the older pieces needed cleaning and occasionally restoration, so she hired a professional conservator away from the Yale Center for British Art. To outfit a lab for art conservation represented a considerable financial investment. But Alana believed that to be successful she had to be bold.

Alana had no new "visions" following the events in Germany and Switzerland. The old visions would always be there, but over the past year she dwelled on them less and less. Strangely, the ordeal of "the trap" allowed her to admit her psychic ability and finally accept it into her life. She now regarded it as a gift rather than a burden.

She was also convinced that if her father had known the whole story of her dreams, he would have embraced them as well. Perhaps he might have looked at his grandmother's psychic gift differently too. Alana reflected proudly that she may have inherited the gift from this ancestor she never knew. This new acceptance of her visions led her to the possibility of investigating her southern roots and perhaps introducing herself to her father's family.

But for now the success of the gallery kept her busy. She sold the home she had inherited from her mother and bought a house overlooking a beach on Long Island Sound.

Andrew stopped by her gallery when he lectured in the States. Their friendship grew stronger with each visit. She knew he was recommending people to her gallery, and she was grateful for his interest. He had, in fact, been her largest single sale when he purchased a painting of the Wailing Wall by a local artist, which he then donated to the Israeli Embassy in Washington, D.C.

The last time Andrew was in town to lecture at Yale, he came out to her beach house for dinner. Alana learned that Sigmund had spent months in Moscow. It was an exciting time for researchers because the Russian government had opened many of their intelligence files to inspection for the first time in history. Sigmund gained new insight into the events of the last fifty years, which, of course, included the years that overlapped with the secret hidden in the trap.

Sigmund's son was still living in Switzerland. He was in college and competing with his show jumpers regularly. Now, completely retired from the Griegg business with no misgivings, Andrew was enjoying the life of a country gentleman. His job was caring for the horses and planning transportation to horse shows. All William had to think about was his school work and riding. He had trained with the top riders in England, and now, though he anticipated a career in the family business, he wanted to fulfill his show-jumping dream first.

Alana queried, "Every time I ask you about your experience with a psychic during World War II, you avoid giving any explanation. When are you going to tell me the story?"

Andrew looked at his watch. "It's a long story, and I have to get my head around how best to tell it. Next time, I promise, but now I have to ask for a ride to the train station. I'll arrive in NY with little time to get to JFK. I'm off to Helsinki to meet up with an old friend." Andrew stood up with a smile. "Come on, bring your doggie, and get me to the train on time!"

Andrew had replaced the void in her life since Kirk died. He kept Alana abreast of the news from Zurich. Niedermeyer had experienced a health scare. It was a mild heart attack, from which he quickly recovered, but the doctor ordered him to reduce his workload; begrudgingly, he allowed Boris to help him in the library. Niedermeyer was slowly introducing Boris to his contacts. To the surprise of everyone in the office, the two men were getting along. Boris even persuaded the older man to leave the building a few times to have dinner, including one night out for pizza. Niedermeyer claimed he had never eaten pizza before.

Ian had expanded the firm's cyber operations and had taken on an assistant whom Sigmund had recruited during his time in Russia. Cyber security would be the focus of their services moving forward into the twenty-first century. Ian was thrilled with this development and began the hunt for even more staff.

Chris and Sabine were now engaged and planned to marry at the end of the year. They were so right for each other that no one questioned the fifteen-year age difference. It was the first marriage for each of them. Alana was invited to the wedding and, as much as she wanted to leave the past behind, Andrew had convinced her to attend. She had already commissioned a painting of the Griegg office, number 96 Hochbaumstrasse, as their wedding present.

In all her chats with Andrew, Alana never asked about David Rosen. The truth was neither Andrew nor Sigmund had seen David since that last meeting after the events at the church. Alana didn't know how that meeting had ended, but David always sent an associate in his stead.

Time went on and the first anniversary of Kirk's death and all that it entailed came and went. Alana refused to dwell on it.

The gallery closed early on Wednesdays. Alana walked with her dog along the water's edge, breathing in the salt air and absorbing the solitude of the beach on an autumn evening. She cut up through the reeds in back of her home and climbed the stairs onto the deck. Inside the house, she turned on the kettle and clicked the TV to CNN Headline News. She caught the tail end of breaking news that startled her, and she quickly switched to the new Fox News channel for more details.

"Breaking this hour on Fox News, I'm Catherine Crier. Stunning revelations out of Israel today as Prime Minister Benjamin Netanyahu announced the discovery of personal letters between Adolf Hitler and the head of the SS, Heinrich Himmler.

"In one letter dated 1937, Hitler acknowledges that he needed the turmoil of war to deal with what he called the 'Jewish problem.' In another letter, written well into the war, Himmler documents a plan for Hitler to escape Germany should the war be lost. A photo of Hitler standing with Himmler and labeled *Secretly photographed at Auschwitz in 1944* is also among the documents."

"Israel's Prime Minister Netanyahu released these comments."

"These letters represent the most convincing acknowledgement of the Holocaust attributable to Hitler himself. The contents of the letters and the photograph are of astonishing historical value."

"The Prime Minister refused to say how they came into possession of the documents. He reports that Israel plans to release the full contents of the letters in the coming weeks."

The whistling of the kettle broke Alana's concentration. The events of the previous year filled her thoughts. She made tea and took it out to sit on the deck with her dog at her side. The CD player filled the air with Enya's haunting voice as the sun sank low on the horizon.

Alana wrapped a blanket around her shoulders and stared out over the water, now dark in the last rays of sunlight. The incoming tide crashed waves against her neighbor's boat launch. Yet nothing broke her concentration on the secret hidden in the trap.

Alana felt elated and yet disheartened, gratified yet betrayed. But most of all she felt closure. She hated the way the word *closure* was bantered about, but in this case, it implied that there could finally be an ending to the horrible events in Germany.

With closure came the memory of how generous the Grieggs had been to her. Now, in light of the day's news, it made her question why?

Alana turned her head when motion near the house drew her dog's attention. She saw Sigmund walking around the corner of the garage.

"Okay Dizzy, stay." She stood and walked out to meet him. Sigmund hadn't changed; he was dressed in the same blue suit he had been wearing when she first told him her story about the letter. Dizzy watched from his vantage point on the deck.

"Hello," he said, "There was no answer at the door; I thought I might find you outside on this beautiful evening."

"Sorry, I didn't hear the bell."

"Alana, we need to talk."

"You're too late, Sigmund. It's all over the news."

"I'd like to explain."

"Come on in." She turned, "I need a drink."

They walked into the house with Alana's German Shepherd keeping a close watch on Sigmund. She poured two glasses of brandy and handed one to him. "I'm afraid this is all I have to offer."

"You should introduce me to your dog before he takes my leg off."

"He's okay. His name is Disraeli. We don't get many visitors."

Sigmund accepted the brandy. "How long have you known the letters were hidden in the trap?"

"About an hour, it's breaking news on every channel. It hit me like a bulldozer." She took a drink. "Part of me has known something was wrong all along. But I never allowed myself to dwell on it. Why are you here?"

"As I said, to explain."

"Explain what? Because I'm pretty sure I understand it now: I led you to the documents, and you gave them to the Israelis. The moment I heard the news I knew it was the secret hidden in the trap. Why did you wait so long to release it?" her voice cracked. "I'm trying to wrap my mind around the significance of the Israelis' story when all I can think of is how you manipulated me! Why didn't you tell me?"

Sigmund stared at her without answering.

"I know this will sound selfish. I thought my business was successful, now I think it is just a sham! Did you send business my way to make yourself feel better for not telling me what you found in the trap? You bastard," Alana slammed her glass down, "You're all bastards." She pulled a tissue from a box on the counter; she didn't want Sigmund to see tears run down her cheeks. "I don't want your money."

Sigmund just stood there looking into his glass.

"I know I'm not one of your 'types,' " gesturing air quotes, "but why couldn't you tell me the truth? Didn't you trust me with the truth?"

"Alana, I know this is hard for you to understand at this moment, but we couldn't. You're a smart woman. Once you get over the shock of hearing the news, I'm sure you will agree that these documents are bigger than any of us. That's why we couldn't be involved then or now. Just let history be history."

"What history?" she snapped back. "History the way you want it? Your altered version of events?"

"It is important that you let this go. I need to know that I can count on you to keep things the way they are."

"How did Andrew get the letters? I was there. I saw everything that happened." She shook her head. "But now it turns out I didn't see anything at all!"

"Alana, the church was dark. Andrew was able to pull material from the tube. He didn't get it all."

"Would you have ever told me if I hadn't figured it out for myself?"

"No." There was a long silence. "If I had come here today, and you didn't suspect anything, the plan was for me to say nothing. I needed to see you to understand what you did or didn't put together."

"Why did you have to make a mockery of my business? I thought Andrew was my friend and sent business to me because of that friendship. Now it seems to be some sort of payoff. "

The assertiveness and confidence Alana had gained over the past year disappeared, and she cried openly. She walked through into the living room and sat on the couch. Dizzy didn't know what to make of the commotion. He kept close to Alana. His job was clear: He was there to protect her.

Sigmund followed and sat in a chair. "We owed you a great deal. It was our way of…" He stopped. He drank the remains of the brandy and placed the glass on a table between them. "I'm sorry. Hurting you was the last thing we wanted to do. But I can't apologize for what we did, because both my father and I believe we made the right choice. We both care deeply about you. We want to make peace with you."

"My visions stay with me." She shouted at him, touching her hand to her chest. "It's not something that goes away. It's as real today as it was in the safe house when you came into my room. If I allow myself to think about it, I am right back in the church and it frightens me. That's how real it is, and that's how real it will stay for the rest of my life." Alana couldn't look at him. "I hate myself for crying like this, I feel like you'll think it is a sign of weakness, but it's not, it's that my visions are so emotional." Her dog still restless; he stood up and stationed himself between her and Sigmund.

"*Weak* is not a word I would ever associate with you." Sigmund tried to get her to look at him.

"You don't have to worry." She blew her nose, "I'll keep your secret. When I stayed in your home, I felt as though we became friends. As odd as it may sound, Andrew is the closest thing I have to family. I would never disappoint him. And for some strange reason, I don't want to disappoint you either." She finally looked at him.

"Alana, this is a matter of great magnitude. Once you are over the shock, I hope you will be proud of what happened. Finding the letter, believing in its importance, and having the fortitude to find answers are all things to be proud of. This was the dilemma we found ourselves in when we made the decision to remain anonymous. As researchers, we wanted the historic value of the letters to stand on its own. You had made clear that you didn't want your psychic ability to define your life, and we believed you.

"I understand we made that decision for you, and you have every right to be angry. It's emotional for you right now, but in time I believe you will see it differently. The notion that the success of your business has been tainted is just not true."

Alana stroked Disraeli as they sat in silence for several minutes.

"I have more information to share with you. May I buy you dinner?"

"You can't fix things over dinner, Sigmund."

"No, but there is more to talk about, and neither of us have eaten, right? You can despise me if you like... you can do that over dinner."

There was another long silence before Alana said, "We have a local Chinese take away or we could drive into New Haven."

"I'm just back from months of Russian take away. Let's go for a nice dinner."

"Don't you have any casual clothes?" Alana stood in her faded jeans and baggy sweatshirt.

"I am who I am, Alana. In fairness, I was in New York on business when I learned that the news would break at any moment. I boarded the first train to come here."

Alana went upstairs to change. Her dog kept his eyes on Sigmund. When Alana was recovering in Zurich, Sigmund had insisted that she take anything she liked from Evelyn's closet. "It was time," he said. Then he donated the remainder of her personal belongings to charity.

Now, a year later, Alana walked downstairs in an exquisite designer dress that had belonged to Evelyn. It probably cost more than the sum total of her wardrobe. The moment Sigmund looked up at her, she felt petty for making the choice.

Alana took him to Café Pica, a new tapas bar and restaurant on the town green in New Haven. It was just around the corner from her gallery. The reviews were great; the style of tapas dining was making news.

After the waiter brought drinks, Alana said, "So what more do you have to say?"

"Have you heard of the 'Gold Train?' "

"No... Wait, it was about Nazi treasure, right?"

"Yes. At the end of World War II it was rumored that the Nazis had filled a train car with confiscated gold, art, and other treasure and then buried the whole car somewhere in the hinterland. It was called Der Goldzug. In the 1950s and 60s, people started talking, giving deathbed confessions claiming they had seen or played some role in hiding the 'gold train' or 'ghost train,' as it was sometimes called. But their stories could never be validated, and any serious research produced nothing of substance.

"But that didn't stop an avalanche of treasure hunters who started looking all over Germany and Poland for a place that could conceal a buried train."

"Are you telling me that in addition to the letters and the photograph, information on this Gold Train was hidden in the trap?"

"Yes."

"So why are you telling me? If I hadn't made the connection to the letters, you said you wouldn't have told me anything. I knew nothing about this train."

"Talking with you today has changed my outlook. You figured out the first piece of the puzzle, and I now believe you should know it all. Alana, I'm trusting you now, 100 percent."

"So the train is real?"

"Yes, the legend of the train is real, but there's an interesting twist. Every effort is being made to keep it a secret—let me tell you the whole story."

"A memory of a small notebook just came into my mind." Alana stated with confidence.

Sigmund smiled, "Yes—a tiny black and white notebook that details the contents of the Gold Train. We turned it over to the Israelis, with an agreement that they follow specific guidelines for the distribution of the treasure. Alana, the Israelis are returning all the items to the families from whom it was stolen, or to their heirs in most cases."

"I don't understand."

"Well, first of all, the treasure is large but not as large as what the legend has led people to believe. The majority of the treasure is comprised of jewelry and artworks confiscated from Jewish families before and during the war."

Alana spoke up, "May I ask where the treasure is now?"

"The notebook documented that the train went to Książ Castle in Poland. The castle was confiscated by the Nazis to serve several purposes, one of which was as a future residence for Hitler.

"As part of this massive repurposing project, the Nazis created a complex of tunnels under the castle. Those tunnels exist today and form a network that stretches for kilometers through the Owl Mountains. Treasure hunters have long suspected that the train was buried in one of these tunnels. Since additional tunnels have been discovered in recent years, seekers of the treasure keep increasing in number and zeal. And rightfully so. We've proved that the legend was true.

"One tunnel was started beneath a building in the town of Walbrzycg just down the mountain from the castle. All indications are that it was meant to link up to the castle, but the Nazis ran out of time—the war ended.

"The little notebook labeled *Der Goldzug* itemizes the contents transported on the Gold Train and identifies its destination as the Walbrzycg tunnel. You see, the

Nazis never intended to bury the train at all, just its contents. If the Nazis initiated the rumor that the train was buried, it was a brilliant redirect. If that was their intention, it worked. Everyone has been looking for places where train tracks lead to a tunnel that could have accommodated a train. It was a bogus assumption. They just moved the treasure into a tunnel."

"Wow. So how will the Israelis get their hands on the treasure?"

"They already have it. Through an intermediary, the Israeli government has purchased the building on top of the tunnel in Walbrzycg along with some surrounding open land. Working covertly, they have already opened the tunnel, found the treasure, and verified it with the notebook. Now they can estimate its value.

"But let me go back," he said enthusiastically, "because this will interest you. We believe the handwriting in the Gold Train notebook is that of SS Commander, Siegfried Schmelcher. He was one of the architects who worked with Albert Speer at the castle complex in Poland.

"It seems Schmelcher may have been more an opportunist than a faithful Nazi. He is most likely the man that Franz saw stuffing documents into an archive box, which was then transported to the vault in the Führerbunker outside of Berlin. Schmelcher's later work at the castle in Poland meant he had an intimate knowledge of the tunnel system and might even have known that the Gold Train treasure was destined to end up there. Documents from Albert Speer's office revealed that Schmelcher had been temporarily transferred to Berlin, placing him at the right place at the right time. We believe Schmelcher acted out of personal greed; he simply wanted to profit from the treasure.

"We now know that the Führerbunker Ziegler was building outside Berlin, the one in your vision, was real, and that Schmelcher was killed when it collapsed. The date of the collapse is consistent with the Franz letter."

Alana queried, "If the bunker that was intended as an evacuation route collapsed, do you think Hitler could have escaped by another route? I just say that because every so often you hear about a claim that Hitler survived the war and escaped to Argentina."

"We don't believe that. There's no doubt there was an escape plan. But there is no evidence it was ever implemented, even without the new bunker outside Berlin. But we will probably never know all that went on."

The waiter came to take their order, but Sigmund asked for more time.

"I'm just blown away by all you've told me. How can the Israelis keep this secret?"

"It will be difficult, no doubt. The project will take a long time, years, and even then not all the items will be connected to a rightful heir. They are working on a number of cover stories on how these items were found without connecting any of it to the discovery of the Gold Train.

"For example: Some pieces with specific provenance could have been 'found' during the renovation of a house anywhere in Europe. This is not uncommon. Every few years since the war, artwork has been discovered in all sorts of places. In some cases the heirs can just accept items back with no need of an extensive cover story. But if a family wishes to sell an article returned to them will need a well-researched provenance that will hold up to scrutiny. No one is being told anything about the Gold Train—only that their object was found in accordance with what the Israelis deem appropriate.

"The Israelis understand that the treasure has to be distributed a little at a time from unconnected sources otherwise rumors might start to circulate about the discovery of the Gold Train."

Alana then questioned, "What about the gold and currency? Perhaps the jewelry and artwork might be traceable, but surely not the gold or any currency."

"You're right, but contrary to the legend of the Gold Train, the treasure included little pure gold—there was, of course, gold jewelry perhaps a few gold coins. But the stacks of gold bars and hard currency as envisioned by the treasurer hunters never existed."

Alana pulled the band from her hair. "I sound like a broken record, but I really don't know what to say. That night in the church, I thought what we went through was all for nothing, so I'm glad that's not true. Something good will come of it after all."

"Well, that's another reason why I'm telling you the whole story. At some point, after the treasure has been distributed, the Israelis may decide to go public with the story of the Gold Train. You can be part of the story if you want to.

"Alana, there is just one more thing. We asked the Israelis to pay us for the notebook, not for the letters or the photograph, just the notebook. We asked for and they agreed to pay us two-million Deutsche Marks. We have already received the first million and expect the second million soon. Some of that money compensated us for the cost of our investigation. We shared a portion of the balance with you through purchases in your gallery. When we referred business your way, it was entirely based on our friendship. We plan to share more of the first payment, and when we receive the second payment, we plan to share that as well.

"Alana, please consider the money we've paid you for artwork a finder's fee of sorts. I realize it may sound strange to you, but it is commonplace in our business. I admit that the circumstances of our investigation were anything but commonplace. The Israelis could never have paid you directly, not to the extent we intend."

"I don't know what to think about that. I don't want to profit from someone else's misfortune." Alana looked at Sigmund, her clenched hands up in front of her chin.

"As we told David, we don't look upon it as profit. You risked your life to discover the secret hidden in the trap."

"But I didn't know about the treasure. We didn't know what we would find."

"How is that relevant?" Sigmund reached to touch her forearm. "Nothing has to change. I'm just asking you to think about it. My father tells me you are coming to Zurich for Chris and Sabine's wedding in December. We can continue the discussion then. Agreed?"

Alana looked at Sigmund. There was so much to think about. There was a moral issue to wrap her head around. What decision would she have made a year ago if they had included her in the process?

Sigmund and his father were correct that she never wanted her visions to define her, so for that reason alone, anonymity would have been a prime consideration. She also understood their belief that the issue was bigger than any of the individuals involved. Therefore, who better to return the treasure to the rightful hands than the Israelis? Would it be so wrong to let them control when and if the story would ever be made public?

After the contentious exchange of words between Alana and Sigmund earlier at the beach house, their conversation over dinner relieved the tension that had defined their relationship since their first meeting in the Zurich office. By the end of the meal, the barriers each had levied were drawn down and put away like a letter never needing to be read again.

"I agree to think about it." Alana said softly, "We'll talk in Zurich."

Back in Germany, people awoke to the news. Horst Wilhelm read through the first excerpts, wondering how his group could refute the validity of the Hitler letters. He had no reason to connect the letters to what happened with Dr. Altmeyer, the Schmidt family, or the letter Albert had asked him to retrieve the year before.

Horst had purchased the contents of Albert Schmidt's library from Helga's sister, who was the only living heir to the family's estate. The group continued to meet and propagandize out of Wilhelm's home. He had hired a computer expert proficient on Internet protocols to develop their online presence. Even so, Horst and the group were unable to increase interest in their revisionist theories.

Both Wilhelm and Galiena pled guilty to their part in financing arms deals, and although they paid hefty fines, they never went to jail. The Bosnian conflict changed the climate for those types of crimes; greater tolerance reigned the day. Their businesses had turned around with the infusion of illegal cash and were strong enough to sustain the fines and the bad publicity. Galiena even kept her marriage intact.

Like Horst, Stark made no connections with the news. She didn't even read the articles plastered across the front page of every newspaper. She was in the midst of a murder case, which consumed all her thoughts. Gruesome photographs of a body found on the sidewalk in a pool of blood cluttered her desk. Stark's life hadn't changed.

Brandt left the police force soon after that night in the church. Stark's outburst with him at the Schmidt home made him think it was time to move on. He was now in law school. Obsessed with the news of the letters, he read every article.

Weeks later, when the Israelis released pictures of the letters, it fell into place for Brandt. The newspaper ran the letters in color and he remembered the yellowed fragments of paper scattered amongst the debris at the church. Before the medics arrived, Brandt bent down to give aid to Andrew; he'd caught a glimpse of him slipping a wad of the same yellowed paper into his pocket.

Now, on a chilly autumn morning, Brandt sat in a café sipping hot coffee, thinking about the yellowed colored paper. He smiled. Of all the players, he was the least likely to link the sensational news of the day to the fifty-year-old secret Franz had hidden in the trap.

THE TRAP

To be continued... Find out what happens to the Gold Train treasure when the Griegg/Eastwood Mysteries enter the horse world and International Show Jumping with book two, *Zen.*

ABOUT THE AUTHOR

Andrea Wilson Steele was born in England and lived in Canada as a child before her family immigrated to the United States. An accountant by profession, she was an officer in two insurance-related businesses during her corporate career.

A life-long equestrian, she teamed with horse trainer, Mark Russell, to write *Lessons in Lightness: The Art of Educating the Horse,* published by the Lyons Press in 2004.

In 2008, Andrea founded the video production company, Advanced Equine Studies, to produce a series of college-level DVDs and online learning experiences for equestrians and equine caregivers worldwide. Advanced Equine Studies received the prestigious Best Educational Program award at New York City's EQUUS Film Festival in 2015 and 2016.

An avid reader of mystery thrillers, Ms. Steele conceived the plot of *The Trap* while commuting to her job in slow-moving rush-hour traffic. The Griegg/Eastwood Mysteries enter the horse world and International Show Jumping in book two, *Zen.*

Andrea lives on a horse farm in rural Connecticut with her husband, horses, and dogs.

Facebook.com/Author-Andrea-Steele